A METAL HORSE nuzzled my finger. No taller than my hand at the shoulder, he was the most delicate little toy I had ever seen . . . and yet more than a toy: he moved of his own volition, and the way he regarded me was more than lifelike—it was life itself.

He was made with too much care, too much precision, to be intended only as a plaything. His head and neck were copper gone a bit green, and his flanks were blown glass. Through them, I could see his clockwork musculature turning back and forth as he pranced beneath my fingers; there was even a tiny clock face that looked as if it had been taken from a small pocket watch. Etched into his right flank was the name *Jules II*. Subtle puffs of steam blew from his nostrils.

The chest that held little Jules was, in fact, a sort of stable in miniature. There was a bottle of oil and a rag in one corner. A crinkle of green patina, his outline, blossomed in another; he had clearly lain dormant for years. How had he known to awaken?

And what else could my entrance have aroused in my mother's world of mechanical wonders?

Mechanica

BETSY CORNWELL

HOUGHTON MIFFLIN HARCOURT
Boston ✷ New York

www.hmhco.com

The text of this book is set in Spectrum.
Hand-lettering by Leah Palmer Preiss.

The Library of Congress has cataloged the hardcover edition as follows:
Cornwell, Betsy.
Mechanica / Betsy Cornwell.
p. cm.
Summary: "A retelling of Cinderella about an indomitable inventor-mechanic who finds her prince but realizes she doesn't want a fairy-tale happy ending after all."—Provided by publisher
[1. Fairy tales. 2. Magic—Fiction. 3. Inventions—Fiction.] I. Title.
PZ8.C8155Me 2015
[Fic]—dc23
2015001336

ISBN: 978-0-547-92771-8 hardcover
ISBN: 978-0-544-66868-3 paperback

Manufactured in the United States of America
DOC 10 9 8 7 6 5 4 3 2 1
4500597998

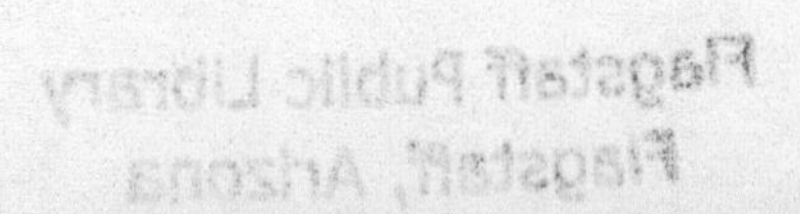

For Elizabeth Wanning Harries:
my teacher, Betsey

"Go and seek your fortune, darling."

—Angela Carter, "Ashputtle *or* The Mother's Ghost: Three Versions of One Story"

Mechanica

PART I

Take the key from behind your grandmother's portrait. I am certain your father still keeps it in the foyer — no one will have touched it in years, I hope. But you, darling, will be able to find the key.

Walk to the end of the hall and open the cellar door. It has no lock; do not fear closing it behind you. Go inside.

Be careful when you walk down the stairs; the wood is weak and treacherous. Bring a candle. The cellar is very dark.

At the bottom of the stairs, turn left. An old writing desk lurks there in the shadows. Push it aside. No doubt you've grown up a good strong girl and won't need help.

Look: there is a door in the wall.

You won't see a keyhole, but run a finger over the place where one would be. I know no daughter of mine will mind the dust.

Twist the key into the keyhole. You might need to worry it a little.

There, darling. You've found it. Use it well.

✷

My mother was wrong about one thing: the cellar door did have a lock. Stepmother had locked me inside enough times for me to know.

She was right about everything else. I was plenty strong enough to push aside the writing desk; I only cursed myself for never having done so before.

Of course, I'd thought Mother's workshop was long since destroyed. I'd seen the fire myself.

Besides, that desk had been my dearest friend. The first time Stepmother locked me in the cellar, a forgotten stack of brown and brittle paper in its top drawer and a cracked quill and green ink bottle underneath provided me with hours of amusement. I drew improbable flying machines and mechanized carriages; I drew scandalous, shoulder-baring gowns with so many flounces and so much lace that their creation would have exhausted a dozen of the Steps' best seamstresses.

Not that Stepmother hired seamstresses anymore. I provided her with much cheaper, if less cheerful, labor. I sewed all of their dresses, though my fingers were not small or nimble enough for the microscopic stitching she and my stepsisters required. I took care not to show how much I preferred fetching water and chopping wood to sewing. Stepmother considered "hard labor" the most punishing of my chores, so she assigned it often.

I never told her how those chores offered me precious, rare glimpses into my memories of Mother. I could see her face, covered in a subtle powdering of soot, laughing at my disapproving father as she carried an armload of wood or a sloshing pail of water down to the cellar. Until recently, those memories, and a few of her smallest inventions, were all I had of her.

I needed to hide her machines from Stepmother, of course: the whirling contraption that dusted cupboards for me, the suction seals that kept mice out of the drawers, the turn-crank in one closet that polished shoes. Mother had taught me enough to keep her machines in repair. When she was alive, she'd dreamed of my going to Esting City for a real apprenticeship, as she herself had always longed to do. But Father would never hear of it.

Anyway, neither of them was able to help decide my future anymore. Now that they were gone, all I knew was that I could not abandon their house to the Steps.

I digress. Father always told me not to worry over things that can't be helped, but I never took his instructions to heart.

He died on New Year's Eve, the year I was ten. I wept noisily over the dispatch letter that announced his death, smearing tears onto the sleeves of what I didn't know would be my last new dress for years. Stepmother stood silent behind me.

He had taken his new wife, with her two mewling, puny daughters, only a few months earlier. I'd tried to befriend Piety and Chastity at first, to beguile them into joining me for a horseback ride, a walk, or even a simple game of boules on the lawn.

I tried talking about books with them too. They responded with glazed expressions and derisive giggles, and when I finally had the chance to look at the beautiful collection of leather-bound books Stepmother had bought them, I found the pages ripped out, and replaced with magazines and catalogs.

Then I knew for sure we'd never understand each other.

After Father died, the Steps grew so much worse. Within a day of his death, they ousted me from my lifelong bedroom, and I was too stunned with grief to argue. My room was next to my stepsisters', and Stepmother said they needed the additional boudoir space. She liked everyone to think that she would never grant her daughters any excess, but in private she spoiled them as if they were the Heir's famously beloved horses.

On the night after she dismissed our housekeeper, she told me to wash the supper dishes. Then—the only time I've done it—I did rebel. I screamed at her like a child, like the child I still was. My position in the family was all I had left to tie me to my parents' love. Though I'd felt it slipping away, until that moment I had chosen denial.

Clearing my eyes of tears, I stared my stepmother down. She looked back at me. Though I had only seen coldness and distance in her face before, I saw something else then. I saw challenge. We both knew what she was doing: she was making me a servant. But I began to think she might be testing me, preparing me for some sacred rite of entrance into her true family. Making sure I was a good daughter.

So I nodded, and I looked down, and I retreated to the kitchen. When your heart is broken, it's easier to follow rules.

I kept waiting, too, hoping I might pass her test. I carried that hope with me like a rosary, counting the worn beads each time she assigned me some yet more menial chore.

If it was ever a test, I must have failed.

Despite what she had reduced me to since Father's death, though, I still could not believe Stepmother was entirely evil. Do not mistake me: she was cruel and sharp, and she spoiled her own children to a fault while denying me any scrap of affection. She took a hypocrite's great pleasure in her own abstinence. She enjoyed denying herself more than she ever relished an indulgence. I could list her flaws for days.

But she gave me my mother's letter. I didn't know why she did, or why she didn't read it first. Perhaps, I thought, it was because she loved her own daughters too much to disrespect another mother's wishes; perhaps I would never know the reason.

It must have been Stepmother, I thought when I found the envelope slipped under my door one autumn morning.

for Nicolette
on her sixteenth birthday

She even gave it to me on the correct day.

Late that night, I crept through the hall to the portrait of Grandmother. She cut an imposing figure atop her huge black stallion, Jules. Mother's family had long been famous for their hunt horses, and Jules was the greatest stallion they ever produced. There were even rumors that the blood of Fey horses ran in Jules's veins—but if that was true, any records of it would have been destroyed after King Corsin's quarantine on Faerie. No one would admit to the least association with the Fey anymore, not after a Fey assassin had killed the previous Heir.

Our country had to learn how to live without magic after that. We were still learning.

Still, with his long, powerful legs, streaming mane, and brightly gleaming coat, Jules looked as beautiful as Fey horses were said to be. Mother used to tell me that together, he and Grandmother could put the men to shame at the fox hunt—I always loved hearing that story.

No key hung on the wall when I took down the picture. Annoyed, I squinted at the letter again.

Take the key from behind your grandmother's portrait.

I puzzled for a moment—then had to laugh at my own stupidity.

I dug a ragged fingernail into the paper at the back of the frame. It exploded in tiny brown fibers that blanketed my hand to the wrist and suffused the air with feathery antique dust. I grinned, feeling rough metal against my finger. I hooked my fingertip around the key and pulled it from the frame.

It was a skeleton key, quite large. The prongs on its shaft were many and complex.

I pocketed it quickly and rehung the portrait, feeling like the heroine in a twopenny storybook. Grandmother watched me from her gilded frame.

I kept near the wall as I walked to the cellar door. I could hear Piety's snores and Chastity gibbering in her sleep. Stepmother slept even more deeply than they did. Still, I stayed silent as a huntress, creeping toward the secret I could sense just ahead of me. Any false move might wake the Steps and pull it out of my reach.

I double-checked the lock on the door and crept down

the stairs. I held my candle high. I had chosen a plain kitchen candlestick—Stepmother would miss the scented beeswax. So it was by a crude and greasy light that I found my mother's gift.

It was easy enough to push the desk aside; finding the door was harder. The flickering candlelight revealed nothing until I practically had my nose to the seam. I was covered in spider silk before I saw it.

But there it was, obscured behind seven years of grime . . . and something else. Something not quite a shadow—something I might have thought, before the quarantine, was magic. Dark, with a darker shine. But it vanished as I put out my finger to touch it, and I thought I must not have seen it at all.

I stepped back, relishing this last moment of mystery. I put a fair amount of force behind the key, expecting rust to have diminished its fit.

But it slipped in like a foot into a slipper, and I stumbled against the opening door.

A rattling overhead drew my attention. There were round, spiked shadows in the darkness of the ceiling, rotating at the same rate that the door was pulling open—*being* pulled. Inside the room, a hissing sound stopped and started in a heartbeat pattern.

I picked up my candle and entered.

The door swung shut behind me, as smoothly and

quickly as it had opened. I didn't feel trapped; I felt welcomed, wrapped in my mother's love. I surveyed my inheritance with awe.

There were charts on the walls, mapping the inner mechanisms of a thousand wonders. There was a coal-powered loom, a sewing machine—*thank goodness,* I thought, my finger still stinging from the last time my needle had slipped—and an automated rocking chair and cradle. This last made my heart ache with loneliness for her and for my own childhood, but I could not stop to examine it further; I was too curious about her other designs. I was particularly drawn to an acidic rainbow of dyes painted into a line of circles, next to long notations of their formulas. I could smell the oil lubricating the gears that had swung open the door.

A bookshelf on the far side of the room completely covered the wall. It sagged into a smile under the weight of its leather-bound occupants. Stuck in amid the books, a desk sat draped with haphazard stacks of paper and half-finished diagrams. A pair of glass and leather goggles rested on top of one blank sheet, still dusted in soot. I recalled the pale rings around Mother's eyes.

I jumped when the room's thick silence broke. A small chest on a low shelf thunked once, and again, in a determined beat.

I sighed, relieved that no one had discovered me. But what lay in that dark box?

Years of unhappiness had made me fearless. I expected a family of rats, and when the thing in the chest scurried into shadows as I opened the lid, I assumed I was correct.

Then I heard the soft whirring of gears, and my nervousness dissolved into delight. I had found another of Mother's creations.

I lowered my palm gently into the box. I found myself cooing and nickering to the thing inside, as if it were a shy cat.

"Come on, now," I said quietly. "It's all right. I won't hurt you." I turned my gaze politely away.

I felt a delicate nipping at my little finger and had to laugh at the sensation. Something rounded pressed against my palm, and I looked down.

A metal horse nuzzled my finger. No taller than my hand at the shoulder, he was the most delicate little toy I had ever seen . . . and yet more than a toy: he moved of his own volition, and the way he regarded me was more than lifelike—it was life itself.

He was made with too much care, too much precision, to be intended only as a plaything. His head and neck were copper gone a bit green, and his flanks were blown glass. Through them, I could see his clockwork musculature turning back and forth as he pranced beneath my fingers; there was even a tiny clock face that looked as if it had been taken from a small pocket watch. He had no mane, but a tail of silver chains that he flicked back and forth and lifted for balance when he moved. Etched into his right flank was the name *Jules II.* Subtle puffs of steam blew from his nostrils. When I stroked his belly, I felt the heat of some inner furnace.

The chest that held little Jules was, in fact, a sort of stable in miniature. There was a bottle of oil and a rag in one corner. A crinkle of green patina, his outline, blossomed in another; he had clearly lain dormant for years. How had he known to awaken? And what else could my entrance have aroused in my mother's world of mechanical wonders?

I lifted Jules from his confinement and set him gently on the floor. He reared up on his steel haunches and looked at me pointedly. We regarded each other.

Then he set off at a canter toward the far corner of the room. I followed—though I paced him easily, of course, even when he broke into a jingling gallop. I felt as if I'd stumbled into Faerie.

Jules halted in front of yet another door, just as subtly set into the wall as the first had been. This one was wider, and streaked in places with dried grease.

I saw a smudged black handprint among the streaks. When I placed my own hand there, it matched exactly. I knew even before I pushed the door open that here was where Mother kept her workshop and the first room was simply a designer's studio, a repository.

I opened the door, and more gears sprang to my aid. The hissing was louder in here, and the air was humid with steam.

Jules pranced eagerly at my feet, his metal hooves clacking against the stone floor. Before me lay a world of possibilities.

It was hard to breathe, at first, in the steam-thickened air, and harder still to see. I stumbled a few steps farther inside as that door closed itself behind me too, and reached down to stroke Jules. Somehow the touch of his hard, warm back made me stand a little surer on my feet.

The rumbling quieted, and the air began to clear. I caught sight of an orange glow at the far side of the room, growing slowly brighter.

Jules saw it too. He let out a pleased whinny—an odd, scraped-glass sound that made my spine tense—and cantered toward the glow.

A furnace. Heat radiated from it and pressed against my face as I approached.

Squinting, I could see where the fire continued to grow and grow at its center, colors changing from deep orange to yellow to white, and something whiter than white in a spot at its very middle, almost blue. The warmth felt good on my skin, seeping through my thin linen dress, as if it were opening me up somehow, readying me to be molded and reworked, like metal.

I saw gloves hanging on an iron hook to one side of the furnace, and I put them on. Of course they fit, just as Mother's sooty handprint on the door had.

Next to the gloves, a series of iron wheels sat built in among the furnace's bricks. I touched one and found I could rotate it easily. It clicked as I spun it down. The furnace rumbled again, its heat lessening slightly. The rough warmth left my cheeks and forehead, and I immediately missed it. I was in love with the furnace already.

I knew, though, that there were other things left to discover, so I turned away and tried not to long for its almost-burn on my face.

I let the fire heat my back as I surveyed the rest of the room. There was a huge leather bellows attached to pulleys that ran up into the low ceiling. I was sure I could control the bellows with one of the iron wheels on the furnace's other side.

Steel and copper sheets lined one wall, somehow mostly unoxidized, even after all the years since Mother's death. Beyond them were shelves stacked with boxes labeled in Mother's spidery handwriting or slotted with glass windows so I could glimpse their contents. I saw more gears, screws, nails, hinges and joints and pistons, bottles of oil and grease and paints: everything that a mechanic of Mother's caliber might need.

Between the shelves and the far wall were dozens—no, probably hundreds—of cubbyholes and drawers, tiny and tinier. I opened them, of course. I wanted to see everything Mother had left me, absolutely everything.

But they contained only drifts of ash, pale gray and so

fine, it flowed like liquid when I pulled the drawers open. Metal label holders under each held drawings, rather than the neatly scripted labels on the larger boxes and shelves.

They were pictures, sketched in worn black ink, of animals. The first were of insects and other crawlers—spiders, beetles, butterflies—then came lizards, fish, canaries, bats. Larger animals, too: cats and hounds and birds of prey. Horses.

And the ash in the drawers I'd opened . . . it *moved.*

I thought I'd imagined it at first, but as I looked closer, it rippled and swirled, then rose into ghostly shapes too vague for me to recognize. It trembled upward, toward me. I put out a hand to meet it, but it cringed suddenly backwards and settled again.

Warm as I was, I shivered.

I looked down toward my feet, but Jules hadn't followed me to this side of the room. He was backed against the furnace wall, his bright ears flat against his head. His slender clockwork legs stood straight and unmoving, and if he'd had muscles, I would have sworn they were tense. I hadn't been much around horses in years, but anyone could have seen he was frightened.

"All right, boy." I hadn't been much around horses, true, but I still knew how to speak soothingly to one. "We don't have to stay here; don't worry." I crossed to the furnace and picked him up, wincing as the fire-heated glass of his flanks met the thin skin on my palm. I hoped I wouldn't blister.

I could feel him . . . *relax* . . . in my hand, as if he had muscles after all. The whirring ticks of his mechanisms, what I would almost have called his heartbeat, slowed down.

He calmed further when I brought him back to the studio. I reluctantly laid him in his stable-box, and he settled down in his corner.

He glanced up at me through those intelligent eyes just for a moment. I caught myself thinking he was sad to see me go.

Then he closed them, and I watched his clockwork wind down. Framed there in his little stable, he was so much like the ink-drawn horse on that drawer in the other room. Both of them, I thought, looked almost lonely.

I was being foolish, of course. Mother's most lucrative trade had been in mechanical creatures like this: automated beetles and butterflies that fashionable ladies wore in their hair or pinned to their dresses. Her best insects could be trained to do simple things like light candles and draw curtains. She always insisted that the insects were simply machinery, though—she said only her most gas-headed customers treated them as pets. I, too, had grown fond of the little ratcheting creatures Mother showed me when I was young, but I'd always believed she was right. Even the trainable ones were no more responsive or affectionate than any real beetles or dragonflies I'd seen.

But I'd only known she made insects, not larger, more intelligent animals. Not horses.

And the look in Jules's glass eyes . . . but I turned away.

It was verging on daybreak, judging by the thin, gray streaks of light starting to leak through the workshop's one narrow window. I retreated to the door and turned the handle, letting the gears overhead take most of its weight.

Leaving the workshop was like pulling away from my mother's embrace. My skin prickled, and my clothes seemed to hang looser on my frame now that I'd left the warmth of the furnace behind. But I had no time for dallying. It was silliness to start missing Mother again, when I felt closer to her than I had since her death.

I climbed the stairs slowly, so they wouldn't creak. Before I closed the door, I took a last moment to peer down into the shadowed well of the cellar.

I took a breath, and blew out my candle.

MOTHER wrote that letter seven years before I read it. She knew she was dying; she had time to prepare. She didn't give me the same luxury.

But beginnings should go at the beginning. Let me start a bit earlier.

The beginning for me, really, was my mother.

She died when I was nine years old.

She was a great mechanic, and a greater inventor. Father made his fortune trading her work in Nordsk and the Sudlands—even in Faerie, before the quarantine. But he did good trade here in Esting, too; her little mechanical insects, set with jewels and forged from precious metals, were cherished in court. By the time I turned six, I had started helping her repair them.

The first time Father came home and saw Mother and me working together in the library, our arms smudged with grease, her brown and my blue eyes bright with interest and excitement, he laughed.

"She's not a miniature of you, Margot, you know," he said.

Mother glanced at me, dark hair falling in her eyes, and she brushed my own brown hair from my face. "Isn't she?" she asked.

Father laughed again, but his laughter was hard. "Surely we should think about a governess for her soon. She'll need to be ready for finishing school in a few years."

Mother looked up. "Certainly she will not," she said. "Nicolette will never be ready for finishing school. My parents shuffled me off to one of those places, and it nearly finished *me.*"

She always did love dramatics.

Father knew when he was bested, and with Mother, that was often. He nodded slowly, turning over the idea of an unfinished daughter in his mind. "A Sistren governess, at least," he countered.

I was looking down at the silver dragonfly in my hands, at the wing joint I'd been oiling, and I did not look up. But even very young children know their parents this well: I could *hear* Mother shake her head.

"I won't have those fastidious zealots under my roof, and you know it, William. I'll finish Nicolette myself, in my own way. I can teach her more than those simpering wimple-clad governesses ever could."

I could hear Father raise his hands in surrender too. "All right, Margot. The Lord knows she's more your child than mine, anyway."

I was. I am.

And so Mother became my teacher—though in truth, she was already. Ever since I could remember, she had read to me from her notes, had drawn blueprints based on the fanciful ideas I whispered to her in the library, and had given me gears and tools to play with. I was never allowed in her workshop, though. Father insisted it was too dangerous, and in this, at least, they managed to agree.

But even after her longest days in the shop—days I'd spend trailing after our kindly half-Fey housekeeper, Mr. Candery—Mother always visited me before I went to sleep. She came to my room to tell me her versions of bedtime stories. Instead of parables or Faerie tales, she fed me biographies of great scientists and mathematicians and philosophers, or histories of Nordsk, the Sudlands, and Faerie.

"When did we first discover Faerie?" I asked Mother one night, snuggling down into the large—ocean-huge, to my small self—bed in which I then slept. My stepsisters claimed it, like so much else, after Father died.

Mother nodded, knowing she'd told me a dozen times before. To get her to repeat a story, though, I had to find a different question every time, a different angle from which we could enter the tale. It was like fixing a machine so it ran better than it had before it was broken, she said; you had to be willing to forget what it had done before and look for what it *could* do.

I'd never asked quite that question before, so I knew I had won.

"Two hundred years ago," she began, "we discovered it. The Heir commissioned a ship and crew to find him a worthy bride, and they set out to voyage over the world. Nowhere in Nordsk or the Sudlands had they found a lady who met his exacting standards, and he held fast to the belief that the perfect wife waited for him in some as-yet-uncharted country.

"They sailed for months, Captain Brand and his crew of brave men and women—women were allowed at sea then, you know." Mother's eyes sparked. "At last, after months of empty, desolate ocean, they sighted land, a tall mountain rising up from the waves, its peak lost in a haze of sky.

"They set toward it at once, and they drew up on a beach of coarse blue sand. They anchored the *Bridegroom* and took the longboats ashore, and the first thing they did was plant Esting's flag in the ground.

"Beyond the beach, a lush jungle stretched out on either side of them. They had discovered not a small volcanic island as they'd first thought, but a whole new continent."

"Faerie." I sighed the word and settled deeper into my pillow.

Mother nodded. "They set off through the jungle, not

knowing what they would find. It took weeks to hack through the dense vegetation, and their naturalist, Lady . . . ?" She trailed off, eyeing me expectantly.

"Lady Candery!" I answered—easy to remember, because the lady in question shared her name with our housekeeper. This was part of our unspoken agreement too, Mother's and mine: she would tell me a story at bedtime, and I would prove how much I remembered from my lessons.

"Yes, Lady Candery. She recorded as many of the new plant species as she could, though she was bound to miss some, for they were all new to us. Do you remember any that she discovered?"

I nodded eagerly. I was always eager—almost desperate—to please Mother, to impress her. "Lovesbane, shadeblossom, Candery's bounty . . . um . . . silver orchid . . ."

"Good." She offered me a small, rare smile like a gemstone. "And after more than a month of struggling through the jungle, they finally came to its end. What did they find?"

"They found a road."

"And they followed that road for a night and a day, until they came to the Fey capital, to the tall, spiraling palace carved from the same gold-veined blue stone that made up the sand on the beaches."

Father came in then—he listened to the end of Mother's stories whenever he was home. She liked us to keep the beginnings to ourselves.

"And when they arrived in the court?" he asked, slipping his arm around Mother's shoulders and pushing his other hand back through his thick blond hair.

"They drove the flag into the floor in the courtroom, too," I replied, a recitation from the official state history books he'd brought me after his last trip. "They knew the Heir would find no bride there, only savages."

Father nodded. "And how did they know that?"

An easy question to my young self; the answer had been in that same history book. "The Fey are not truly people. They do not look or act like civilized men. The Lord made them to serve us and made us to care for them."

Mother stroked back a stray lock of my brown hair. "You've learned your new books' lessons well, sweeting. So Captain Brand and his crew claimed Faerie as a colony of Esting."

"And we have lived in peaceful dominion over them ever since." Father ended the story.

Mother looked up at Father for a long moment. She stroked my hair again, and though it seemed as if she wanted to speak, she said nothing.

Father dimmed my lamp, and they left the room.

"Those history books are wrong about at least one thing," Mother told me over tea the next day. She'd come up from the workshop for a little air, she said, and a little respite. I knew that respite for her meant a lesson for me, but I didn't mind. I always wished Mother would spend more time teaching me, not less.

Mr. Candery had told me to meet her in the library, and there he brought us a pot of clary-bush tea and thin sandwiches layered with radish and white goat's butter. I crunched happily through the sandwiches and drank the strong, colorless tea, relishing the warmth and energy it gave me. These days, Father was always complaining about the expensive Fey imports Mother insisted on keeping stocked in our kitchens. After their last argument about it, she'd stopped ordering Fey wines or dried fruits, but I was grateful that we still had the clary-bush. It was always my favorite tea: floral and sharp, at once a courtier's handkerchief and a knight's armor.

"What are the books wrong about?" I asked, tucking into another sandwich. Thin radish, sweet butter, speckles of salt. An unladylike swig of clear tea.

Mother usually paused to think before answering any of my questions, but this time her response was immediate. "Esting's dominion over Faerie is *not* peaceful." She spoke even more forcefully than usual. "There are rumors of—look at me, Nicolette, when I'm talking to you."

I glanced up guiltily. "I'm sorry, Mother." I'd been watching the painted fish on the inside of my teacup as they flitted through their china world, making tiny ripples and bubbles in the tea. Another Fey treasure, this tea set, one that Father had paid dearly for when he and Mother were still courting.

He never liked to see that tea set himself anymore, but it was special to us, to Mother and me.

To prove I'd been listening, I added, "There's talk of something, you said?" I had not yet begun to fathom that when Mother and Father disagreed about something, it meant that at least one of them had to be wrong; it had only recently occurred to me that they fought more often than they did anything else.

Mother's lips pursed. "The Fey have grown selfish with their magic, they say," she said. "They're not nearly so willing to give it to us as they used to be. I imagine they've begun to realize how valuable it is here, much as people like your father have tried to hide that fact from them. They're not *animals*, for the Lord's sake. They can think. And if they keep thinking, it won't shock me or anyone else with a brain if they decide to rebel."

People like your father . . . She'd always called him William before, even to me. To hear her say "your father" seemed distancing in a way that frightened me, in a way that I didn't like to think about.

"But can you still use magic, Mother? Can you still make the buzzers?"

It was the name I'd used as a toddler for Mother's mechanical insects, the ones that Father sold all up and down the continent, and that for years had been the height of style in the Estinger court. My methods for fixing them had improved rapidly in the last months, and I was longing for the day when Mother would decide I was ready to start building my own. I was convinced that day couldn't be too far off. But if she stopped making them entirely . . .

I'd always loved magic. It was just another tool, really, like coal power; it simply wasn't fully understood here. But I couldn't believe that it was as bad as Father's books seemed to suggest, and as some Estingers seemed to think it was.

I looked at Mother pleadingly.

"Oh, don't worry, darling," she said. "It would take much more than high prices to stop me."

She gestured casually toward Mr. Candery, who was conducting a pair of wheeled feather dusters around the bookshelves and mantel with small flicks of his elegant fingers. She'd been making more and more helpmeets for him lately, things that made his duties around the house easier. Mother's inventions and Fey magic—it was hard for me to imagine one without the other. "You might not always mention my new, ah, ideas to your father, though." She spoke as if she were joking, but there was something haughty, almost angry, in the way she smiled. She'd said "your father" again too.

I didn't like to think what that kind of smile meant. I'd never seen anything like it on her face before.

Father returned from his trip to the Sudlands a few weeks later, his trunks still full of Mother's insects and oddities.

"I sold barely a dozen, though the trade in mechanics

was the busiest I'd ever seen it," he said. "People don't like magic the way they used to."

"Nonsense," said Mother. "This country thrives on magic." She looked at him sharply. "So does this family."

Father grumbled and looked down; there was not much he could say to that. The house, Lampton Manor, was his family's, but he—and I—both knew well enough that Mother's inventions were what afforded us our wealthy lifestyle. It was even Mother's workshop, rumbling away under us, that heated our fireplaces and kept the household running with only Mr. Candery and a part-time maid serving us.

But then Father changed tactics. "There were Brethren everywhere in Esting City," he said. "The square was crawling with them. They were carrying banners, holding signs, preaching to the crowds. Saying magic was against the Lord's glory, against man's endeavor. Saying that the specks' tricks had made Estingers lazy and stupid, unable to do anything for ourselves. That we'll be sitting ducks when they turn against us."

Mother sucked in her breath at *specks* and *tricks,* and I knew enough to be shocked by Father's words myself, even if the sudden, feverish light in his eyes hadn't frightened me already. *Specks* was the worst Estinger word for the Fey, referencing their heavily blue-freckled skin, and to call magic *tricks* was an insult to the honesty of anyone who used it.

I waited for Mother to raise her voice, to ask whether Father was calling her a trickster. But she didn't; for a long while, she didn't speak at all. Then her face seemed to open up, like curtains, and what I saw behind her eyes was immensely sad.

"You used to love it too," she said. "What happened?"

Father kept looking at the floor. Finally, his voice measured and carefully neutral, he said, "Sometimes one finds one is wrong."

He stalked past us into the sitting room, where he stayed for the rest of the afternoon.

His next trip was only to Esting City for a few days, but when he came back, he said things were worse yet. There were rumors of an uprising in Faerie, and Fey brigands were attacking Estinger military and trade ships alike.

But it was not until the year I turned nine that I understood what the tensions with Faerie truly meant. That spring, Mother came home from one of her very rare social calls earlier than expected, her face ash-gray and sober. She called Father and me into the library, and Mr. Candery, too. Our housekeeper stood deferentially at the edge of the sofa where Father and I settled ourselves. Each of us tried, in our ways, to pretend patience while we waited for Mother to collect herself and give us her news. I fidgeted with my skirts; Father bit his nails. Only Mr. Candery's composure seemed unruffled—he stood there as quiet and stable as ever.

"The Queen has been poisoned," Mother said. "She is dead."

"Poisoned?" Father pulled his hand away from his mouth. A dot of blood grew on his ragged thumbnail. "With what?"

Mother looked at Mr. Candery, her eyes soft; I had rarely seen them softer. "Lovesbane. Her doctor gave her too much."

It was an herb that grew only in Faerie. Its medicinal properties were their own kind of magic, and it was the only cure for Fey's croup, a disease that had come back with Faerie's first explorers. Queen Nerali had been abed with the croup for months; a Fey doctor had been imported to treat her.

But if one takes too much lovesbane, it becomes a deadly poison.

Father shook his head. "I knew no good could come from Faerie," he said.

Mother stood. "No good?" she demanded. "And what of my work, then? What of the money you bring in selling my insects?"

Something she didn't say hung in the air too: what of Mr. Candery?

Father stood as well. They eyed each other, neither willing to concede.

Finally, he spoke. "Well, what will happen now?" His voice was flat, cool; he was speaking of the Queen's death, not our family's future.

Mother nodded, though not in agreement. "He's banished the Fey," she said. "King Corsin. He's banished all of them. They have to leave in a fortnight." Her gaze ticked for a moment toward Mr. Candery, then back to Father. "The part-Fey may remain. Mr. Candery will have two weeks' leave to stay with his mother, to say goodbye."

Father had all but applauded when Mother spoke of the banishment. Now he turned toward our housekeeper and frowned. "He can say his goodbyes in a day or less," he said. "That parent of his lives in Esting City, not two hours' ride from here."

"Mr. Candery says 'Mother,'" my own mother retorted, "so it is only right that we do the same."

Father gave her the kind of look that suggested what he wanted to say in reply was not fit for my ears.

Mother looked to me now. "I want to give them some time together," she said. "He'll likely never see her again."

"None of us will see any of them again, Lord willing," Father muttered. "Not in Esting, at least."

"William." Mother's voice was nearly a whisper now, but full of warning. She looked at me again, and so did Father.

He shrugged, stood up, and left the room.

Mother stared after him for a moment, all softness gone from her expression. Then she stormed out too, and a moment later, I heard the cellar door slam open and shut.

I never liked to see my parents argue; of course not, no child does. But I thought this was something worse, something of a different kind, than I had ever seen before.

Neither Mother nor Father returned to the library, though I waited there for them.

It was Mr. Candery who stroked my hair, and told me it was all right, and took me to my room. He gave me a book of old poetry to read and told me not to worry.

Our housekeeper came back from his goodbyes two weeks later, as quiet as ever. I wanted to ask him about it, but our friendship had never been founded on pressing questions—or on any kind of conversation at all, really.

So when he returned, I waited for him at the servants' entrance, silently regarded him as he hung up his hat and coat, and then reached up—he was still so much taller than I, though I was nearly nine and starting to grow faster—and took his hand.

He looked back at me, smiled a smaller smile than usual, and reached into his breast pocket. He pulled out a small, thin book: Faerie tales. He pressed one long finger to his lips.

I nodded. I understood what he did not say: I must keep the book secret, especially from Father. I would realize later that the book, like the Fey, had become illegal; then it just seemed like a secret between friends.

I knew that he wanted to be alone. I hurried up to my room to spend the afternoon in one of the ways I loved best. Soon I was immersed in a long story about a brave girl, a cave, and a magic fish.

I finished the book not long after supper; I've always been a quick reader. I crept back downstairs to the library, hoping to dig through Mother's engineering tomes and find something I hadn't yet devoured.

A wand of yellow candlelight lay along the floor where the library door had been left slightly open. Faint whispers followed the light's path, coming from inside.

I could not help myself: I stood behind the door, listening. I hoped I might overhear my parents reconciling, but the voice I heard was not Father's.

" . . . Brethren preachers on every street corner of Esting City," Mr. Candery murmured, "railing against magic, saying it rebels against the glory of the Lord. They insulted my mother and her kindred as they took to their carriages — and little better than cages they were. I shudder when I imagine what sort of Estinger ships will carry them home."

I heard Mother sigh. "What is there for us to do?"

Mr. Candery's voice grew still softer. "What is there for us, ever?"

Just then one of her beetles buzzed past me on its metal wings, flying through the cracked-open door into the library.

"Is the door open?" Mother asked. I heard the rustle of her skirts as she moved toward me, and I scurried away.

I came down to the library for lessons as usual the next day, but Mother was not there to meet me. I waited nearly an hour, ticked out on the elaborate mantelpiece clock Mother had made before I was born, but no one came.

Finally I decided to go to the kitchen to see if I could help Mr. Candery with anything. As I walked down the corridor, though, I saw him emerge from the cellar, closing the door silently behind him. When he saw me, he jumped as if startled—I'd never seen him even close to unsettled before.

"Your mother is ill," he said gently, handing me a large book Mother usually kept downstairs. "She wants you to spend the day with Copring."

"What's wrong with her?" I asked bluntly. I knew it had to be something serious if it kept her from our lessons, and even more so from working.

Mr. Candery looked down at me, his eyes kind and concerned. The fine lines in his blue-freckled face were deeper than usual; I had the sense that a less composed person would have sighed. "Fey's croup," he said.

I nodded and tried to look calm, but all I could think of was Queen Nerali, who'd died after contracting the same disease.

After Mr. Candery walked away, I realized that he hadn't told me not to worry.

I turned the pages of L. Copring's *Second Treatise on Mechanical Engineering* all morning, but for once I couldn't focus on my reading. I was overcome with anxiety, but I knew I was never to disturb Mother when she didn't want me.

My hands would not stay still, so I left my book and spent the afternoon fiddling with a mechanical beetle I'd nearly finished repairing the week before. At last I fastened the new wings I'd made to its back. I wound the tiny key at its head and watched it buzz, lopsided, out through the window.

For weeks, Father forbade me from visiting Mother; Fey's croup was especially dangerous for the young, he said. He wouldn't even enter their chambers himself, for fear of infection, but slept in one of the guest rooms. He had Mr. Candery methodically burn her dirty sheets and clothes. Everything she'd touched, he said, was at risk of contamination.

I couldn't stop thinking about our dead Queen, or the cure that should have saved her.

"Why hasn't Father bought any lovesbane?" I asked Mr. Candery one day over breakfast; Father and I rarely ate together.

He stared at me. "Have you asked him that?" he said.

I looked away, though I couldn't tell myself why. "No . . ."

"Good." His voice grew heavy with relief, but just as quickly turned sharp. "Never mention it, Miss Lampton. Never again."

It was the first time in my life that I felt I couldn't ask the question: *why?*

He knew me well, though, and he saw what I was afraid to say. "Remember the Queen," he said. "Remember what your father's been saying about my—about Faerie. He would be very angry if he heard you talk about buying lovesbane."

I felt something harden inside me. "He would be frightened, you mean." And then, with a flash of boldness: "Why don't you get it for her?"

He turned away. "I gave my savings to my mother when fe left," he said. "It would be years . . . and your father . . ."

When he turned back again, his face was as impassive as ever. "I shouldn't be telling you these things, Nicolette," he said. "Please don't ask me to. And now"—he gestured at Mother's elaborate mantelpiece clock—"I have to see to your mother."

He left before I had the chance to say anything else, but I didn't know what I would have said.

It was always Mr. Candery who tended Mother. He said he couldn't catch the croup himself, because of his Fey blood (though my books later told me that wasn't true).

Neither he nor Father would tell me how she was faring.

I spent all my days in the library, reading more and more and practicing as many repairs as I could on the mechanical insects and small machines that no longer interested Mother. I thought if I could only learn enough, only understand enough of her work, I could bring her back to health somehow. By fixing her machines, I hoped I could fix her, too.

But no one even let me see her.

One night, I crept up to her room. I needed to see her for myself, to see her sickness. . . . On some level I simply couldn't bring myself to believe that she was seriously ill. She was too vibrant, too strong, for that.

The door to her room seemed heavier than usual when I tried to push it open. The hallway was oppressively dark, but a shifting red firelight flickered over me when I crept inside. Was the fire kept high to speed Mother's recovery, perhaps to break a fever? I knew almost nothing about the symptoms of Fey's croup.

I stepped futher in. A too-clean metallic smell filled the air, and suddenly my eyes were watering. There was the huge, red, roaring fireplace, and there was Mother's old witchwood wardrobe. And there, across the room, shrouded in gray canopies, was Mother's bed . . .

Over the roar of the fire, I couldn't even hear her breathing.

Panic rose in my chest, and I flung myself not onto my sleeping mother, but back out the door and into the hall.

There was something terrible happening in that room. I knew Mr. Candery had been right to keep me away. Whatever it was, I couldn't bear to face it. Sometimes I think I still can't.

*

My memories of those last weeks splinter and scatter when I try to gather them up. The last weeks of Mother's life.

*

It was the smoke, finally, that told me. Not Father, who never knew how to talk to me to begin with, and not Mr. Candery. I smelled it from the library, where I was resetting the season hand on Mother's mantelpiece clock. It had been lagging a little in winter, though spring was fully come.

Then I turned and saw it, a dark calligraphy curling in through the open door: the wet, dirty smoke that comes from burning things that aren't meant to burn. Metal smoke, oil smoke.

All Mother's linens had been burned outside on the lawn that stretched between the back of the house and the beginning of the Woodshire Forest. That was clean gray smoke, cotton smoke, nothing like this.

I'm not sure how, but I knew. Right away, I knew the smoke was coming from the workshop. Perhaps it was the smell, oil and metal and coal, a perversion of the mechanic's scent that always hung around Mother.

My body tensed, and I stood still for a long moment, my hand still stretched up to Mother's clock. Then I ran.

I remember Mr. Candery there, in the cellar. Calm. Putting out the fire, now that its work was done.

Mother had taught me what to do with the different

kinds of fires that might result from her experiments. She always said I had to learn how to be safe before I'd be allowed in the workshop.

I knew how to help him, and I did.

I did not think about what the fire must mean until afterward, when we had put it out, to stop it from consuming the rest of the house.

I did not understand until Mr. Candery wiped the soot and sweat from his blue-specked cheeks, his usually smiling face racked with grief.

He'd been burning Mother's clothes and sheets for weeks, on Father's orders, but all those things could be replaced. Burning the workshop could mean only one thing.

"It's . . . she's . . ." I couldn't get the words out.

Mr. Candery opened his long arms, and he held me tight as I slumped against him.

He said nothing, but then, he had always been a quiet man.

FATHER had grown quiet in the weeks leading up to Mother's death, keeping to his new room and barely speaking. But now he was loud, with relief, I think, at his own survival—whether of the disease or of Mother herself I was not sure. He shouted every time he spoke.

I listened to him through a gray haze like smoke, thick in my chest and my eyes.

"We're safe," he crowed. "The worst is past. Nothing in the house can infect us now."

He'd thought the whole workshop must have been rife with infection, and he'd had Mr. Candery burn it all. Mr. Candery then rebuilt and walled over the rest of the cellar, work he insisted on doing himself. From that day until my sixteenth birthday, I had thought Mother's workshop was, like her, lost to me forever.

Sometimes the haze drifted away, and when it did, I knew Mother would want me to mourn her by learning from her.

I couldn't bear even to look at the cellar door, and I didn't want Father to know that I still loved the work Mother had loved—he was sure she'd contracted her disease from "some Fey trifle" he'd brought her. Even my beloved clary-bush tea had been burned.

But those things didn't mean that I stopped working. I still read her books that had escaped the fire, the ones kept in the library or that had happened to be in my room. She had taught me so much, even though I was only nine, and I taught myself more. Without her workshop supplies, I could not build new machines, but I could repair the little helpmeets that were left in the rest of the house. I had a small toolbox and several partially completed models that she had kept in the library to teach me, and I hid them from Father. I could do enough to keep learning.

In a burst of energy the night before Mother's funeral, I stayed up until dawn removing, oiling, and replacing the series of pistons that operated the large linen-folding machine she had installed last year in an upstairs closet. It ran off of some of the excess heat and smoke that rose up the chimney, so I decided that the chimney needed cleaning as well. I knew that needed a spell, not a machine, so I trotted downstairs to open the secret cupboard in the kitchen, the one where Mr. Candery kept his Fey cleaners—the cupboard he thought I didn't know about.

I knew it was there, even though I couldn't see the seamless place Mother had built into the wall and Mr. Candery had disguised. I pressed my hand against it as I'd seen Mr. Candery do a few times when he thought I wasn't looking. I waited for the metallic *pop* of springs that would precede the opening of the door.

Nothing happened.

I pushed harder, trying not to get frustrated. I knew it was the right spot, just to the left of a framed botanical illustration of silver orchid, one of Lady Candery's discoveries in Faerie. I never knew what had become of Lady Candery; she hadn't returned to Esting with the *Bridegroom*'s crew, and the one time I'd asked Mother, she'd dismissively said that she didn't know.

Candery was a common name, especially among the part-Fey, but I always liked to think that Lady Candery was one of our housekeeper's ancestresses, and that perhaps she shared his long, thin face and nose (though undecorated with Mr. Candery's sprinkling of blue freckles), as well as his quiet and gentle demeanor. I imagined her strolling through the jungle and caressing each new blossom or leaf the same way Mr. Candery handled Mother's finest Fey china.

This was the picture; this had to be the place. Maybe, I thought, I had to visualize it. I imagined the dusty bottles and jars and tins on their dustier shelves behind this hidden door, the slight glow of some, the way others seemed to suck away the light around them.

I pushed as hard as I could; still nothing. I slapped the wall in frustration.

There was a gentle coughing sound behind me. I turned and faced Mr. Candery, who was standing in his black nightclothes and cap with a glowing orb in his hand, watching me with a bemused expression.

"I—I'm sorry," I stammered. "I didn't mean—"

"Didn't mean to wake me, or didn't mean to prowl around my cabinets?" he asked quietly. "If it's the latter, I must say I disagree. You certainly did mean it."

I blushed and wondered if I would be punished . . . but then I saw that he was smiling.

"You are most welcome to prowl," he said. "It's only healthy in a child your age, and I'm delighted to see you do anything healthy these days. Here, let me assist you."

He stood beside me and placed his long, blue-spotted hand over mine. His skin was very warm.

"Allow Nicolette Delacourt Lampton," he murmured, "if you please."

I heard a pop and a whir, and the door to the cabinet opened.

"I was just looking for chimney powder," I muttered, embarrassed. "I knew I oughtn't to have—"

"It's all right." Mr. Candery smiled at me. "It's for the house's use that I keep these things, of course. It's really your father who—well." He shook his head slightly, and his smile faded. "I'm glad you can use these things, in fact, Miss Lampton. I think they may serve you well in the future."

He pressed the shaker of chimney powder into my hand

and closed the cabinet door again; it faded into the pea-green-painted wall. The orb he carried quenched in his grasp, and he walked away.

I wanted to ask him why he thought these things would come in handy; I'd once read that some of the Fey, even part-Fey, could occasionally tell the future.

But what my future could be now, without Mother, I didn't think I wanted to know. Besides, I thought Mr. Candery probably meant only that I might find a use for the chimney powder again.

I soon did; it seemed the chimney's heat powered many of Mother's helpmeets. But much as I enjoyed fixing what she had left behind and treasured the inventions themselves, I valued her library's books most of all. I never took them out of the room, for fear that Father would notice, not that he came home much after Mother's funeral. He wasn't interested in anything but trade now, especially since his most lucrative business, Mother's insects, was gone along with her. With King Corsin declaring ever-increasing tariffs on international trade, he struggled just to get by. I knew that if I had been older and had not needed looking after while Father was away, Mr. Candery would soon have been gone as well.

Neither of my parents had been eager hosts; now, with Father so often absent, no one ever visited. It was only Mr. Candery and me. Lampton Manor began to run a little wild . . . and so did I. The furniture grew faded and old-fashioned;

the windows warped. I forgot all my studies but Mother's books, and I lost the few acquaintances I'd had among the local children, the manor hidden away behind the Woodshire Forest as it was.

I became not a finished or educated young lady in any sense that Father would recognize, but educated far beyond my years in my own way. I read everything else in the library that interested me—mostly explorers' biographies and histories of Faerie. Between the books and Mr. Candery's stories, I fell in love with the very idea of the place.

My favorite thing about the Fey was their families; perhaps that was because of Mr. Candery, who felt as much like family as anyone I'd known. The books said the Fey thought of family differently than we did: they lived with friends instead of with a spouse and children. If a group of them wished to have a child, they all decided together who would bear it, and together they willed or wished—the translations differed—the child into being. Their rulers were Fey that everyone in the whole country had wished into existence together; they had traits and parentage from everyone they ruled.

When Estingers came to Faerie, they found that the same thing happened: if a human and a Fey both longed for a child together, soon one or the other would find themselves pregnant. This baffled the Estinger scientists who wrote about it, and their descriptions were filled with condemnation.

The historians who wrote about the Fey described this as a kind of savagery too, but I loved it. I wanted to believe that there were friends who loved each other enough to live together, to be families together. That the love between friends could create life too, just as romantic love could in Esting. I wanted to believe in such a family.

So when Father came home from one of his trips to tell me he was engaged to a woman with two daughters, I was thrilled. I thought I'd found the sister-friends I had dreamed of, the kind with whom I could make a new family.

It had not taken Father long to remarry — but, he explained to me, he didn't have much of a choice.

"We would be on the streets soon enough without the Halvings," he told me, pulling me onto his knee. I was ten years old then, and Father hadn't held me in years. He spoke as if he were addressing a small child, and I had to tell myself not to squirm away from him.

"Lady Halving will provide for me — for us both — and that's not nothing. Her love, and her money, might just be enough to get us back on our feet." He sighed. "And she is beautiful. My God, I never thought I could catch such a one. You'll see, Nicolette. It's nigh impossible not to love her on sight."

I spent months anticipating that love, waiting impatiently for Lady Halving and her daughters to arrive.

The day of the wedding, I was breathless and nervous. I couldn't stop my gloved hands from trembling.

I didn't see them until the ceremony, which was small

and simple, it being both Father's and Stepmother's second marriages. Piety, Chastity, and I were the only ones there with them, besides the Brother who performed the ceremony. Stepmother had dressed beautifully and modestly for the occasion, in a high-necked gray silk dress with a long line of tiny buttons down the back. She wore a simple headpiece, too, with a gauze veil that covered her face and tucked snugly under her chin. It was pinned in such a way that Father could not lift it, though at first he tried; in the end, he kissed her through the veil.

My new stepsisters, though, were opulent—that was the only word I could think of, watching them. They both wore elegant green dresses, Piety's the color of moss, Chastity's of unripe apples. They were beautiful girls, and from the moment I saw them, I was consumed with a longing . . . not to be them, precisely, but to learn from them. Their hair was shiny and curled; Mr. Candery and I barely managed to keep mine brushed. My dress, too, was nothing compared to theirs, a simple beige cotton Stepmother had sent me. I had appreciated the gesture, thrilled over it, even; but the color did not suit me, nor the cut. Watching my new sisters made me feel, for the first time, that I was plain.

Father and Stepmother left for their honeymoon directly after the wedding, and Piety and Chastity still had the rest of the year at their finishing school in the city, so I didn't get to have my new family quite yet. Instead, I went back to my solitary life at Lampton Manor with Mr. Candery.

I buzzed with energy for that month, fixing every insect I could get my hands on and helping Mr. Candery with anything he asked of me. My most special joy, though, was arranging the two adjoining guest bedrooms that would become Piety and Chastity's suite.

I agonized over how to decorate their rooms, what would please them best. I hung dried flowers in the corners for scent and color, and I fitted everything up with the little conveniences I'd learned to build with Mother: a lever by the heavy closet door opened it for them; a crank turned the vanity mirror so they could see themselves from different angles; a rotating wheel in the dresser moved their clothes so they could reach all of them easily. I even placed a simple clock of Mother's on one bedside table. It was a way to connect my old family with my new.

After the rooms were finally ready, with weeks still left before my new family would arrive, I started spending my time there, curled against the wall with whichever book I was reading that day. I would look up from the huge pages with their dense lines of tiny text, and I would picture Piety, Chastity, and myself lying on the floor together, reading to each other or inventing stories of our own. Those rooms were the site of so much imagined friendship; I was sure the reality would only be sweeter. I felt I could not wait for it a moment longer.

As it turned out, I did not have to wait long. They arrived at Lampton a full week before they had planned.

I was in the library when Mr. Candery told me my new family was home. I bounded to the sitting room in a joyful dither.

When I saw them, though, I stopped and stood still, and only stared.

Stepmother's face, though still lovely, was thin and strained. The lines around Father's mouth were deeper than they had been even a few weeks earlier, and he glanced around nervously, his gaze never resting anywhere for more than a few seconds. He paced the room, while Stepmother sat in the alcove and stared out the window.

They were frightened. I did not know why, but I could see that much.

Piety and Chastity were not with them.

"I always knew this would happen," Father muttered, shaking his head.

Stepmother nodded, her hand at her throat. "I know it, William. The Fey are not to be trusted; the Brethren have been telling us so for years. For centuries."

"Aye," said Father. "It was only a matter of—" He turned and saw me standing in the doorway. He rushed to me and swept me up in his arms—something he could barely do anymore, now that I was getting so tall. But he never seemed to notice that I grew.

Besides, he seemed to enjoy adding some drama to our reunion. "Nicolette, darling," he said.

Only Mother had called me darling before.

"I'm so glad you're safe."

I pushed back to look into his face, frowning. "Why wouldn't I be safe?"

He shook his head and put me down. "We have something to tell you girls." His eyes flicked toward Stepmother, then out the door. "Get your stepsisters, won't you?"

I had assumed Piety and Chastity were still at school. I hadn't seen them since the wedding, where they had kept to themselves, whispering and giggling. I had waved then and tried to smile through my shyness, but had not quite been brave enough to approach them.

Even though I was still nervous, I trotted eagerly back upstairs and knocked on their door. I could hear my own quick heartbeat.

I heard that giggling again too, coming from inside. At my knock, it silenced.

"Who is it?" one of them called. That voice's especially dulcet tones, I would later learn, were Chastity's; Piety's voice was always a little thinner than her sister's.

"Your sister," I called through the door, unable to keep the smile from my face or my voice. "Father wants us all to come to the sitting room."

The door opened. Piety and Chastity stood there, shoulder to shoulder, though Piety was shorter.

"Sister?" said Piety. "Who's that?"

"I think Nic-co-lette means herself," sighed Chastity, drawing out the syllables of my name until they sounded absurd.

"Oh." Piety smirked. "Goodness me, I didn't know who she meant. I think one sister is quite enough, don't you?"

Chastity lifted one dainty foot and kicked Piety in the shin. "Yes," she said, her voice cruel, and her sister winced and pressed her shin against her other leg.

"All right, Nic-co-lette, we'll come down," Piety grumbled.

I stepped back, intending to hold the door open for them. They pushed past with such force that it knocked against me, leaving what would ripen into a bruise on my arm.

I thought I should probably follow them downstairs right away, but I couldn't resist looking into their rooms first. I was dying to know how they had nestled themselves in with the decorations and arrangements I had made for them.

But the rooms were not as I'd left them. The dried flowers I had so carefully arranged were crushed into dustbins. The levers I'd made for their mirrors were pulled out, screws scattered on the floor. They had thrown open the dresser, but the rotating wheel was wrenched out—to make more room for all their clothes, it seemed, which even that huge dresser could not contain. Several more trunks, and hat- and shoeboxes by the dozens, littered the room. Stuffed animals cluttered the bedspreads Mr. Candery and I had chosen from the attic; the little embroidered pillows from Grandmother's time were strewn on the floor. Mother's clock was nowhere to be seen.

And the books I'd left for them were in a pile next to the fireplace, splayed open, pages crumpled. I rushed forward to gather them up. There wasn't even one that hadn't had a page ripped out already. And in the fire I saw a few smoldering scraps of green leather, of the board that went underneath it, and I knew that some of the books were already lost entirely. I knelt at the hearth, and before I could stop myself, I reached into the fire to gather up a few of those scraps. Of the books, at least, I would save whatever I could.

My eyes stung—from the smoke, I thought. Even kneeling by the fire with ashy, blistered fingers, torn-up books in my lap, I lectured myself that I shouldn't make too much of what Piety and Chastity had done. If I had moved somewhere new, I told myself, I would have wanted to make it my own too.

But I was ten years old, and lonely, and preparing my new sisters' rooms had become my special delight. I had spent so much time there, dreaming of them, making the rooms just the way I would want my new room in my new house to be, if our places were reversed.

I was embarrassed to find tears pricking at my eyes. I closed the door and started down the stairs to rejoin Father.

It was only that they didn't know, I told myself. They couldn't have guessed that it was I who had done all of that for them.

I walked back to the sitting room. Piety and Chastity had settled together on the love seat at the far side of the room. Father was still pacing; Stepmother was still perched on the window seat. I took the brocade-backed chair near the fire, the one Mother used to sit in. It felt much too big for me.

"All right, children," said Father. "We have to tell you something."

Piety and Chastity looked to Stepmother. I kept watching Father.

"You thought we would be gone another week or so, I know," he said. "I hope that at least you are glad to see your parents home so soon."

"Mother pulled us from school," Piety said. "We were just about to start our dance lessons."

I was filled with a sudden curiosity and envy. Dance was hardly something Mother would have taught me. There wasn't much time for it between engineering and theoretical physics, and neither she nor Father had been much for dancing.

"Oh, I know, darling," Stepmother said. "Worry not. I'll have you both finished nonetheless. We simply wanted you out of danger."

My stepsisters' eyes widened; mine stayed fixed on Father. My curiosity about dance lessons had lasted only a moment, and now I just wanted Father to tell me why he had come home.

"Danger?" I asked. "Father, what happened? Why are you back so early?"

Father nodded. "We came back because of some news from Esting City. Heir Philip has been killed."

"Murdered," Stepmother said, raising her long, elegant hand from her neck to her mouth. "Assassinated by one of those Fey savages. It seems there's nowhere safe now."

"No need to scare the children," Father said.

I needed no looking after in that respect; I didn't think there was any reason why a Fey assassin who had killed the Heir might come after powerless young girls living in the country.

But Chastity, to my surprise, broke into tears.

"Philip!" she cried. "He—he—he would have been bride-searching just when we—" She buried her face in the upholstery of the love seat and sobbed.

Piety managed to contain her woe better than her sister, but her lip trembled as she turned toward her mother. "What an awful thing," she said, but I could tell she meant awful for her, not for the young man who had died.

Stepmother nodded resolutely. "I know, girls," she said, "but I think, truly, that this may turn out to be a blessing. The younger prince, Christopher, will be of age to start the Heir's training in a year and a half, and he's closer to your own ages, only thirteen now. Besides, Heir Philip was likely to search out his bride abroad, as so many of them have done—as his own father did, the fool." She frowned. "Perhaps this will serve as a reminder that foreigners are not to be trusted, not to be brought into the palace."

I finally looked away from Father, toward Stepmother. "There were really Fey in the palace?" I asked. "I thought King Corsin had banished them all."

Stepmother looked at me with something between condescension and suspicion. "And what do you know of it?" she asked, but kept speaking before I could answer. "King Corsin invited the Fey ruler to the palace for negotiations—he's always been softer on them than Philip, and it seemed he was reconsidering the banishment. The Brethren protested against the invitation altogether, of course, as well they should have." She looked up at Father.

He nodded and continued. "Just days after the Fey arrived," he said, "Heir Philip fell ill. Lovesbane works in a sneaking way like that—an overdose will spread through the body and kill you slowly. Who else could have administered it but the Fey, especially after what they did to Queen Nerali? King Corsin listened to the Brethren after that. The Fey ruler is in prison, and the judgment on whether he will be extradited or executed will come soon enough." He sighed and adjusted his collar.

I noticed how he pointedly used *he* instead of *fe,* the pronoun that most Estingers use when speaking of full-blooded Fey, who are neither male nor female in the common sense.

It wasn't as insulting as calling them specks, but Mother would never have stood for it.

Did he remember nothing of Mother, of her predictions that something just like this could happen, a rebellion among the Fey? Or did he only remember her disease, her stubbornness, the way even I had to wonder if she had loved him in the end?

I thought I ought to say something, but in that room, at that moment, I was suddenly afraid to speak my mind. I wonder sometimes if I should have guessed, even then, what was to come.

Stepmother rose from the window and went to stand behind Piety and Chastity. "I did not want my daughters anywhere near the city with that murderer there, locked up or not. It's not safe for them until he is gone. It's not safe for anyone."

"We'll be safe here," said Father, walking to her and putting an arm about her waist. "Don't worry, dearest."

They stood there, framing Piety and Chastity on the love seat. I watched from Mother's chair, not quite able to stand and join them.

I had hoped that the first few weeks with my new family would be a blissful haze of new friendship and bonding; instead we all spent it nervous, quiet, waiting for news from the city.

After Heir Philip's funeral, King Corsin extradited the Fey

ruler back to Faerie on a prison ship—Father was surprised that fe had been allowed to live, but it seemed the younger Estinger prince, Christopher, had asked for leniency. Still, once the Fey ruler was delivered home, King Corsin imposed a total quarantine on the country. Father had just left on his next trade route when the news came out. No ships, Fey or Estinger, were allowed in or out of the Faerie ports; no Fey goods or magic could be traded at the markets. Whole bushels of lovesbane were burned in town squares, like effigies.

We heard—or I overheard, from the visitors Stepmother entertained—about part-Fey all over the country rising up against the King, decrying the new law, even whispering of a full revolution.

But King Corsin, Stepmother's visitors assured her, had sent his troops out to quell the uprisings. These same friends reported back that the near-revolution had been tamped down with very little bloodshed.

There was some blood, though. There was Father's.

Mr. Candery answered the door that day, as he always did. The black-liveried courier at the door, though, took even our staid housekeeper by surprise. I heard him gasp from where I was sitting in the library; it was the only room I could retreat to with any hope that Piety and Chastity would not disturb me. I was reading one of Mother's engineering books.

I rose, but Stepmother reached the door before I did, coming from the front sitting room. She gestured Mr.

Candery away; he retreated to the kitchen. I stood still behind her.

"Madame," the courier said, saluting her solemnly. He handed her a thick black envelope, *To the wife of William Lampton, Lampton Manor, Woodshire* inscribed on it in an official-looking silver print.

I knew the ritual from a few novels I had read. It was one accorded to the widows of men who had died in battle.

All I could think, at first, was that Father had been a trader, not a soldier, and that there had never been a less warriorlike man in the world. Father was smart and slick and quick-thinking; he could talk anyone into anything, except Mother. He had never had to fight in his life.

But Stepmother took the letter and nodded, then swept the deep curtsy that was her part of the ritual. She opened the letter and read it silently and excruciatingly slowly.

Her voice, when she spoke, was even and low. "Thank you for delivering this news," she said, "much as I regret to receive it." It was as if she were reciting lines from a play.

"Madame," the courier said again, with another salute. He turned away and mounted his waiting horse.

Stepmother closed the door behind her and turned back into the hallway. She stared at the letter for a few moments. It seemed to me a very long time.

Then she looked up at me, and her face did not change at all. It was still that perfect, cold mask, that lovely icon.

She swept past me, down the hall and then up the stairs to her room.

I stayed there, in the doorway, staring after her.

Then I ran to the kitchen, where Mr. Candery was standing by the table, and threw my arms around him. He had held me when Mother died, and I knew he was the only one who would hold me now.

And he did. Tears bled down my face, and my ribs racked with huge, shuddering, painful breaths that I could not control. I was vaguely aware that it was not just grief I felt—not entirely—but also panic. What would happen to me now? The thought only frightened me further, and I collapsed entirely, sobbing and wailing. Mr. Candery kept holding me close.

I don't know how much time passed. At last the panic began to subside, and I felt myself go still as a haze of exhaustion came over me, too thick to see through.

Mr. Candery lifted me up and carried me, nearly sleeping, to my room.

When I finally woke up late the next morning, that fog still surrounded me, denser even than the one that came after Mother's death. I remembered the violence of the last day's sobs, how my body had shaken inside Mr. Candery's gentle hold, but I could not find the place in myself where that violence, that grief, had come from. I did not even want to know how Father had died. I didn't want to be able to see him that way in my mind: his body still and cold, torn apart or shot, simply for being in the wrong place at the wrong time. . . . Any thought of that just made me pull the blank fog tighter around myself again. For the first time in my life I didn't want to know, or understand, anything.

Everything was gray inside me, and quiet, and thicked with haze.

✷

I stayed in bed until Mr. Candery called me down for lunch; after I ate, I went to the library, always my safest place. I opened one of Mother's books and stared at the first page, still wrapped in the blankness that had settled over me while I slept.

Some time must have passed, and then Mr. Candery came in. I thought he would tell me it was time for supper.

Instead, he sat down on the couch and gestured for me to sit next to him; I did. He smiled sadly at me for a long moment, but said nothing.

"What is it, Mr. Candery?" I finally asked.

"Miss Lampton," he said gently, "I'll be leaving in the morning."

I stared at him. My first thought was *of course he will.* It was what people did; it was how my story went. Mother, Father, and now Mr. Candery. Everyone left.

"Why?" I asked, nearly whispered.

Mr. Candery shook his head. "They won't keep anyone but you now." He looked at me carefully, but I didn't yet understand his meaning. He sighed and started again. "Be careful of her," he said, serious and gentle as he always was. "Of your stepmother. Don't let her wear you down. Mr. Lampton would have said it's not my place to say so, but—well, it's someone's place, and there's no one else to say it. Be careful, Nicolette."

He touched my hand where it lay on the page, a finger under the line I had stopped reading. Everything was a broken line for me in those days. I was slipped into the empty spaces between words.

"I've tried to make things as easy as possible for you, after I leave," he said. "I've thought something like this might happen, ever since Heir Philip . . . well. But you'll find the house easier to manage than it might otherwise be, if you let the spells, and your mother's machines, do their work. I've locked them all away from everyone but you, like that cupboard was locked, do you remember?" He smiled fondly for a moment, then grew somber again. "I know Lady Halving won't hire anyone else to help you."

"Help me?" With the haze in my mind, I wasn't sure what he meant.

He nodded. "You'll be taking over care of Lampton, I'm afraid." He went on before I could say anything. "She won't hire anyone to help you, but you can help yourself, Nicolette, more than you know." He wasn't smiling now, and his quiet voice was urgent. "You can build things, fix things. Don't forget."

I hadn't forgotten, of course, as Mr. Candery well knew. He had brought me worn-down gadgets of Mother's to fix often enough, and had always gone to the village to find me little notions I needed for the small projects and experiments I dreamed up from reading Mother's books. I couldn't do much without a workshop, but if Mr. Candery hadn't been there, I couldn't have done anything. He had not been averse to continuing Mother's brand of education, at least.

"I know," I said, slowly. "I'll be all right." I said it disaffectedly, but I thought it must be true. I had survived through all of this, and I would continue to do so; I just had to wait out the days, the empty spaces. All the days until something better might come.

Mr. Candery smiled at me, gently, one last time. He stood. I thought he might say goodbye, but he only turned away and said, "don't stay up too late."

After Mr. Candery left and Stepmother made it clear that I was to replace him, I fell easily into a new routine at Lampton—much more easily, perhaps, than I should have, barring that one screaming fit the first night I cleared the table. Rules fit in nicely with the haze I walked through; I didn't really have to think about anything. Not the deaths of my parents or losing Mr. Candery, not the way my new family had turned me into a servant.

Years passed in that haze, and I hardly noticed. I took everything in stride; even when Stepmother decided to convert the library into a receiving room, I simply rescued a few favorite volumes before the booksellers came, hid them in the kitchen, and continued about my chores. Some smothered voice inside me might have been crying out at the loss of the library, the last place in the manor where I'd felt really safe, but I paid that voice no mind. Now was a time not for anger, but for survival. I would survive. I knew that was all I could do.

I woke early every day, added new wood to the fires, and went out to fetch the eggs and milk for the Steps' breakfast. I kept the supplies in a cupboard that was cooled by a small tin fan I'd made myself; a drop of Fey cooling water once a month, just behind the fan, was enough to keep milk from turning sour. What I would do when the cooling water—not to mention Mr. Candery's other Fey supplies—ran out, I did not know, because they were all illegal now. But I wasn't running low yet, and I was too sad, too bored, too . . . too passive . . . to address the problem before it began to press on me.

I took the dough for the day's bread out of Mother's kneading bowl with its twin wooden fists, shaped the loaves, and put them in the oven. While the bread baked, I measured tea leaves into another machine and listened to it start to heat. I laid out breakfast carefully, and any spills or crumbs I left were swept up by another small spell.

Sometimes, in passing, it occurred to me that I should worry about all the little illegal magics I used, but Mother had trusted them, as had Mr. Candery. I'd never been able to see them as anything but blessings.

When I had spare moments, I would read the few books I'd hidden away, or repair and maintain the machines that were showing signs of wear. I had not forgotten Mr. Candery's advice to do whatever I could for myself. I had to be good at repairs—if Mother's machines had stopped polishing the boots or cleaning the fireplaces, I would never have been able to do everything.

So I led a busy, if haze-smothered, life for the years between Father's death and my sixteenth birthday, when I found the workshop. I never expected much of anything to happen, and nothing much did. I was in a constant state of waiting for things to begin.

PART II

I OPENED my eyes to Jules standing on the desk, butting my arm with his glass forehead. He looked up at me, and I could hear the gears inside him ticking. His glass-on-metal whinny scraped my ears, and tiny curls of steam puffed from his nostrils. I smiled down at him.

It was only my third night in Mother's workshop, and I hated that I'd wasted time by drifting off . . . even though I had been exhausted since that first sleepless night on my birthday, because I'd spent all the time I wasn't cleaning for the Steps down here. I realized, looking at the little mechanical horse on my desk—something like a dream himself—that I hadn't dreamed, or slept much at all, in three days.

Still, there was a part of me that didn't feel tired, that in fact felt awake for the first time in years. I wore myself out reading through the engineering books in Mother's studio, more advanced than anything she'd kept in the upstairs library; cataloguing her supplies, the pistons and rods and screws, the hammers and wrenches and counterbalances; and learning to work the furnace, the glassblower, and the mechanized drills. This was a bright, sharp kind of exhaustion I felt, the kind that comes from excitement and engagement and *work.* It was the very opposite of the vague haze I'd moved through for the last six years, nearly as asleep as Jules had been in his stable-box.

Besides, I told myself that my chores would get easier with each passing day, as I could now repair Mother's machines much more quickly, and much more effectively. I even hoped to supplement them with a few inventions of my own.

The first few months after my birthday passed in that buzzing, vibrant exhaustion. I was perhaps most grateful for the sewing machine, which helped me speed through my least favorite chore. It handled in a flash the long seams that used to take me hours, but I still had to step rhythmically on a pedal to power it and guide the fabric with my hands. I did this in the studio, but I would often glance up from my work at the second hidden door, dreaming of the drawers full of gears and washers and screws that lay beyond it, and the tubes and sheets of metal leaning against the walls, calling to me. The glassblower in particular attracted my attention. Jules stayed at my elbow, and every few hours, I fetched him coal, for I'd found there was indeed a tiny furnace in his belly.

Every day I sorted through another corner of one of the

two rooms that made up Mother's workshop, hoping to learn more about all the projects she'd left behind for me to finish. I started by cataloguing her books, and because I read them each as I went, it was a long and slow process. Nearly two months passed before I shelved the last of them.

Most wonderful of all, I found other survivors from Mother's insect-making days, the buzzers I'd so loved as a child, hidden in little boxes between her books or forgotten at the backs of drawers. By my fourth day in the workshop I had discovered two fat, gold-plated beetles; a week later, a many-jointed caterpillar that made loud ratcheting noises as it crawled across my desk joined their ranks. Within a month, I had found three spiders with needles for legs and steel spinnerets loaded with real thread; a large copperwork butterfly, so light and delicate that even with a metal wingspan the size of my two hands, it could glide and flutter about the room; and a little fleet of five dragonflies, their wings set with colored glass. They flew or crawled or buzzed about just as real insects and spiders do, but they did not seem as intelligent as Jules—just as, I supposed, real insects compared to horses. Jules himself adored them; sometimes he would nicker at the buzzers, and they would seem to do what he told them. I began to think of them as his minions. They were as much of a mystery as he was. They lit up the workshop with their glittering, metallic movements, and it was almost like having bits of Mother back again.

Mother's fortune had come from little clockwork bugs

like these, and I dared to think that if I could learn her secret, I'd be rich enough to buy my own workshop in no time at all. But I couldn't find anything in her books or journals that explained how she'd made them come to life . . . and I couldn't begin to fathom how I might recreate machines that moved of their own volition, not without understanding whatever magic she had used. Besides, whatever her secret had been, I knew it had to be illegal now.

But even though I couldn't replicate her automata, I loved the ones I found. And I loved Jules most of all.

The first time I donned Mother's goggles, I laughed at my bug-eyed reflection in a metal sheet. When I removed the goggles and glanced in the warped surface again, I looked enough like my memory of her to make me think I had seen a ghost.

I found her journals as I went too, scattered among the encyclopediae and dictionaries and manuals and books of engineering and theory and philosophy. I only ever found one journal at a time, never two together. I began to see that she had written them along with the books she was reading and that the spidery handwriting lining the margins of her books matched up with daily entries in her journal, over a span of at least ten years.

Scattered in the journals were more personal accounts as well, tales of my father early in their marriage, later subsumed by her pregnancy, and then by my infant self. These were all secondary, marginalia to the more important work of her life, which was clearly always her *work.* I had known this as a small child, and sometimes I'd wished I had been her center; now I thought I understood. She loved me—I'd always known that—but she loved her work too, and her inventions would not spring up without her, the way I would grow whether she spent every moment by my side or no.

Nicolette grows so quickly. Already she is not content to sit in her crib, napping or cooing at the mobile I made her. Already she wants to explore, so William has convinced me to keep her above stairs, where the furnace and the metals and the tools cannot hurt her. I miss my girl, but she is so quick, and certainly she will grow without me. My other children will not.

Her other children. I did not know what to make of that. I put Mother's journals down and decided to focus on building, not reading, for a while. I pretended my heart didn't ache.

One evening, after I put Jules and his minions away, I had my first revelation. I'd turned away from the shelf that held Jules's stable-box and back to the sewing machine. It was large, covering a good third of the drafting table that I'd pushed against the wall opposite my desk, but both machine and table were dwarfed by the absurd, frothy volume of fabric for Chastity's newest dress. I was glad for the machine, but I still hated sewing for the Steps. I resented it for the time it took away from my reading and my inventions. But that night, as I stared at the machine's iron frame, I realized that with a few modifications, Jules and his minions could do my sewing for me.

After consulting Mother's books, I selected my tools. I built Jules a harness from the leather laces of Chastity's too-small winter boots. A pulley system with a weight on the pedal allowed Jules, moving at a steady walk, to power the machine as quickly as I had done. With the minions' help to guide the fabric, he could at least do my straight seams for me—and depending on how much I, and he, could teach them (for it seemed that just as I could speak to and teach Jules, he could speak to and teach the buzzers), perhaps they could eventually sew curved seams too, or even detailed work.

All those hours of freedom I'd gain . . . I was breathless with relief just imagining them. They were hours I'd spend working, mostly, but doing *my own* work. And—oh, miracle—I could sleep.

As it turned out, they were natural tailors. Soon all I had to do were the finest details, the buttonholes and pleating, which took far less time, though still too much for my taste. I hoped they would learn even those before long. But I also needed to make the Steps believe the work was mine, so I sewed whenever I had to linger in their presence.

I still spent one hour with them each evening to hear Stepmother read Scriptures. This nightly ritual was a remnant from Father's time, the last lie that kept us a seeming family.

I stitched as easily as I could with my clumsy hands—or, rather, hands that I had often thought clumsy, but that created the machines of my mother's design with an ease that still felt foreign. Every time I drove the needle into my fingers, I had to remind myself that I was not truly clumsy, only unskilled at this particular craft.

Piety and Chastity sat opposite my little stool, alternately lounging on their purple fainting sofa or staring bluntly out the window. Stepmother read each night's Scripture with a sensuousness that never entered her voice when she spoke her own words. She had used the same tone to recite her wedding vows to Father—soft and dark, full of hidden seductions. What a lie, her voice.

On one particular evening, though, there were to be no Scriptures. Instead, Stepmother drew an envelope from her apron pocket—though she never lifted a finger for housework, she nearly always wore an apron. It gave her the appearance of constant dutifulness.

She pulled a thick, square card from inside, so rich that it was almost cloth. The edges ran with a tastefully subtle pattern of angled lacework, punched into the paper by no human hand, surely, but by magic or machines.

"His Highness King Corsin," she announced to a suddenly attentive audience, "invites us to a Cultural Exposition Gala, to be held at the start of the New Year. The judged Exposition will celebrate and support, through a generous Royal Endowment, the advancements of Esting's most brilliant inventors and artisans, as well as . . ." Her voice trailed off as she scanned the invitation.

Piety and Chastity leaned forward, rumpling their full skirts. My ears tingled to hear what Stepmother so casually omitted. A judged exposition, with funding for inventors!

" . . . a ball on New Year's Eve, at the palace, to commence the Exposition festivities." Here Stepmother's voice trilled, and a tremble came into her elegant fingers. "My dear girls, your chance has come."

Piety and Chastity clasped hands and nodded heads, their respective chestnut and yellow curls bobbing in unison. Their faces, Piety's oval and Chastity's heart-shaped, equally lovely and equally vacant, shone with rapture.

An Exposition . . . Royal Endowment . . . inventors and artisans . . . I cringed as my needle stabbed under a fingernail. I looked down at the bloodstain spreading into the pleats on Piety's chemise. The pain soon fled—as would the blood, with a good scrubbing.

I pulled my work close, hoping to keep my accident from notice.

I had no such luck. "Mother," Piety whined, "Nick's ruined my chemise. I need a new one." Her plump cherry of a mouth turned to pouting.

She and Chastity refused to call me by my full name, Nicolette—I think they were jealous of its cadence, or its lack of implied virtue. They had christened me Nick at Father's funeral.

"Then of course you shall, sweet one," crooned Stepmother.

"Me too," said Chastity, for probably the twentieth time that day. Her words were usually an echo of Piety's. "Me too, if Pie gets one." She narrowed her eyes at her sister. Piety wrinkled her nose.

Stepmother silenced them with a raised hand. "My dear girls, you will both have new wardrobes in full by the Exposition," she cooed.

I barely managed to contain my horror. Was I expected to produce these wardrobes, and by the New Year? Winter was nearly here already. Even with Jules and the minions, I couldn't see a way.

That night, I doubled my usual hours in Mother's workshop. I worked so intently that I didn't notice time passing until a ray of sunlight issued through the one narrow window in the study and hit me square in the eye. It was too late for sleep then—I had to have breakfast on the table by the time Stepmother came down at seven. Even so, ideas buzzed through my head, and I wouldn't have been able to sleep even if I'd gotten the chance.

Stepmother was clearly excited too. She ate her poached egg on toast with pleasure, even enthusiasm. She usually liked to act as if eating were beneath her, a necessity she only suffered through to stay strong for her dear daughters.

She even talked to me as she ate. "Go into town today," she said, pricking open her yolk with the tines of her fork, "and consult the milliner. You'll need plenty of fabric for the dresses Piety and Chastity described to me last night." She shook her head fondly. "They always know how to look their best, bless their hearts. They'll grow out of this vanity when they marry, as I did, but Brother Lane says there's no harm in letting girls be girls."

She looked up at me as she said this, the first time we'd made eye contact all morning. I was expected to look at her whenever I was in her presence, of course, but she rarely returned the favor.

She scowled. "Put your hair up," she said. "There's no need to let it hang down your back like a harlot. Whom are you trying to attract?"

I pulled my worn shawl over my head and wrapped my hair inside it, then tied it in a large knot behind my neck. Visions of Piety's waist-length hair sprang to mind, but I ignored them. Never mind that binding my hair up tightly gave me headaches—in Stepmother's eyes, my only motive was to lure away one of her daughters' many suitors.

Piety and Chastity appeared at the top of the stairs. They walked down slowly, gracefully, posing for each other as they went. Their soft cotton nightgowns floated around their ankles. I scratched at my rough linen bodice.

"I want bacon," yawned skinny Piety. She smirked at Chastity, who was watching her plump figure and would have only dry toast this morning. Each sister secretly envied the other's shape, but of course they would never admit it.

"My dear girls," crooned Stepmother, "Nick is going into town today. Please tell her your wishes for your new wardrobe—particularly your ball gowns. She'll want to start working on them right away."

Oh, yes, I thought. *I can't wait.*

Piety wanted a white gown, cap-sleeved. "Bridal," she sighed, her eyes glazing over. "Cream lace all over and orange blossoms in my hair."

Chastity cut in. "Satin for me," she purred, "bright white, like an angel."

Piety prodded Chastity's round arms. "She'll want long sleeves," she snickered.

Chastity yanked Piety's hair, and they both shrieked.

Stepmother glared at them, and they sat down quickly and silently.

"I should go," I said. "I'll need as much time as possible."

Chastity snorted. "You'll get as much time as we give you," she said.

"Where's my bacon?" asked Piety.

THREE hours later, I finally walked out the door, wondering when I would ever have time for my own work. As I hurried to the Woodshire town center, one meager street of little shops, I contemplated ways to get supplies. There was more than one abandoned machine along the overgrown road into Woodshire: I passed a rusted-out water heater, a chisel plow, and a small, bent carriage frame. I eyed all of them eagerly, but the metal was too degraded to be reworked or even salvaged. The only parts worth saving were the thin rubber tires on the carriage wheels, but even they were dubiously weathered; besides, Mother's workshop was fairly well stocked already. And I needed plenty of things for the Exposition that I'd never find at the side of a road: fine cloth for a new dress of my own, for instance, if I wanted anyone to take my wares—and me—seriously. Stepmother had credit at the milliner's, but she'd receive an itemized list of her charges at the end of the month. I couldn't add anything extra for myself without her knowing.

I realized as I thought these things that I had already decided to attend the Exposition, that I wasn't just daydreaming about it. The ball didn't interest me as much, but if I could show my work, the designs I had begun conceiving during late nights in the workshop, maybe I could finally become a real inventor, like Mother had been.

The milliner and tailor was a dour middle-aged man named Mr. Waters, slow to speak and rather joyless. But he was always honest and fair in his trade, and I respected him.

He looked up through a scruff of lank salt-and-pepper hair when I entered the shop. The bell on the door frame rang a second time as the door bounced shut behind me. Curtains covered the windows, protecting the many-colored bolts of fabric from sun damage. I consulted my scribbled list, depressed by the Steps' lack of imagination.

"Good morning," I said, as cheerfully as I could muster. "I need white today. Lots and lots of white."

Mr. Waters didn't answer. At first I assumed this was only his customary curtness, but his silence continued much longer than usual. He was staring down into his hands; when I looked closer, I saw that the object of his attention was a broken length of grooved rubber. I recognized it immediately as a timing belt, larger than the one on my own sewing machine, but functionally identical. It was a crucial part. If it had broken, the rest of the motor was likely in utter shambles. Mr. Waters' trade had already suffered in the years since the quarantine on Faerie, and I could guess from his expression that he couldn't afford to have his machine fixed.

As he gazed down at the belt, I watched his usually expressionless face melt into despair. "It's those confounded new machines," he said. "Coal powered, you know. Chap who sold it to me said I'd sew seams ten times as fast. Said even my poor arthritic mother could use it painlessly. He was a good salesman, that lad. Paid him a fair portion of what this shop's worth for the damned thing not a month ago." He let out one brutal laugh. "Course he was a Nordsken lad, wasn't he? Long gone now, back to his prairies. Not that I could afford a mechanic anyway, not with what I paid out."

He squinted up at me through light brown eyes magnified by thick glasses. "I'll sell you the fabric," he said gruffly, "but I can't do much more for you, Miss Lampton."

I admit that part of my goodwill toward Mr. Waters came from his tendency to call me that: my father's name, a small reminder of what I had once been. Of course, back when everyone called me Miss Lampton, I'd never had occasion to set a patent-booted foot in his shop. Things were different now.

Mr. Waters was a stickler for class distinctions, and my family's past wealth kept me above him in his eyes. This was the one aspect of his personality I did not respect, though

I had to appreciate it when everyone else insulted and harangued me. Once in a while, he even helped me with my sewing, free of charge and free of Stepmother's knowledge. I would have helped him even without my pressing need to barter for extra fabric.

And all at once, I knew how I would obtain the extra fabric I needed to attend the Exposition.

"I could repair your sewing machine, Mr. Waters."

His doubting guffaw caught me off guard. "Oh?" He chuckled, all class distinctions gone for the moment. "And how will you manage that?"

I cleared my throat and, straightening my spine to its full length, I looked Mr. Waters in the eye. "That's the timing belt," I explained calmly, reminding myself that he did not yet have any reason to think me capable. "The rubber's snapped, see? When the belt broke, it would have thrown off the timing of every cog in the motor. I'd say most of them are damaged now, too. A needle or pin, or some such thing, must have broken while you were sewing and flown in between the main pulley and that belt."

"A pin broke . . . that's so," Mr. Waters said quietly. His face had resumed its usual neutral expression, but there was respect, even admiration, in his eyes.

I felt myself starting to smile. "Skill with machines runs in my family, you see."

"Really?" he said. "I don't remember your father being

much good with moving parts." His eyes lowered. "He was a good man, don't misunderstand me. A real good man."

This touched me so deeply that I wasn't even tempted to explain—besides, there was a reason Mother had kept her inventions anonymous. Few people thought a woman capable of mechanical brilliance like hers. I could hardly expect Mr. Waters to believe that my mother, not my father, had been the expert mechanic.

"Thank you," I whispered.

"Well," he said briskly, handing me the part, "you can't do more harm to it, at least, and I'll thank you for trying."

Turning the long, ridged bit of metal over in my fingers, I took a deep breath and sent my mother a silent prayer to help me prove myself in this.

Mr. Waters ushered me behind the counter and through a doorway into a back room I had never noticed before. There an old woman sat knitting in a rocking chair, her foot tapping on the floor to keep her chair moving. She lifted her toes and rotated her ankle, and I heard her worn joints grind and click.

Her stitches were tiny, and a length of elegant black lace drifted from her needles down over her lap. The wrinkles around her eyes had molded into permanent squints, and she glowered at her delicate work through thick half-moon spectacles.

"Miss Lampton, meet my mother," said Mr. Waters. The woman looked up at me, and her eyes brightened.

"Is that Nicolette Lampton?" she asked. "Forgive me, dear, for not standing to greet you. It's getting hard for me to move around so much." She held out her hand, and I shook it gladly.

I thought of my mother's automated rocking chair, and of how easy it would be to design a knitting machine, and my smile widened. I knew now that I would be able to barter my skills and inventions for anything at all I might need.

"Lovely to meet you," I said, and meant it. "I'm here to fix your son's sewing machine."

The woman nodded. "Wonderful! Wonderful." Her voice faded away as she focused once more on her lacework. Her hands resumed their quick, pained movements.

I turned to Mr. Waters. "Now, where is this troublesome beast?"

He pointed to a corner of the room, where lurked a larger sewing machine than I'd ever seen before. It ran entirely on coal power; there was a small stove under the table, where the pedal would usually be. It would be lovely and warming for the feet, too, I thought, making note for my own designs. A rectangle of red fabric lay strewn over the workspace, scrunched up tight around the huge needle. A deep tangle of thread bloomed like mold between the needle and the motor's main pulley.

I fingered the broken timing belt in my hand: I could see where it had come off the machine, and the carnage it had left in its wake. I had a wrench in my apron pocket, and

I requested a mallet and a file, which Mr. Waters supplied from his button-making and corsetry cabinets. Before I set to work, I handed him the list of fabrics and notions I would need for Piety and Chastity's new wardrobes.

I lay down on my back so I could look up into the machine. First I examined each cog, filing down any damaged edges. Each moving part on the motor had a small timing mark; I held my breath while I matched them with their twin marks on the engine's housing. They all needed to align in total precision before I could replace the belt itself.

The one Mr. Waters had shown me, I finally decided, was past repair: the rubber had torn in more than one place, and too many of the grooves would be lost if I melted it back together. Ordering a new belt, from Nordsk no less, would take months that neither Mr. Waters nor I had to spare. But I already knew what to do.

"I'll be back shortly!" I called, standing up. I hurried into the shop room and out the front door. The bell clanged behind me as I fairly skipped up the road, mallet in hand. I was *good* at this, I knew I was, and I loved doing it, too. This kind of confidence felt strange, like waking up healthy after a long illness. I was grateful for the feeling, both to Mr. Waters and, I realized, to myself.

I found the carriage frame waiting for me at the roadside, and I carefully pried off the two small front wheels. The left tire was brittle from exposure to the sun, and it started to crumble even as I held it; but the right had been shielded by the rest of the carriage frame and was still fairly pliable. It would have to do.

Back in the shop, I used Mr. Waters' measuring equipment—in this, at least, the tools of his trade and of mine intersected perfectly—to carve meticulous notches into the rubber. I had to adjust the main pulley slightly to accommodate my improvised timing belt, but just as I'd known it would be, the wheel was close to a perfect fit.

Finally I emerged from under the machine. I straightened the fabric over the board and threaded the needle. Trying not to cringe in anticipation, I touched my foot to the pedal.

There were three things that could still go very wrong: the timing marks might be misaligned, so that the machine would fly apart again as soon as it started; I might have carved the grooves into the new belt imprecisely, in spite of Mr. Waters' measuring tools; or the old rubber might have perished after all, so that it would crumble under the pressure of the motor. I'd learned the hard way, during my years as Mother's pupil and in my own recent experiments, how irreparable each mistake could be.

I pressed down on the pedal and heard the motor rumble. The fabric danced under my fingers, and the flawless whir and slip-slip of the needle and thread sounded like music. The machine was perfect.

"Mr. Waters!" I called, smiling so broadly it nearly hurt. I had fixed something for someone else, and I was on my way to escaping the Steps and a life that already felt too rusty and small for the new opportunities that lay before me now.

I heard Mr. Waters walk up behind me. "Amazing!" he cried, suddenly effusive. He clapped me on the shoulder. "I hate to admit, Miss Lampton, I didn't think you could do it." He smiled warmly. "Now, what can I do for you in return?"

I had to laugh—this was going so much better than I'd hoped. "Well," I said, "the fabric you've just cut is for my stepsisters' ball gowns."

He nodded.

"Though I don't care so much for the ball, I would love to attend the Exposition that follows it . . . but I don't have anything suitable to wear."

He frowned and would have started in about the Steps' injustice, as he'd done several times before, but I shook my head at him. I wiped my hand, still holding the wrench, across my hot cheek. Hardly daring to hope, I spoke quickly: "Do you think I might have some fabric of my own?"

He laughed, and for a moment I feared he might be laughing at the absurdity of my question. But he led me back to the front of the shop, sweeping his hand in a grand gesture toward his merchandise.

"Anything you like, Miss Lampton," he said, his smile nearly as wide as mine. "Anything for the lass who saved my business."

I took in the rainbow in front of me, and for the first time in years, I was spoiled for choice. The green silk? The gold brocade? I needed something that would look respectable at the daytime Exposition, but that I could perhaps dress up later on. Finally I saw a bolt of sky-bright blue percale, the color of a cloudless spring. My hand reached out of its own accord, but I saw the grease on it from the sewing machine and pulled away before I touched it.

"A fine choice," said Mr. Waters. "I'd prefer you to your sisters even if I didn't know you, just on that pick." He pulled the softly shining fabric from the wall and unfurled it across his cutting board, marking off the yards with a bit of white chalk. He fished a spool of matching thread from a drawer, then opened his cabinets of ribbons and buttons and once more offered me my choice.

Recalling the beauty of his mother's black lace, I chose small, shiny jet buttons and black grosgrain ribbon. I decided that my next lesson for Jules and Company would be in buttonholes.

Mr. Waters, usually so reserved, folded me in his arms, lightly crushing the paper-wrapped bundles I held. He and his mother thanked me twice more each before they let me leave.

The shadows leaned east as I walked back home, and I knew Stepmother would wonder why I'd dallied. I wiped the grease off my hands onto the dry leaves that covered the grass at the side of the street and carefully inspected my dress. When I deemed myself presentable, I turned onto the drive.

I could hear the three of them at tea inside, their quiet simpering giggles and hushed gossip. A young male voice mixed with theirs: Fitzwilliam Covington, one of Chastity's more talkative suitors. They'd never know how long I'd been gone.

"I've heard rumors of a Fey ship slipping through the quarantine," Stepmother was saying.

I paused by the door to listen. Piety's and Chastity's conversations with their suitors were usually terrifically dull, but if Stepmother was present, she would occasionally talk politics with the young men. I got most of my news by eavesdropping this way, and news of Faerie particularly intrigued me.

When Heir Philip had been killed, King Corsin had said Fey evils and barbarism made their betrayal inevitable. He'd cut off all remaining trade with Faerie, increased Esting's military presence there threefold, and finally imposed a quarantine on the entire continent. Our coal-powered armada was more than a match for Faerie's bright-sailed flotillas, and before long, all of Faerie's borders were locked down. It had been seven years since any Fey ship had left port.

To hear Stepmother tell it, though, the worst effect of the quarantine, of King Corsin's fear, was that Christopher—the younger prince and now the Heir—was sequestered from public view, quarantined, too. There was no chance of Piety and Chastity meeting him at high teas or garden parties or balls. Fey assassins could lurk anywhere, King Corsin insisted, despite the supposedly airtight seal on Faerie's borders. So the Heir stayed safe and secret behind the palace walls, and Esting's eligible maidens pined with curiosity.

I stood there in the hallway, concealed behind the closed sitting room door, lost in my thoughts of Faerie and then of the royal family. The Steps' conversation had wandered in the same direction—little wonder, given their obsession with the Heir's every move and with the upcoming Exposition and ball.

"Mrs. Hellifer tells me the festivities will last a week at the very minimum," Stepmother said. "She is sure the Heir himself will even be present to help judge the Exposition and to dance at the ball."

There was a rustling of silk skirts, Piety and Chastity fidgeting with excitement. "Just think," I heard Piety sigh, "actually to see the Heir, to dance with him. Do you think he'll be handsome, Chas?"

"Of course," Chastity replied, her tone almost offended, as if she thought Piety might be insulting her future husband. "Mother always says how beautiful Queen Nerali was."

"Painfully beautiful," Stepmother added, as if the Queen's loveliness had been a personal affront.

Chastity continued, "Well, how could her son be anything but beautiful, too? Besides, princes are always handsome, and charming, and brave, and romantic—"

"Oh, don't talk of the sodding Heir so," Fitz groaned, and I could practically hear his eyes rolling. "Here you've got such a strapping specimen just before you, living and breathing and eating biscuits in your parlor, ready to serve your every whim. Who needs some pasty, shriveled prince stuck behind palace walls?"

Chastity simpered, mollified. Piety sighed—none of her suitors were present today, so she was free to swoon over the Heir as much as she wished.

Honestly, I agreed with Fitz. What use would it do any girl to marry the Heir if it meant she'd be stuck in hiding with him for who knew how long? The palace was a lovely prison, certainly, but never to be able to leave . . . It was all too familiar a situation to me. I had just started to imagine a kind of life for myself: making a living of my own, having a home and a workshop—even buying back Lampton from the Steps, if I was extraordinarily lucky. Maybe even traveling, once I had my business established. Nothing could make me give up the freedom I longed for, not even the heir to a kingdom. Why marry someone if that marriage is only another trap?

"You know, Mr. Covington," Stepmother began, in an even tone that indicated she planned on showcasing her intelligence, "I hear tell from Brother Lane that the Heir differs quite spectacularly from his father on several important issues. He is apparently opposed to the quarantine and has been campaigning for some time now for a different relationship with Faerie altogether—perhaps even a withdrawal."

"Yes," Fitz said, his voice turning tight and cold. "Lord knows where he got the idea—the board always appoints the royal tutors so carefully. Heir Christopher thinks we should treat the Fey as we do our fellow men. If he has his way, there could be tariffs, trade regulations, even a Fey ambassador. And we all know where that would lead."

It was easy to picture the Steps' shudders. King Corsin had decreed that anything less than a total quarantine and a complete lockdown on Faerie would mean allowing the Fey's worst natures to take over. Eventually, he insisted, such leniency would lead directly to an open war.

I decided I'd listened long enough, and I made my way past the parlor door, ready to start on my machines again. I couldn't go back to the workshop until the Steps were sleeping or gone, but there were still plenty of chores to finish upstairs.

Just before I reached the kitchen, the parlor door swung open. I almost didn't notice, as it no longer creaked the way it used to—thanks once again to the supplies I'd found in Mother's workshop.

Fitz appeared in the hallway. Tall and slim, with auburn hair and creamy skin, he was a handsome young man, and he smiled and winked at me as he closed the door behind him. Fitz was a jovial presence at Lampton, and his quick wit often made me wonder why he bothered to tolerate Chastity's simpering idiocy. But she was beautiful, and I knew well enough from Father that beauty can make a lover tolerate any number of shortcomings.

Still, Fitz was nearly always civil to me, so his regard for Chastity didn't lose him quite all of my respect. I greeted him with a demure nod and a bob at my ankles, the way Stepmother had taught me to acknowledge my betters.

"Ah, come off it, Miss Nick," he said, grinning, sliding his hands into kidskin gloves.

Fitz always called me Miss Nick, and my pulse always gave a quick flutter when he did. I wouldn't have said I fancied Fitz . . . precisely, but he was indefatigably charming, and I was not immune.

"We've known each other long enough that you needn't curtsy every time we meet." He leaned in conspiratorially. "We might be close to family soon enough, you and I. Step-in-laws, you know." He tapped the side of his nose with a gloved finger. "Trade secret, though. Don't go telling Goldie on me yet."

"I won't tell, Fitz." My fancy vanished. I wondered if I was doing an adequate job of hiding my disgust. *Goldie.*

He smiled, whether condescendingly or kindly I could never quite tell. "I knew I could count on you to keep secrets from them," he said.

He retrieved his hat from the stand, doffed it at me glibly, and was out the door.

I frowned. What did he mean, he knew I could keep secrets? I told myself it was only idle banter—such banter was Fitz's stock in trade, after all. His father was a very minor noble, and I knew Fitz hoped his quick mind and quicker tongue would help him push through the ranks at court.

Still, for the first time in my life, I had secrets that were precious. His comment shook me enough that it took an hour of dull cleaning in the kitchen and a long time talking to Jules that night to stop the gears of my mind from spinning with worry.

THE spiders took to buttonholes like naturals. Jules and the minions' work was improving and refining even faster than my own. That very night, as I was laying out the pattern for Piety's ball gown, I felt Jules's muzzle nudge against my wrist. He pranced over the design, pawing at it, snorting steam.

"You don't like it? Neither do I. It's a bit stodgy, I think." I chuckled. "At least it suits her." I used to love drawing up gowns when I was a child. They were their own kind of blueprints, their own kind of architecture and construction. But Piety and Chastity were uninspiring subjects.

Jules trotted to my inkwell and dipped one copper hoof inside. Walking carefully backwards on three legs, he returned to my sketch and dragged new lines into the pattern.

I stepped back to see what he'd done. I laughed again, but in amazement this time, almost in disbelief. He'd drawn the neckline lower and the sleeves fuller, with an elegant ruching at the shoulders. My boorish, matronly design suddenly gained life, youth, and even a certain flirtatious decadence.

"You do know," I informed him, "you've just assigned yourself the task of designing every single one of the Steps' dresses." I stroked his glass back. His gears turned in pleasure, and their tiny movements vibrated under my hand.

I looked at him more carefully then; I stared, really, until he looked quizzically back at me and pressed against my hand, as if to ask what was wrong.

I patted him gently, then scooped him up and carried him to the sewing machine. With a whistling neigh, he called over two of the dragonflies to pull him into his harness.

Through the door into the furnace room, I could just glimpse the sky-blue fabric of my Exposition outfit draped over my adjustable dress form. I knew I'd have to start on the Steps' new wardrobes soon—or rather, Jules and the minions would have to start—but every time I saw that blue percale, I could see myself at the Exposition so clearly, a successful inventor, admired by all. Never mind that I didn't yet know what my great invention would *be;* in my mind, my dream had already come true.

I turned back to the cluttered comfort of the designer's studio. Standing underneath the gray-curtained window, I could look upward and see the almost-full moon in the clear, cold night sky above me. I stared at it determinedly. I would never have let it show on my face, not in the workshop with Jules there . . . but he'd frightened me.

I'd known that Jules was affectionate and dutiful, and I'd thought he was intelligent. Yet those were traits that would describe any good carriage or hunting horse. And I'd grown fond of him, much fonder than even the silly court ladies were of Mother's insects. I knew Mother would probably laugh at me if she knew how affectionate I'd become.

But a horse who could think both spatially and artistically—a horse who could understand the structure in the lines of a gown, who could *draw?* It was laughably absurd. Only humans had such power. Logical design, incorporating geometry and engineering, was a human kind of magic even the Fey didn't possess; Mother's and Father's books agreed on that much, and it was what King Corsin wanted to celebrate at the upcoming Exhibition. It was part of what made some people—Stepmother, the Brethren, even Father—believe that humans were better than Fey.

Something else from one of Mother's books came to mind: Fey animals, it was said, possessed more wisdom than those in Esting. I'd thought that only meant sharpness, ability to be trained, but perhaps . . . perhaps there was truly *more . . .*

I hurried back across the studio and walked up to the many small drawers in the far corner of the furnace room.

But I stood there for at least ten minutes, unable to open the drawer labeled with the drawing of a horse so much like

Jules. The small brass handle was cold on my fingers, despite the warmth of the room.

When finally I opened it, I waited with dread for the ghostly shape to rise up from the fine gray ash again. But the substance there was still; it didn't even ripple in the liquid way it had done before.

No ghosts.

I shook my head; whatever Jules might be, I knew at least that he was good and that he loved me, too. And even if he was somehow connected to the ashes in these drawers that made me shiver every time I came near them . . . well, that was still Mother's work, and I loved and trusted her above all. I had to.

I closed the drawer and turned its cold handle to secure the latch. It was all too easy to pick up Jules in my hands, press him to my chest, and cuddle him like any cat or dog. He rubbed the top of his head against my collarbone and nickered softly, and the butterfly hovered in front of us, as if it were watching.

He was my Jules, and my mother had made him. That was all that mattered.

The dressmaking whirred by after that. I would start the design, Jules following my pen and tracing in small corrections. Then he would steer the fabric through the sewing machine while the insects applied the smallest details.

While they worked, I spent my time improving my skill with the glass blower. Within a few days, I could turn sand into transparent glass spheres, and in another week, I'd added slim holes to turn the spheres into beads. I even blew a few small bowls and jugs.

Jules seemed to approve: he chased the beads around my desk like polo balls. I managed to copy the shape of his glass flanks and belly, and soon he had a shiny, jointed new coat that would have been the envy of any show pony.

I quickly filled a large sack with beads. I amended my mother's dye formulas to create deep jewel colors, practicing on the extra fabric from the Steps' new wardrobes. I soon had stacks of colored silk, velvet, and satin scraps, mostly in my favorite hues of purple and dark blue, folded on my shelves. I had no idea what I'd use them for, but they were beautiful.

I kept some black seed beads for myself and vowed to take the rest to Market. I had already begun drawing up ideas for my Exhibition display.

My only trouble lay in finding a Market Day when I could sneak out and wouldn't risk meeting the Steps on the street. They went to Market nearly every week, dressed in their finest, to parade their wealth and buy unnecessary, gaudy trinkets. Last time, Chastity had returned wearing a four-inch gold brooch of two embracing, piggish-faced cherubs, and Piety had a long, emerald-studded serpent woven into her hair. I'll admit I admired the serpent. The craftsmanship was excellent, and I do love emeralds, but the way she wore the thing, it looked like Satan lurking in the tree of knowledge.

The very next week, they were invited to a tea at the palace. The way Stepmother went on about it, you'd almost have thought it was a private invitation rather than one sent to every fine house in our country. The royal family hosted a tea for what Stepmother called "the good families" every year.

This year, however, it was rumored that the Heir himself would join them. Even I had to admit an interest in that. Since Philip's death, when Christopher had become Heir at only thirteen years old, no one but his family, his Brethren tutors, and the court physicians—and, I imagine, a few trusted servants—had laid eyes on him. Even his image on Esting's five-crown coins remained that of a round-cheeked child, not the young man he surely must be by now, three years my senior. At nineteen, he could start to search for a bride.

And for the first time in generations, the Heir's bride would be an Estinger. Through nearly all of our country's history, since long before that particularly picky Heir sent Captain Brand and his crew in search of new lands and new beauties, Esting's royalty had chosen spouses from abroad. It had been a way of ensuring good trade and diplomatic relations with other countries—kings don't tend to invade their children's new love nests. Less officially, but widely acknowledged in whispers, it was an excellent way to avoid the inbreeding common in some royal families as well.

So while Esting's commoners tended to look almost like cousins, with fairish skin and hair ranging from yellow to nut-brown, our nobles' and royalty's looks showed much greater variety. Those with ancestors from Nordsk were ice-pale, with light eyes and lighter, sometimes even white, hair. Those who traced their roots to the Sudlands—the birthplace of Heir Christopher's mother, Queen Nerali—had rich brown skin, curling black hair, and long-lashed dark eyes.

Of course, some commoners had started to show these traits too, over the years. But no one tended to speak of it, because foreign looks in a commoner usually meant illegitimacy. It wasn't polite to mention such things.

Piety and Chastity insisted that this year's tea reception was special, since, they said, the hopeful Heir could make an appearance himself. They had to look their best. Of course they immediately demanded new outfits, and Stepmother only barely convinced them that they shouldn't go all white just yet. So I made—or really, Jules and his minions made, for I hardly needed to help them now—a pea-green jacket and bustled skirt for Piety and a similar blush-pink ensemble for Chastity.

"Really, Nick," murmured Stepmother one night, stroking a long finger over Jules's perfect seams, "your sewing is much improved lately . . . almost tolerable, in fact."

I smiled blankly and trotted down to the cellar.

✷

On Saturday, I packed an old carpetbag with beads and a display model of my new lace-knitting machine. Jules followed me around the workshop like an anxious puppy.

"I'm sorry, Jules, but I just can't take you," I said, reaching down and stroking his copper ears. None of his copper was green anymore. He worked so hard that he'd worn off all his patina, and every Sunday I polished him to a mirror shine.

I picked him up and hugged him to my chest. "I wish I could," I said, "but Stepmother will have my hide if Chastity's dress isn't finished tonight. You can make it so much better than I ever could; you know that."

He bent his head and nudged my thumb gently, moving his legs back and forth inside my hand. I set him down, and he immediately cantered over to the sewing machine. I'd rigged an even more elaborate setup for him and the minions over the past weeks: a slender ramp ran from the floor up to the tabletop, and tiny harnesses hung from the sewing machine. There were small levers attached to my best fabric scissors, so they could be moved by even the most delicate hoof or insect leg. Little wheels under my pincushions gave them the look of tiny, round carriages.

Jules hooked his neck through his sewing-machine harness and started to trot, steering a perfect seam into Chastity's bodice. Then he looked back at me plaintively.

"That's my Jules." I petted him one more time. "I'll bring you back some quality charcoal. Top-notch, I promise."

His tail flicked with pleasure, and a delicate jewelry clinking echoed in the air.

I crept back upstairs and toward the parlor, listening for the sounds of the Steps. The house was silent; when I looked out the door, I saw the fresh tracks of a rented carriage on the gravel drive.

I went into the kitchen and pressed my hand to Mr. Candery's secret cupboard. I used to worry that as my hand grew I wouldn't be able to unlock it anymore, but it still clicked open for me years after Mr. Candery had first let me in. I dug through the—emptier now, but I couldn't worry about that—cabinet and found a tiny, dusty vial at the very back of the bottom shelf. *Ombrossus oil,* it said on a thin, peeling label. *For disguise. Consider enemies and apply one drop as needed.*

I had never used the oil before; I'd never had a need to disguise myself, and there was only a shallow, viscous puddle left at the bottom of the little vial. I pulled off its cork stopper and raised it to my nose; it smelled spicy and complex, like the dense sinnum buns Mr. Candery used to bake.

I pressed my finger over the opening and slowly tipped it upside down and back again. A little whiskey-colored drop remained on my fingertip, and I raised it to my forehead, thinking of the Steps. Piety and Chastity's lovely, vacant faces; Stepmother's sharp hazel eyes, full mouth, and high cheekbones.

But I stopped before I let the ombrossus touch my face. There was so little left, and I knew the Steps would be at the palace all day. I wanted to protect myself at Market, but I knew each remaining dose was precious.

I sighed, looking down at the drop on my finger, and I reluctantly scraped it back into the vial. I took one last breath of the warm sinnum scent, then placed the little bottle in my apron pocket. I had no idea how many times I'd have to hide myself from the Steps, and I'd need at least one drop for the Exposition.

Another problem I couldn't bring myself to deal with yet. Sighing, I fetched my bag and gathered my hair into a kerchief for the journey to town. On my birthday, I'd thought I'd found all the answers in Mother's workshop, but sometimes I wondered if my new work had given me more problems than it had solved.

Yet as I stepped out the door, my worries—about Mr. Candery's supplies, about Jules and the minions' true nature, about all the work I had to do—rose up and off my shoulders. I was leaving the house not on an errand for the Steps but of my own volition, for my own purposes. I couldn't remember the last time I'd gone farther than the edge of our back lawn by my own choosing. Who knew what the day could bring?

My heart began to beat faster, and I found myself almost running, my heavy carpetbag slapping against my legs. I was so full of hope and expectation that the seven miles' walk around the edge of the North Forest to Esting City seemed to take no time at all.

I debated with myself how to organize my wares—by color? by size?—and whether I should mark my price beforehand or haggle with every customer. I had no idea how much beads sold for, so I decided on the latter.

I heard the Market before I saw it: wagons rumbling, birds squawking, and scores of vendors hollering. Good smells called to me, too—sweet pastries and roast meats, exotic perfume oils, spices and smoke.

Then I turned a corner, and I was in the middle of everything: a brightly colored, fast-moving current of shoppers jostled me from all sides.

I stood shocked and still, blinking like an imbecile. I'd not been among so many people at once since . . . well, not ever. I'd been too young when Father was alive, and the Steps kept me well hidden. I was only allowed to run errands on weekday mornings, when the shops were relatively deserted—and even that was just to the nearby, but tiny, village of Woodshire. This was Esting City, with the hulking, blackstone palace itself in its center, and the Market was no less grand than its setting. The streets swarmed with shoppers, and every stall was bursting with cloth or jewelry or spices or foodstuffs. I couldn't see a single open place for me to set up my own display. I glanced around helplessly, confused and suddenly nervous, and feeling very, very small.

A large man with a shock of yellow hair knocked hard against me as he pushed through the crowd. "Ow!" I cried, and without thinking, I dropped my carpetbag to clutch my shoulder. The man didn't apologize; he only laughed at me, with a hard, appraising look in his eyes that I didn't like, before moving on. I groped downward for my bag.

It was gone.

My heart gave two great stuttering thumps, and I looked around, panicked, but I knew it was already lost in the pressing river of people that surrounded me. I felt all my work, all my dreams, the legacy of Mother's workshop and Mr. Candery's kindness, slipping away on that river.

Someone tapped my shoulder.

Turning, I was confronted with a pair of liquid-dark brown eyes, crinkled at the corners. I glanced down and saw my carpetbag held easily in a strong, brown hand. I snatched the bag into my arms, and he offered me no resistance.

I pulled back a step, so I could see the eyes' owner.

He had a squarish face, with a wide, strong jaw, full mouth, and a broad nose, and his skin was a rich, dusky brown. His eyes were large and deep-set, and crinkled not from age as I'd first thought, but from his broad smile—he could hardly have been older than I was. Sable curls fell over his forehead, and he ran his hands through them, trying unsuccessfully to push them back.

"Good morning, miss," he said. "You almost lost your goods, there. I thought you could use some assistance."

I felt my face color; I had needed help, I knew, but I didn't like to think that I showed it so clearly. "I'm fine," I said, trying to sound confident. "But I mean—um—thank you."

When his smile broke out again, I knew I'd failed. "Sure, you're fine."

I sighed. "I'm just looking for a place to set up my wares."

He raised one thick brow. "You're new to Market, are you not?"

I was beginning to find him rather condescending.

A new voice joined his. "So what if she is?" A very round, very golden sort of girl shoved the boy aside and smiled at me. "I'm Caro. Caroline Hart."

She stuck out her hand, and I shook it.

"Nicolette La . . ." I trailed off, unsure of how many connections the Steps might have at Market. The last thing I needed was some chipper girl or handsome boy mouthing off to Stepmother about my new business venture. "Lark," I finished lamely.

"Pleased to meet you," she said. Neither of them seemed to doubt my nom de Market.

I smiled at Caro, feeling a little worn around the edges, and looked up at the clock in the main square. I had hours left before the Steps would arrive home, and I intended to make the most of them, tired or not. I straightened my shoulders.

"I'm pleased too," added the boy—the young man, really—and he winked at me, or at least I thought he did, though it may have been a trick of the light. "And my name's Fin."

"Nicolette," I said again. For the first time, I felt as if my name was too fancy, too snooty for these people and their familiar, short nicknames. The Steps' "Nick" started to seem not so bad after all. Had I given myself away with my aristocratic name?

"Call me Nick, if you like," I added, reddening again. "That's what my . . . sisters call me."

"Sisters, have you?" asked Fin. "I've always wanted a sister. A brother is a fine thing too, of course, but a sister would be especially nice."

I resisted letting out a derisive snort; *nice* would not have been my word of choice. I looked from Caro to Fin. They didn't look at all alike: Caro was plump and ruddy and golden-haired, while Fin had a linear, almost geometric look about him, and was much darker. Yet I'd assumed they were family. I wasn't sure why, except for their easy, affectionate manner with each other.

"And what am I to you, then, but a sister?" cried Caro, gently shoving him again.

Fin cast an odd, shadowed look at her for a moment, but it passed under the light of another sudden smile. "That you are, I suppose," he said. "That you are."

Caro put her arm around my waist—I winced a little, unused to such friendly contact—and she pulled me out of the flood of shoppers and into the cool shadow of the awning over her and Fin's booth.

"I reckon you didn't reserve a stall, did you?" she asked.

I didn't register her words at first. I was too busy admiring their merchandise.

There were two distinct halves to their display: on one side were lifelike sculpted figures of our country's folk heroes, and on the other, little metal boxes that played music at the turn of a handle. Some had been recently wound, and I recognized our national anthem in one and a sweet, lilting love song in a second. The boxes were shockingly small for the intricacy of the sounds they produced—it was as if a minuscule Royal Orchestra hid inside each one.

I turned to the sculptures, which were all as intricate as the music boxes. My favorite depicted the Forest Queen, a woman who'd lived two and a half centuries before my birth. Legend had it she'd built a whole city in the heart of Woodshire Forest, high up in the trees, where all those who'd lost their homes or their livings to the then king's high taxes could live.

The Forest Queen's molded face gleamed in the sunlight, and her dark blond hair shimmered over her shoulders so that it almost seemed to move in the breeze. She even looked a bit like Caro, with her arched brows, round cheeks, and pointed chin. Her hands pressed elegantly over her heart, their sun-browned skin so true to life, I thought she would be soft when I touched her. But no—she was cold, hard, crafted from some metallic compound even I did not recognize. Both the music boxes and the sculptures were so skillfully wrought that any artisan in the country would have been proud of them.

"Well," said Fin, "did you reserve a stall, or didn't you?"

"No," I murmured, coming out of my reverie. "I didn't know I had to."

He scoffed, but Caro patted my shoulder again. "Don't worry," she said, "you can split with us." She glanced over their already crowded table. "Sorry there won't be much room."

"Oh, sure, you can share with us," Fin cut in. "Just make sure you share the rental fee, too." He smiled again, but it was a sharp, closed smile.

"Fin!" Caro snapped. "It's her first time at Market. Be a little kind, won't you?"

I couldn't help taking a step or two back, away from the budding anger between them.

"Caro, please, we both know you need that money, and you won't let—" Fin cut himself off abruptly. When he turned to look at me, his false smile was gone. "You're welcome to share with us, of course." He sighed. "Forgive my rudeness, Nick. Please."

I blinked. My name was sweet in his mouth.

"Thank you both," I mumbled, but I looked at Fin when I said it. "I'll certainly pay my share of your fee—once I earn it, that is."

Caro grinned. She began rearranging the little music boxes, and Fin stepped in beside her and moved some of the figurines to one side. His hands were broad and capable-looking, their skin slightly callused. He wrapped a few of the sculptures in brown chamois cloth and tucked them into a shelf under the table.

I realized that the sculptures were his, and the music boxes Caro's. I reprimanded myself for thinking the art had been a woman's work, and the machines a man's. After all, I was a mechanic myself, and not ashamed to admit I had become quite skilled—and Mother was the most brilliant inventor I'd ever known.

Caro swept a rounded hand over the now-empty space in the center of the booth. "All yours," she said.

I walked around to the back and took my place between them. I was surprised to feel myself relax, my breaths growing deeper and steadier, my spine unlocking. It felt natural, having Fin and Caro by my side—as if we'd been standing together our whole lives and I'd only just noticed it.

I pulled apart the kissing-style clasp on my carpetbag and fished out my knitting machine. It stood as high as the length of my forearm, and I decided it should stay at the back of my display, lest it block the view of my beads.

I replaced it and took out my bead satchels and bowls instead. The clear bowls looked well against the deep green fabric Caro and Fin had spread over their table, and my many-colored beads glittered in the noontime light. I arranged four small bowls toward the front of the booth, and two larger ones behind them. I'd brought more, but couldn't fit anything else in the narrow strip my new friends had cleared for me.

"Ooh," murmured Caro. "Nick, those are lovely."

Fin nodded. In the shadow of the awning, his eyes gleamed black, and his long lashes cast shadows over the planes of his cheekbones.

"Thank you," I muttered. Suddenly unsure what to do with my hands, I dove back into my bag and found the knitting machine. I'd folded it for transport, and now I clicked the steel supports together. The gears slipped into place, and I pulled the glass-handled crank out to the side. The two needles in the center looked bare and aggressive, like teeth.

"What is it?" Caro breathed. She reached out and brushed her fingers against the handle.

I smiled at her. "You'll see." I dipped my hand into the bag again and found a skein of white tatting cotton, left over from when Chastity decided her spring dresses needed smooth lines, not lace. I hung the skein over two hooks on the side of the machine, then looped a few starting stitches onto the left-hand needle. I pushed the right-hand needle inside the last loop and turned the crank.

The needles clicked and whirred together. A train of lace frothed out from the top of the machine. It was a simple pattern, yarn-over stripes and spiked edging, but it was the best I could do so far. Floral lace, I'd vowed to Jules that morning, would come soon enough.

When I'd spun out a few handbreadths, I looked up to see what Fin and Caro thought of my invention.

To my surprise, there was a well-dressed gentleman standing in front of us—and he was staring intently at my machine. He wore a pinstriped jacket and stroked his huge, elaborately curled mustache, all the while squinting downward through a thick monocle. A few darker freckles were scattered across his dark brown skin.

"Wonderful," he said under his breath. "Just wonderful." He looked at me, his brown eyes sharp. He raised one eyebrow (the other stayed firmly in place, securing his monocle) and I saw surprise in his glance. I supposed that, like many Estingers, he'd assumed inventors were always men.

His surprise vanished quickly though, and when he spoke, his voice was businesslike and brisk. "How much for the machine, lass?" His monocle glittered.

"Um." I cleared my throat. I'd hoped someone would offer a sum first, so that I could get some idea of how to price things. As it was, I had no idea. "Well, sir, this particular one isn't for sale. It's more of a . . . display model."

As I spoke I realized: I am a terrible saleswoman.

"I see, I see . . ." He twirled a cane between his gloved hands. "How much for one of my own, then?"

I made a few quick calculations: Mr. Waters usually

charged half a crown per hour for his labor as a tailor, and I supposed my skill was about as valuable as his. I added the cost of the materials to the time I'd spent building the machine.

"Ah, six crowns?" I squeaked. I glanced to my left, to see if Fin agreed with my price . . . but he'd vanished, along with several of his sculptures.

I looked to my right and was relieved to find Caro's solid form still next to me. She offered a reassuring nod, and her golden curls bobbed against her round cheeks.

The man grinned and extended his hand for me to shake. "Excellent," he said. "I'll take it." He pulled two fat coins from his pocket and placed them on the table, then reached inside his jacket and produced a purple calling card. "Deliver it to this address as soon as it's done, and you'll get the rest."

He turned and ambled down the street. I stayed poised over my wares, my hand crushing the edge of the calling card, my arm still extended. *Gerald, Lord Alming,* it read. Somehow I thought the name sounded familiar . . .

Caro clapped her hands and brought me back down to earth.

"Two crowns now," she cried, "and four more to come! That's near the rent for the whole booth!" She shook her head and leaned in. "Though I'd wager you could get eight or even ten crowns for such a thing. My arthritic grandmum would weep with joy if she owned one."

I smiled. "Consider yourself my second customer. I'll bring your grandmother's machine to the next Market Day."

The ruddiness blanched out of Caro's skin, and the friendly smile I'd thought was permanently lodged on her face faded. "I don't take charity," she whispered.

I cringed at my own tactlessness. I reached toward her quickly, then drew back, not knowing what I should do. "I didn't mean to . . ." I said, unsure how to finish my sentence. "I don't—I'm not—" I struggled with how to explain, especially because I knew what Caro meant. My pride was all I'd had left, after the Steps stripped me of my wealth and privilege and belongings. I would've hated for someone to come along and help me out of pity—that was part of why I'd kept to the house so much all these years, even more than Stepmother required.

I felt the beginnings of tears prick at my eyes. I looked in Caro's face, begging her to believe me.

She must have, at least a little, because she reached out and touched the hand I'd withdrawn. "No, I imagine you're not," she said, and a tinge of color returned to her face. "I have an idea. I'll forget about the booth-sharing fee until I've paid back for a machine for my grandmum. Call it a trade between friends."

"Friends," I agreed, relieved. I squeezed her hand and couldn't help grinning like a fool.

There were several customers in front of our booth by

then, and they all wanted to try working the knitting machine. By the end of the hour, I had five orders and I'd sold more than half my beads. I had to hide my display model eventually, for I knew I couldn't build more than that, keep up with the Steps' wardrobes, do my chores, and come up with something for the Exposition too. I could feel my face and chest flushed with excitement and success. I thought of how alien those feelings had been until the past few months, when Mother's workshop had brought hope and ambition back to my life.

Fin returned fifteen minutes later. He and Caro exchanged another of their private looks. I wondered why he'd gone, of course, but I didn't think I'd known him long enough to ask.

Market ended too quickly, and I packed my bag with the knitting machine and my empty bowls. All but a few beads had sold, and Fin took them to add to one of his new sculptures. He promised to bring it to the next Market Day so I could see. I wasn't sure when I'd next be able to come, but I nodded happily anyway.

Caro hugged me eagerly before I left, but Fin only laughed and shook my hand.

"It was good to meet you, Nick," he said, and this time he definitely winked.

I walked home quickly, hoping to beat the early snowstorm that was already sending down its first flakes. I skipped every few steps and swung my carpetbag through the air. The day had turned out better than I'd ever hoped—almost miraculously, in fact. With five knitting machines and all my beads sold, and two new friends into the bargain, I thought conquering the Exhibition would be as simple and straightforward as one of Jules's perfect seams.

Jules! I'd forgotten to buy his charcoal. I sighed and scolded myself, and some of the light drained out of the day. I told myself I was silly for feeling so sad.

Still, Jules had done so much for me, and I'd already broken my very first promise to him. I walked more slowly, dragging myself up the long path through the estate's snow-sprinkled front gardens. My new friends were wonderful, but Jules was a more steadfast companion than anyone I'd ever known.

I wondered what I could do to apologize. I was still puzzling when I opened the front door.

Stepmother stood just inside the darkened hall. A tight scowl marred her beautiful face.

"Well," she said, "where have you been, little mechanic?"

SHE grabbed my kerchief and yanked it hard, forcing me inside. I caught sight of Piety in the shadows, her eyes cold.

Stepmother dragged me farther in and twisted my hair to make me face her. Rough pain shocked my scalp, and I heard some strands stretch and snap. I grabbed her wrist and curled my palms tight around it, pulling her skin in opposite directions. She cried out, but didn't release me.

"We've been in your room, Nick," she said, "and imagine what we found there. I should have known you weren't capable of such fine sewing on your own."

"I—" I gasped, the pain still sharp. "I don't know what you're—"

"Shut it," said Chastity, walking down the stairs. Her heavy skirt rustled on the staircase. "We found it, Nick. What, you thought we wouldn't?"

Stepmother gripped me harder, and her long fingernails

scraped against my forehead, drawing a trickle of blood. "She never was very smart. She got that from her father, I imagine." She laughed softly.

Chastity kept advancing until her face was only inches from mine. "Poor Nick," she whispered, and when her mother scoffed, she raised her hand. "Poor Nick, too stupid to keep her soot off the stairs. Why, your bedroom is thick with it!" She waved a black-dusted finger in front of my eyes, then smeared it across my nose. Stepmother produced a handkerchief from her apron pocket, and Chastity delicately wiped her hand.

Soot in my bedroom? I'd been so careful . . .

"And that dress!" Stepmother laughed again. "What on earth! Could you possibly have thought we would let you attend the ball with us? And in *that?*"

The ball? I tried to think, but Stepmother's hold drove too much pain through my mind.

She let go of me at last, and I swung my fist at her face. I landed a punch, but Chastity was already behind me—I'd never have thought her so quick—and she pinned my arms behind my back.

Stepmother touched her cheek, prodding for a swell. "Piety," she said, her voice soft and dangerous, "go find me some ice."

"What?" Piety emerged from the shadows by the door, frowning at her mother. "Let Nick do tha—oh. Right." She trotted to the kitchen.

Stepmother and Chastity manhandled me up the stairs and down the corridors, to the drafty servants' quarters where I slept. Stepmother opened the door, and Chastity shoved me inside.

My only lamp was lit, burning out the oil for who knew how long. I could see a trail of soot on the floor. I crouched down, my scalp still aching too much for me to think clearly, and stroked my finger along the path of tiny hoof prints through my bedroom.

"Nice rat you had there," said Chastity. "Had to stamp on the pest three times before it quit moving." She kicked something by my side; I heard a rattle and clank. A tiny gear rolled into my line of sight, leaving a thin string of oil in its path.

"Jules—" I knelt and touched the gear, refusing to believe. I turned.

A small mess of copper and steel and shattered glass was splayed across my ragged carpet, just next to Chastity's daintily booted foot. The only parts still intact were his chain-link tail and a bit of glass that read *II.*

I kept whispering his name, "Jules, Jules," while the Steps stood over me, watching. I wanted to stand up and pummel Chastity, but my body was sluggish and obstinate, and it kept me on the floor. I stayed still, trying to catch breaths that wouldn't come.

"Mechanic Nick," said Stepmother, moving closer. "It's too perfect, really."

"I think we should call her Cinder-Nick," scoffed Chastity. "After how dirty she is. You know, from the soot."

"You needn't explain," Piety said, coming through the door. She handed Stepmother some ice wrapped in a cloth napkin. "We understand your reference, you nitwit."

"Piety!" Stepmother snapped. "You mustn't speak to your sister like that."

"I'm only saying I like your name better, Mother," said Piety. "Though it's a bit repetitive. I think we should call her Mecha-Nick—Mechanick . . . Mechanica."

Stepmother smiled. "It does have a certain resonance," she said. "And since she'll hardly be able to continue in that line of work now"—I cringed, imagining what else they must have destroyed—"she'll relish her new name all the more."

She reached down and grabbed my chin, pulling my face up so I had to look at her. "Mechanica," she said, rolling her tongue around each syllable, "you will stay in this room for two days; do not think I'll be foolish enough to put you in that cellar again. We are accustomed enough to your incompetence to get by without your services for that long. At the end of that time, you will resume your chores and your dressmaking. Until then, there will be no food, no water, and not a word from any of us. Perhaps then you will come to appreciate your station here, and the company of your family, rather than waste your time with disobedience."

She pushed me down again and left the room, her

daughters trailing behind her. I heard the key turn as she locked the door.

I stayed where she'd left me, crumpled on the floor, clutching Jules's gear and torn between grief and anger. I tried to move a few times, but my limbs shook too much.

When I finally gathered the strength, I pushed myself up and crawled into bed. I pulled my thin coverlet over my head and let myself cry, sure that the Steps would no longer be near enough to hear me.

I hadn't cried in years. My dull, lonely life had been too monotonous for the drama of tears, before today. I remembered almost crying at Market, when I thought I'd lost Caro's friendship before I'd gained it in the first place. And now I'd lost Jules, my very greatest friend.

The quilt soon grew damp and I made myself stop, not wanting it to frost over in the night, my room being so far from the fireplaces.

The snow was picking up, and white sheets drifted across my window. I forced myself to breathe evenly. I dragged my hand across my eyes and buried my face in a rag-stuffed pillow.

I didn't realize I'd fallen asleep, because in my dream I was still in bed, trying not to cry. I was still cold enough to shiver under my coverlet.

I heard a soft clinking on the floor, but didn't look over until the sound grew into a small crash, like a wineglass breaking in reverse. I thought Chastity had come back, and the only thing that gave me the strength to sit up and look was the prospect of getting my revenge for Jules's death.

I saw only the metal and glass scraps on the floor. At first I thought I'd imagined the noise—but then the scraps began to move. I heard the backwards glass-breaking sound again, and a few shards of Jules's body jumped into the air and fused together.

They settled to the floor. For a moment they were still.

Then everything moved at once. Gears rolled forward, nestling inside the healed glass, fastening themselves to rods and joints and each other. A copper ear skittered over the rug, clipping to Jules's forehead, which in turn joined his neck. More glass mingled, more gears clicked. They came together in a crescendo rush, and in a snapping, clanking, shivering movement, Jules was whole again.

He cocked his head to the side, and his ears pricked forward, greeting me. I laughed and felt the corners of my mouth tremble.

Jules cantered over to the bed and reared, pawing the threadbare blanket with his hooves. I bent to pick him up, but he jumped suddenly and I heard another crack. I cried out, unwilling to lose him again so soon.

Fissures appeared on his flanks and back, and his ears flattened to his skull in panic.

I clambered off my bed, trying to reach him, then

stopped, realizing with a dreamer's clarity that there was nothing I could do but watch.

The cracks grew over him like vines, faster and faster. At first he bucked, whinnying metallic screeches. Then he gradually stilled, looking up at me with frightened eyes.

He was growing.

New, molten glass leached out between his fissures, cooled, and hardened only to crack again and make room for more. The gears inside him moaned and creaked, and metal filings gathered at the base of his transparent stomach, then flew up again and formed more joints and chains and gears. Black smoke poured from his nostrils.

Soon he was the size of a large dog, then a man, and still he grew and grew, until he towered over my bed, as big as any plow horse I'd ever seen. Glass dripped down his flanks like sweat, a few rivulets still glowing with heat.

At last he shook his head and huffed, then nuzzled his copper nose against my shoulder to let me know he was all right. He smelled like a smithy.

Jules walked over to my closet, each heavy step making the floorboards creak. He nudged open the door and, finding the closet empty, stomped a rear hoof and butted it closed again.

I wondered what he was looking for; my closet was bare. Then I remembered Stepmother's words when she'd confronted me earlier: "Could you possibly have thought we would let you attend the ball with us? And in *that?*"

"Jules—" I gasped. "You made me a dress?"

He returned to me and knelt by the bed, joints creaking under his new weight. "Get on," he huffed, his voice low and graveled, and in the dream, it was only natural that he could speak.

I climbed onto his back, and then he was running, or maybe flying, and I felt the hum of his gears under me, the heat from his furnace warming my legs. We left my room through the window, and Jules galloped toward the forest behind Lampton Manor.

He halted, finally, beside a tall oak tree drooping with snow. I clutched his neck, my ribs still heaving as I gasped from the thrill of the ride. I knew this tree: my parents' graves lay under it. The snow was so deep, I could not see the gravestones.

"Look up," he said, and I did. A sumptuous ball gown was caught in the tree, all dark and shining, the train sweeping toward the ground. Wind battered the silk and lace, but the branches cradled the dress well, and it looked unharmed.

"It's beautiful, Jules," I whispered, stroking his neck. Tears froze in my eyes before I could cry. "I'm sorry I forgot your charcoal."

Jules huffed sharply and shook his head. "Get down, Mechanica," he said, and coming from him, suddenly I thought I liked the name, even if it had first been spoken by the Steps. Mechanic and Nick: the thing I loved and myself. Mechanica.

I dismounted, but kept one hand pressed to his side. My feet sank into the fresh, powdered snow.

Jules reared and then barreled forward, his head colliding with the oak tree. A sharp crack broke through the air. The dress shifted a bit in the branches, but stayed aloft. He backed up and rammed the tree again, with the same result. He did it again, and a third loud thud echoed through my dream.

"Stop it, Jules," I said. "It won't help . . ." And then I realized that the noise I was hearing wasn't right, didn't fit with the dream somehow. Then I knew I slept, and I woke to my cold room and thin mattress, the top of my blanket soaked and frosted stiff with tears.

My hand ached—I opened it and saw that the gear was still clutched in my fist, its spikes piercing my skin and drawing tiny drops of blood. I remembered that Jules was still gone, and I was still trapped.

I heard the thudding noise again and jumped. It seemed to come from outside, and I looked over and saw stripes cutting through the snow on my window.

A rock hit the pane, making another thud and another stripe through the snow.

I scrambled out of bed and opened the window, wincing against the freezing air. It was dark outside, and it had stopped snowing; I hadn't realized I'd slept so long.

Someone waved at me from the ground. "Can you come down?"

I could not identify the whisper, couldn't even tell if the voice was male or female. The view from my window faced the back lawn, just like my workshop did; this side of the house was both the coldest and the most secluded. I could see a white expanse of snow below me, and a dark figure, but I had no idea who it was.

I briefly worried that the Steps would somehow hear our hushed conversation . . . but suddenly I realized that I didn't care. They had killed Jules and destroyed the workshop—nothing else they could do really mattered to me.

I was freer now, in a way, than I'd been before.

"Well?" the rock thrower whispered again.

I stared down. I was on the third story, but exposed wooden beams ran all the way down to the ground, criss-crossing the white walls. I silently thanked whichever of my ancestors' architects had come up with that idea.

"I think so," I hissed back. I pictured the Steps inside, oblivious to my new adventure. The moon was barely up; they were probably reading Scriptures in the parlor right now, safely on the other side of the house.

I retreated into my room and wrapped my kerchief tight over my ears, then found the bulky coat in the back of my closet that used to belong to Father's driver. It hung comically large on me, but at least it was warm. I dug through the pockets and pulled out my old moth-eaten mittens. I wondered, for the hundredth time, why Mr. Candery's cupboard of Fey helpmeets didn't include moth repellant.

The window stuck halfway up. I wouldn't fit through unless it opened all the way, so I put all my weight behind it and shoved as hard as I could. The wood groaned, and I heard a crack, but it opened. I ran my mittened hands over the panes, checking for damage; there was only one small fissure in the glass, toward the bottom. I shivered, remembering my dream.

I climbed outside and let my legs dangle until my foot brushed against the first beam. I stretched my arm up to close the window, but I couldn't quite reach. I left it, knowing an open window wouldn't matter if the Steps found I was gone.

Gripping the window frame, I stepped down. The wall was slick and icy, and my feet wobbled on their narrow hold. I saw a beam to my right and reached for it, then held on tight as I lowered myself again. Snow lay thick on my next foothold, and some seeped through the tops of my boots.

I paused for a moment to breathe. I'd never been afraid of heights, but clinging to an icy wall with almost twenty feet between my body and the ground wasn't particularly appealing. Holding my breath, I felt downward for the next beam.

My foot slipped, and I dropped five feet or more before I managed to grab a windowsill. My ribs hit one of the beams on my way down, and my chest clicked painfully when I breathed in. Still, I wasn't on the ground, and I didn't think I was too badly injured.

I made myself look down. To my relief, I was halfway

there. With about ten feet to go, I took my hands off the beam and fell back.

I rolled on impact and the soft, fresh snow cushioned my landing. I stood up and dusted the powder from my coat. *That was almost fun,* I thought.

The dark figure came closer, and I recognized Caro's short, round body even before the moonlight revealed her face.

"I meant come down by the stairs, you idiot," she said. "You could have killed yourself!"

"Mmm, but I didn't, did I?" I grinned at her. I didn't think I'd ever been so happy to see someone.

Caro crushed me in her arms, and even though she was more than a head shorter than me, I felt comforted and protected in her embrace.

"How'd you find me?" I asked.

She cleared her throat and let me go. "I may . . . or may not . . . have followed you home." She squinted up at me, embarrassed. "You just seemed so broken down and henpecked, Nick. I thought you might need some looking after. And then I saw you get pulled inside like that, and I knew for sure you needed help. I figured I'd come back when it was dark and things had quieted down." She scowled. "Those aren't your sisters, are they? I mean, no one should treat you that way—but especially not your family."

I laughed roughly. I thought Caro must have dozens of siblings and cousins, all as golden and smiling as she, all caring for each other and never arguing.

"They're my sisters all right," I said. "My stepsisters, to be specific."

Caro shook her head. "Well, never mind that." She turned and started toward the forest, beckoning. "Follow me."

I trotted along behind her, trying to step in her boot prints. Her feet were much smaller than mine, though, and her stride shorter, so I often missed.

Once we were thoroughly inside the tree line, she stopped. "I'd like to help you," she said, louder now that we were away from the house, "but I won't give you help you don't want. I know how you feel about charity."

We both grinned.

"Now, I'm guessing you aren't one for running away, or you would have run long ago. Am I right?"

I shrugged. "For a long time I didn't think it was possible. But I don't want to leave my parents' house until I know there's a better life for me somewhere else. This was their home, and it's still mine."

Caro nodded. "And what would be better?"

I closed my eyes, imagining. "A home of my own, a big workshop, actually eating the food I make instead of just the scraps . . . and someday saving up enough to buy this place back from the Steps . . ."

I found myself spilling my whole life story, unsure what it was about Caro that let me speak so freely.

She just listened, barely even moving except to smile or

nod sympathetically, even though I knew her feet must be as numb as mine in the snow.

"That's why I came to Market today," I said, finally. "I want to build something really grand for the Exposition, so that maybe I can get enough commissions to open my own shop. Then I could leave the Steps forever, and I wouldn't have to rely on anyone but myself ever again." I laughed grimly. "Of course, now that they've caught me, I won't be able to go to Market, and I won't save any money, the whole workshop is gone, and the Exposition might as well be in Faerie for all I'll be able to get there." I laughed. "Not that I'd mind seeing Faerie."

Caro said nothing, even when I finally managed to stop talking. The wind hissed around us. An owl hooted overhead.

Finally she nodded. "Well," she said briskly, rubbing her mittened hands together, "I can't give you a new place to live, Nick, and I can't help you cope with the Steps. But I think I know how to get you to the Exposition."

"Really?" As much as Caro felt like a friend, my memories of the last seven years told me I couldn't rely on anyone, let alone a girl I'd only met that morning. Besides, how could someone as young and poor as I was help me?

"Yes," she said, all too patiently. "Since it's likely unwise for you to come to Market without the Steps' leave"—I raised my eyebrows and scoffed, but had to agree with her—"I can meet you here, whenever I'm free, and take your beads and machines and things, whatever you can still make, to Market for you. You can tell me what you need for your inventions, and I'll buy your supplies with the money from your wares."

I thought I'd spent all my tears, but my eyes pricked and burned at her kindness. "Thank you," I said, managing to keep my voice steady. "I think . . . I think that might work, if I can find time to get away." I brushed my face with the rough sleeve of my coat. "Why are you bothering with me, Caro?"

A branch cracked behind us. I stiffened, hearing snow crunch under boots as someone approached. I was certain the Steps had found me, and I spun to face them.

It was Fin. His arms were crossed, his face hidden in a tree's shadow. "Caro's not in it for nothing," he said.

"Lord, Fin," Caro exclaimed, "must you skulk so?"

Fin made a noise that might have been a laugh—or perhaps a growl. He stepped out of the shadow. His face looked serious enough, but the good-humored crinkles around his eyes told me not to worry. "If Caro's going to help you," he said, "she'll need something in return."

Caro's cheeks darkened, their blush so high I could see it even in the moonlight. "I—I thought . . ." She tugged on a curl that had come loose from her red woolen hat. "Maybe I could—perhaps—keep a small portion of the bead money, for my trouble." Her blush heightened still further. "My mum is sick . . . and the . . . the doctors—"

"Of course," I said, cutting her off before her face turned

purple. "I wouldn't think of letting you do this otherwise." I smiled at her, and she tentatively smiled back.

"Good," said Fin. "Mrs. Hart really needs a better doctor, but the only good ones are kept for the royals, doing nothing, and the medicine—"

"Oh, shut it, Fin," said Caro. "It's all turning out just fine, see?" Her voice was strained, though, and I wondered how serious her mother's illness really was. I thought of Mother, dying of Fey's croup, and the illegal lovesbane Father wouldn't buy to help her.

"Well, I can't thank you enough, both of you," I said, hoping to turn the subject away from sick parents and palace greed. "The only problem is, I think the Steps will be watching me very closely from now on. I won't be able to tell you ahead of time which days I can get here."

"Not to worry," said Caro. "Fin and I can get there, can't we?"

Fin nodded. "It'll take some work on your part," he said, "but then, it's for your benefit. We could hardly let you just sit around and be rescued." I could hear the teasing in his voice.

"It would be boring," said Caro, nodding her agreement.

"What does this brilliant plan involve, exactly?" I asked.

Caro beckoned and turned away, walking deeper into the forest. Fin took my hand, and we followed her together. His hand around mine comforted and frightened me all at once, just as Caro's touch had done at Market: simple and kind, foreign in the way it didn't ask anything of me.

The owl screamed again, and its call made me feel immensely far from civilization, even though Lampton Manor was, at most, a mile behind us.

"How do you know where we are?" I asked. In spite of the warm assurance of Fin's hand, doubts were trickling through my mind.

"We grew up nearby," said Fin. "We used to come play in this forest all the ti—"

Caro coughed, cutting him off. Part of Woodshire Forest was Lampton Manor's private property, and the rest belonged to the crown. As far as I could tell, we were walking just along the property line. No one was allowed in without a royal hunting license—or a royal pedigree.

"Er," said Fin, "as long as we're quiet about it, we should be fine."

I shook my head. "I don't care if we're allowed here or not."

Fin squeezed my hand. I squeezed back, but that suddenly felt too bold, and I hoped the moonlight wouldn't show my blush.

Caro stopped after a few more steps—too few—and Fin let go. "We're here," they said, almost in unison.

I looked around, confused. There was nothing "here" that was different from any other part of the forest: tree trunks, snow, and the blank bluish moonlight that cast Fin's brown skin with a deep indigo. My own skin looked bluish-gray, while Caro's had turned into translucent ice. The moonlight suited him better than either of us.

"I don't see anything," I said, feeling singularly dense and a little suspicious.

"Up there," Fin whispered, his breath gentle on my ear.

I looked up.

There were dark shapes in the trees above us, blotting the stars, covered with snow. Some were simple platforms, some boxes with slanted roofs like small tree-hung cottages. Caro stepped forward and brushed aside the branches of a thicket, and I saw a large shed on the ground there, almost completely hidden by the snow-covered bushes around it.

It took a moment, but suddenly I recognized what the shapes meant. They were ruins, and this was the site of the Forest Queen's abandoned village.

My story-loving heart thrilled at the idea, and I felt as if I'd stepped into one of the books I'd read in childhood. I stood still, taking in the moldering platforms around me, filled with a happiness that was almost like worship.

"You can bring your beads and everything here," said Caro. "Hide them in the shed, and we'll come pick them up, you see, and leave the money up there"—she pointed to a nearby treehouse—"once we've been to Market."

I almost asked them how to get up there: there were no stairs, no ladders, not even a knotted rope to climb.

Then I blinked and admonished myself for being so dense. It was a tree, wasn't it?

As if to confirm my thoughts, Fin loped away, grabbed a branch, and nimbly swung himself upward. Caro and I watched him climb. He reached the doorway and stepped in, snow falling through the slats where he walked.

He called to us from inside. "See? Simple." I could hear the smile in his voice.

I ran to the tree. I found I could more easily match my steps to his boot prints than to Caro's.

I jumped for the first branch and just barely caught it. I kicked my legs up toward the trunk, and my boots scudded over the rough bark before finding a hold. Putting most of my weight into my arms, I sideways-hoisted myself up until I could take the next branch. I was in the treehouse in seconds.

"You're right," I said, glad my years of chores had made me so strong. "It is simple."

Fin's laughter blended with mine. We looked out the window and waved, and Caro laughed too, below us in the snow.

We parted in the forest, since Esting City lay to the west and Lampton Manor to the east, each about two miles away. Fin hugged me this time, and he whispered "Good luck," his lips close to my cheek. I shivered.

He turned to leave, but then looked back at me, frowning. "Do those Steps of yours give you any food when they lock you up?" he asked.

I had to laugh. "Hardly," I said, "but I'll manage."

"Hmm." He dug into one of the pockets in his black woolen coat and pulled out a neat twist of brown paper a little smaller than his hand. "Take this," he said. "It's not much, but it's good."

I looked down at the parcel, then up at Fin again. I could sneak in and out of the pantry at home easily enough . . . but there was some code we were all writing there, in the forest that night, and I didn't want to break it. "Thank you," I said. And then, remembering Caro's concern about taking charity: "I'll pay you back after Market day."

Fin's dark eyes flashed. He didn't say anything, but I knew I'd taken the wrong tack. My heart sped up and I tried to think of a way to apologize, but while I was still fumbling with my words, he turned to go again. He and Caro kept a small distance between them as they walked away.

The snow squeaked under my boots, packing farther into the footprints I retraced. I noted odd-looking trees and rocks on my way, hoping they'd help me remember how to get back. I recalled the warmth of Fin's hand on mine, and I smiled as I walked.

I'd made it almost halfway back before I realized the immense flaw in our plan. With my workshop destroyed, I had no place to make beads or to finish that morning's knitting machine orders.

How had I forgotten for so long? I had always considered myself a fairly practical person — how could I not have realized?

I knew the answer already: I'd been caught up at once in Caro and Fin's excitement. I'd caught their hope like a contagion. Perhaps I wasn't so practical after all. . . .

Had Market been only that morning? So much had changed there, and so much had changed afterward, that it seemed ages away.

I covered my face with my hands and groaned. What would I tell Caro and Fin? And what could I do now, with my equipment gone? My new friends had offered me hope, but it had lasted only as long as Jules's reincarnation in my dream.

I couldn't give up, though, I lectured myself. Not yet. I couldn't disappoint my new friends so quickly . . . and what was more, I couldn't disappoint myself.

When I got back to the house, I encountered another problem. I'd barely managed to get down from my third-story window and couldn't possibly climb back up. I didn't dare go through the front door—I was almost sure the Steps were asleep by now, but *almost* hadn't been good enough lately.

At the back wall, facing the forest, the workshop's small ground-level window was buried under the new snow. I didn't want to see my shop in its ruined state, but the cellar was my only safe entry into the house.

I had to break the glass to get in, after I'd dug through about a foot of snow. My mittens were caked with it, so I just closed my eyes and made a fist, praying the blow wouldn't lodge any shards in my knuckles—and that the breaking glass wouldn't wake the Steps. The sound wasn't as loud as I'd thought it would be, thankfully, and it was further muffled by snow.

The cellar was nearly pitch-black. I lowered myself in and stumbled over my own feet.

The inside of the workshop was what I had expected: chaos. Sheets of butcher paper that Mother, and then I, had tacked along the walls, covered with formulas and calculations and little notes, were all torn down, shredded in pieces on the floor or crumpled up and stuffed into corners. Even with the paper that covered the room in brownish snowdrifts, though, it was *emptier:* most of my books were gone. My other works in progress that I'd set on the huge desk or on the bookshelves—oh, the bookshelves—lay in smithereens on the hard floor. I saw with a kind of harsh, hollow amusement that the only thing left intact was the sewing machine. The Steps had been careful, it seemed, not to destroy anything that would affect *them* too much.

With a shiver I realized that my dressmaker's dummy, while still unharmed, had moved: it leaned against the outer door, propping it open, so that I could see into the rest of the cellar. Attached to its wheeled base were tiny shoelace harnesses, the ones the buzzers used to do my sewing . . . and leading away into the darkness, a mincing pattern of infinitesimal hoofprints . . .

Jules, Jules . . . I couldn't think of him yet without shuddering. I knew he was a machine, and that Mother would say he couldn't feel pain, but then, she would have said he couldn't even think, not really . . .

No. I would mourn Jules later. I had to assess the workshop now, to see how impossible my once barely possible dream had become.

It was the empty bookshelves that hurt me most. Not just the odd failed experiments and scraps of dyed cloth I'd piled onto them, and not just the many old texts, invaluable as they had been; at least I'd had a few months to absorb them, and the years of Mother's tutoring before that. I knew enough, at least, to keep going, to get by.

But Mother's journals were gone. They had helped me learn to interpret the oldest of her reference books, they had given me her own ingenious ways of simplifying the sliding motion of a piston or of blowing glass evenly and without extra bubbles . . . and they had been in her voice, always her crisp, demanding, intellectual voice, the voice that had told me the stories and taught me the lessons I'd loved. I remembered the sight of my childhood storybooks burning up in Piety and Chastity's fire, the day they'd moved into their rooms. I knew beyond doubt that Mother's books and journals had already met the same fate, in the gaping central fireplace of the Steps' receiving room, our old library.

I could carry on without the journals, but I'd lost her voice again; I'd lost *her* again.

I wondered if Mother would ever stop dying, if she'd ever leave me for the last time. It didn't feel that way.

Even in her last gift to me, I had failed her.

I righted my toppled desk chair and sank onto it, burying my head in my arms. My temples pounded, my throat clenched, and though my eyes were dry and burning, I shuddered as if I were crying. I had no idea how one day could contain so much happiness and despair at once.

I heard a tiny buzz and clatter, and a light weight landed on my left hand. I looked up. One of the beetles perched on my ring finger, rubbing its wire feelers together. Two small sparks fizzed above its head.

"At least you were saved," I said, though I couldn't manage a smile.

But then I heard more buzzing, more clicks. A dragonfly emerged from a pile of clutter, and two spiders descended from the ceiling. Soon the whole fleet of buzzers had surrounded me, and beetles' legs were stroking my hair, butterfly wings fluttering against my arm, and spiders clacking their steel pincers as if in sympathy.

I stroked each of them in greeting and tried to smile. I was impressed, truly, that they'd known to hide, and I was pleased and slightly baffled that even they so clearly wanted to comfort me. *Why couldn't the Steps have found a dragonfly instead of Jules?* I thought—and then felt ashamed, for the dragonfly's sake. But I could not change my wish.

Still, I was grateful for the buzzers, at least.

And then I heard a sound that made my heart lift a little

more. The furnace rumbled to life in the back room—the room with the door that had no key.

I ran to the hidden place in the wall where the door would open, stumbling over crumpled paper. The sooty handprint Mother had left was long gone, worn off every time I'd moved from one room to the other, barely thinking of what I did. Shaking with hope, I pressed my hand to the place I knew so well.

Immediately, seamlessly, it opened. I let out a breath I hadn't known I'd been holding.

What if there was more to this, to the secret of the workshop, than the false fire of years ago? What if there truly was magic—real, illegal, Faerie magic—keeping this place hidden?

Had that magic sent Mother's letter to me too? I no longer believed Stepmother could have done me such a kindness.

I understood less about this place than I ever had—and I loved it more than ever too.

I hurried out of the furnace room, the studio, and then the cellar, making sure the doors closed fast behind me.

I took off my boots when I entered the hall and wiped the bottoms of my stockings with my flannel petticoat. I didn't want to risk even a speck of soot giving me away again. I took the servants' stairs as I always did, rickety, dusty, and connecting the kitchen to the drafty third floor that housed my bedroom. I pictured Jules climbing up the main stairs to my room and wished I'd told him about this more hidden staircase.

My dream flooded back to me then, just as real as when I'd first had it. I was too spent to cry anymore, or even to mourn him.

But in the absence of those stronger emotions, I felt a tingle of hope. The workshop was intact, or half of it was. And I knew, especially after tonight, that Mother still had some secrets in store for me. Standing there on the servants' staircase, I grew convinced that I'd find her designs for Jules eventually.

I was still lost in a dream of rebuilding him when I got to my door. I opened it—picking Stepmother's locks was always one of my favorite hobbies. Once inside, I could barely keep my eyes open as I forced the lock closed again; but I wanted to maintain the Steps' belief in my imprisonment, if I could.

Enclosed in my cold room once more, I drifted, exhausted, to my narrow bed.

Part III

MY room was flooded with light when I woke, and I couldn't believe I'd slept so late. I'd grown used to crawling out of bed before the first wash of sunrise warmed my window-sill—or to skulking into the kitchen after a night in the workshop without having slept at all.

I stretched slowly, relishing the knowledge that I had no chores that day. It was a Sunday, too, which meant the Steps had been at church all morning, and would be out on social calls for much of the afternoon. They were back for their brief Sunday luncheon by now, but in an hour or so, I could sneak down to the cellar.

Luncheon. My stomach started complaining even as I thought the word. I hadn't eaten since leaving for Market the day before, and even though I knew I'd survive until the Steps left and I could go down to the kitchen pantry, I wanted to eat *now.*

I remembered the parcel Fin had given me just before he

and Caro had left, the one he didn't want me to pay him back for. It was still in my overcoat's left pocket, hanging on a post at the end of my bed.

I smiled with relief, eagerly dug out the twist of paper, and unfolded it in my lap. I discovered a small, glistening pile of what looked like wrinkled garnets. When I touched one it sprung into fresh, purple-red plumpness, as if it had only just been picked.

Rhodopis berries! I hadn't seen them in years, not since before Mother died. They were Fey fruits, more like small, stoneless plums than any berries that grew in Esting, valuable for both their intense juiciness and the way that, if properly dried and stored, they revived at the touch of a finger. They were said to help settle an overworked mind, too; perhaps that was why Mother had eaten them so often.

Like all Fey goods, they were contraband now. I wondered at Fin's boldness and trust in giving them to me; with the king's strict laws, he could be imprisoned if I reported him. But then, I had decided to trust both Fin and Caro last night; I'd had to. Maybe Fin gave me the berries to show that he trusted me, too.

As the fruit burst into sweet, liquor-strong juice on my tongue, I was transported back to the tea times with Mother that I'd loved, a tray of sandwiches or a bowl of berries laid out between us as she imparted whatever lesson she had in mind for the day. The taste of the Fey berries was as vivid a memory as the image of Mother's face or the aroma of clary-bush tea, and I found myself even more grateful to Fin for letting me relive them so clearly.

I ate only a few before twisting the paper closed again. I'd be able to slip into the kitchen soon enough for some plain bread and cheese that wouldn't be missed. The berries were special, not just because they were so hard to come by in Esting, but also for the memories they evoked—and because of the new friend who had given them to me.

My hunger quieted, I looked around my room, wondering what to do until they left. I'd not had such a luxuriously idle stretch of time to enjoy since childhood. My first thought was a wish for books, real books: novels and poetry and stories. I loved my mother's science texts, but those were my work. I longed to read for pleasure. I decided to leave a note for Fin and Caro, asking them to buy me a novel at the next Market Day.

I did have a journal under my mattress—I'd brought it up from the workshop a few months ago, for when I had ideas in the middle of the night. I pulled it out, retrieved pen and ink from my dresser, and immersed myself in writing and drawing, careful to listen for any sounds of the Steps approaching my room.

I kept drawing Jules: diagrams of his hocks, his neck, his ears, the furnace in his belly, and the tiny pistons that surrounded it and made him move. It had never even occurred to me to open him up and learn more about his workings, strange as that seemed to me now. But I knew—I really knew, now that I'd lost him—that Jules had never been an invention to me, never been one of Mother's oddities, or even a tool. I'd no more have split him open than I would a pet cat, or a dog, or a horse of my own. I'd always known, deep down, that Jules held the rights to his body, not me. He wasn't an object, but a being, something really alive.

And that meant he was really dead. I flung my journal aside and lay down on the bed, cold and sad and still again, waiting for the Steps to leave.

I heard nothing for half an hour, and then the whinny of a horse from their rented carriage outside and wheels crunching in the snow. I grew certain they were gone . . . but I decided to climb out the window again, just in case. My little bedroom was on the side of the house the Steps almost never saw. They always used our grander front door to welcome guests or to meet their hired carriages. Here at the back of the house, where the shadows of the forest's tall pine trees sometimes nearly touched the workshop's window, I was hidden and safe.

Snow was still thick on the ground, but the sun was warm, and much of the ice on the wall had melted away. I moved quickly and got to the ground easily this time, though my chest still hurt me slightly.

I entered the workshop through the window I'd broken the night before. My eyes rested on Jules's harness by my sewing machine, and a sharp pain went through me. I sat down at my desk chair and took a shaky breath.

My largest caterpillar—I'd found several in the workshop's seemingly endless secret compartments over the last months—crawled out from behind a stack of papers and onto my hand, clinking a cool, weighty path over my fingers. I looked at the sewing machine again and saw the spiders crawling over it, the other caterpillars and beetles making their way to their assigned places, the dragonflies hovering in the air.

I had a whole battalion of insect tailors, but Jules had been their leader. I'd never thought even to name them—but then, people tend to name horses more often than they do insects. Jules had been my only real friend.

I ached. Jules, Jules. What would my work be without him here to help me? I remembered the jingling sound of his chain tail as he trotted after me along the shop's stone floor, the way his glass eyes always seemed to understand when I told him about the hardships of my life with the Steps. I had no one who would look at me like that now.

And yet . . . dark eyes, crinkled at the corners, with long shadow-casting lashes, appeared in my mind. A squarish face with warm, brown skin . . . an easy, dimpled smile . . . a low laugh. Fin.

I told myself not to be stupid. We'd met only twice, and those times on the same day. Of course it would be impossible for Fin to understand me.

But for all my stern lecturing of myself, I could not quite tamp down the warmth I felt, could not quite turn Fin's face from my mind: his quick smile, the shape of his mouth.

He haunted me nearly as much as Jules did. I almost hated myself for it.

I spent my first precious hour in the workshop making an inventory of Mother's supplies. In part, I wanted to reassure myself that the Steps hadn't ruined everything, that the back room of the workshop was still intact. I also hoped counting the sheeting and gears, the bolts and wires and glass, would lead me to some revelation about what I could build for the Exposition.

At first I imagined a mechanical spindle and spinning wheel—but any large enough to be of interest to businessmen would be far too heavy for me to carry. Then I pictured some sort of loom or an automated glass blower—but again, these would be far too large. This was a problem I hadn't even thought of until now. Anything that would impress the Exposition judges, I was certain, would be too big for me to transport there in the first place.

I sank down into my chair again, reduced back to depression and hopelessness more quickly than I could have imagined. Jules gone, my foolish thoughts of Fin, and now this—I was simple and stupid, not worthy of showing at the Exposition at all.

If Jules were here with me, I could talk to him, and maybe

talk myself through to some solution. But he was gone, and I didn't have the skill or the knowledge to bring him back.

I remembered Lord Alming's knitting machine then, and I forced myself to stand. At least I could do that.

Before I started, though, there was one other thing that I had to do. I took the ombrossus that I'd hidden away in my pocket and stood on a chair so that I could reach the workshop's window.

I looked down a bit reluctantly at the little vial with its tiny pool of brownish oil. If I did this, I would only have enough left for one or maybe two more applications. I would have to choose my days of freedom very, very carefully.

But if I didn't use it here, the Steps would almost certainly find the workshop again. I couldn't even be sure that the ombrossus would keep it safe . . . but it was better than nothing, and I had to try.

I tipped a drop onto my finger and smeared it onto the window's ledge, thinking of the Steps the whole time. The liquid was oily and slick, and the wood absorbed it very slowly. I was able to cover the whole windowsill with one drop.

I repeated the spell at the studio's front door, the one the Steps had found. Once again, a small drop was all I needed to cover the door frame. It felt thinner and more watery on my skin this time, but when I squinted at the vial, what remained was still thick and viscous. I supposed its structure must change to suit one's needs; I'd heard of much stranger things.

There wasn't even enough inside now to make a puddle at the bottom of the vial; a couple of lonely drops clung to its sides. Two more disguises. I would try to wait as long as I could before using it again.

The weight of sadness that had settled over me when the Steps found the workshop, when Jules died, had not yet lifted, even though I was doing my best to make it right.

I dragged myself to the back room and gathered the molds from my knitting prototype, the metals I would need for Lord Alming's machine.

I strapped on Mother's goggles and set to work.

The Steps were invited to dine at Fitz's the next day, so I slipped out my window again—this time to go to the woods. I'd made a list of supplies I would need to build more knitting machines, some other mechanical sundries, and a request for a novel or two, and I wanted to get it to the Forest Queen's ruins as soon as possible, since I didn't know when Fin or Caro would next be there.

It was still early in winter, and the snow's surface had melted during the day and then crusted over at night, so a slick glaze of ice met my boots when I reached the ground. I wobbled and slid across the flat expanse, progressing painfully slowly until I reached the forest. I felt as if I were walking on glass.

Looking back toward the house, I worried about the boot prints Caro and I had left in the snow. There were clearly visible divots tracing our path between the wall and the forest, as well as my return to the workshop's little cellar window.

But the Steps rarely went outside even in the temperance of spring and autumn, and never at all in the heat of summer or in the cold and snow. They preferred their fireplaces and their fainting sofas and their Scriptures, as they always had; the back of the house had never been their territory. I remembered the games and long walks I'd imagined enjoying with Piety and Chastity when I still thought we would be sisters.

They would never see the prints. I turned into the colder shadows of the forest.

The snow was softer here, shaded by the trees so it hadn't had a chance to melt and reharden. My feet sank toward the ground, and as I walked, I began to feel it trickle through the cracks in my old boots, numbing my toes where they stuck through the holes in my thin wool stockings.

It took longer to get to the ruins than I'd expected, though I didn't get lost, because I had our footprints to follow. They were less visible here, but they were not completely gone. I remembered the bent trees and sharp rocks I'd used to mark my path last night too.

The snow-covered ruins looked like clouds caught in the branches, or snowdrifts that had simply forgotten about gravity. I marveled that they had stayed up for so many years. Mother had told me the story of the Forest Queen, but because there was not much science in it, I'd only heard it a few times. I wished I knew more, and then thought of Fin's sculpture. I decided I would ask the next time I saw him.

Then I heard, in the closest ground-level shed, a creak. And another. Footsteps.

I darted behind the nearest tree, startled by the intensity of my fear. But a territorial anger soon took me over. No one was going to take away my hiding place before I'd even had a chance to put it to use.

I stepped forward. "Who's there?" I called, grateful my voice sounded as fierce as I felt.

I was greeted not with a cowardly scurrying away as I'd hoped but with a warm, easy laugh.

"It's only me, Nick." Fin appeared in the doorway. "No need to sound so fearsome."

He walked outside in the smooth, loping motion I'd so quickly learned was his signature. It seemed so natural to him that, had I not seen the clumsiness of some of Piety's and Chastity's suitors, I would have been tempted to assume such fluid and self-assured grace was simply part of being male.

"I was just checking for your Market orders," he said, nodding back toward the shed. His dark curls caught the sun. "And Caro wrote you a letter that I wanted to leave for you." He waved a thick brown envelope.

He glanced at the paper I held, and a grin began to suggest itself around the edges of his mouth. "That's quite the list you have there. You must be planning on some serious inventing."

I wasn't sure how to answer him — I had the sense that he was being sincere and teasing at the same time.

"I take my work seriously," I replied, and when the grin broke out full on his face, I felt my blush all the way to my eyebrows. I knew I'd said the wrong thing.

"Only teasing, Nick," he said, his smile softening.

I tried to smile too. "I know," I said, very quietly. I felt I should be able to tease him back, but I wasn't sure how to do it.

Silence stretched out between us. I looked at Fin, and I longed for something clever to say, but all I could think of was how foolish I must look, my skin pink and flushed, wearing old, worn skirts and a man's coat, disheveled from my climb down the wall and my walk to the woods.

Fin, on the other hand, looked just as at ease and — I reddened again as I thought the word — handsome as he had at Market, and as he had in the moonlight when he and Caro had come to find me. He wore a white shirt, the top loose around the brown slope of his neck, a gray wool buttoned vest and black winter coat and breeches, all tailored to his broad frame, and black, new-looking leather boots. He must not be so poorly off as Caro, then, I thought. I wondered if that was the source of the tension between them over the booth's rental fee—did Fin want to help Caro's family? I knew well that she wouldn't take charity.

At that moment, though, I thought it would be hard to refuse anything Fin might have to offer.

All this passed through my mind in the moment or two we stood looking at each other, during that painful silence.

If I couldn't think of anything to say to him, at least I ought to leave, instead of staring at him like an imbecile.

"Here's the list," I said, offering him my paper.

Fin quirked his thick eyebrows. Another smile. "Thanks," he said, and took it from me. "Here's the letter."

He kept smiling through another moment of silence I didn't know how to fill.

"Come now, Nick," he said. "Don't you want to talk to me?"

"I . . ." Of course I wanted to talk to him. I wanted to talk to him too much, which was precisely why I couldn't think of anything to say.

He smiled more gently now, and the absurd thought that perhaps he understood how I felt passed through my mind. "Back up in the trees, shall we?" he asked.

I still felt as if I should be able to think of something witty to say. Instead, I nodded. "All right."

I followed him up another tree, where there was only a platform, so well shielded by the branches above it that it was hardly dusted with snow. He kicked what little there was away, then took off his overcoat and spread it on the wood. He sat down on one side of the coat, his legs dangling over the platform's edge, and gestured to the space next to him, the motions of his hand elegant and almost formal. I wondered if he and his family worked in the palace.

"If you please, miss," he said, and I smiled. If his father wasn't a butler, or some other kind of high-class house servant, I'd have been shocked. That would have accounted for his nicer clothes, too.

"Thank you, kind sir," I replied, proper as I could, and sat down next to him.

"Well," he said. "Good."

I looked over at his profile. Half his smile, as it turned out, was just as disarming as all of it.

"So I suppose you'll have to go back to those idiots soon, but I thought we should talk a bit, being friends and all." His last word rose a little in a half question.

"Being friends." I nodded to encourage him.

"Why do you stay with them?"

"I . . ." I sighed. "They're still my family, I suppose. But that's not—" My lip trembled; I touched my palm to my chin, and it stilled. "If I left now, it would only be to seek the same work somewhere else. At least this way, I'm still living in my father's house. I can still work with what my mother left me. I am—there are things I love about my life there, in spite of everything. I couldn't give them up to be a maid in some other house that I'd never loved. When I leave, it will be to move to a workshop I've bought with my own money, earned from my inventions. I want leaving the Steps to be a triumph, not an escape. I want to feel like I'm not running away from anything, not hiding. I want to feel as if I never have to hide again."

I stopped. How had I managed to talk so much? And how would Fin possibly understand how I felt? He worked in some grand house he didn't care for, I was certain of it. Had I just insulted him?

I looked down at my moth-eaten mittens. I couldn't look him in the face.

"Not hiding." That was all he said, but it was enough that I could glance up from my hands and over to him again. I was caught immediately in the liquid darkness of his eyes, rimmed with those thick lashes, creased as always with good nature at the corners. But the creases faded now, and his face was serious. "That sounds well, Nick, not hiding. I think I know what you mean."

He did, I could tell. I didn't have space left in my mind to think about how, not while I took in his face, the shape of his eyes and lips, his mouth that looked so kind, even unsmiling—and most of all, the knowledge that he understood.

"I've been hiding too," he said, "or I feel as if I have."

Suddenly it wasn't hard to look at him. I was astonished. "What do you mean? What are you hiding from, Fin?"

He looked at me searchingly for a moment, and then looked down. Was it hard for him to look at me as well?

"There are things I—secrets I have to keep too." His hands, covered in thin black deerskin gloves—a high-level servant undoubtedly, I thought—dusted over his face in a gesture I could only call self-conscious, even from this beautiful, confident boy.

I considered his face again. His dark and shining hair and eyes, his brown skin, his thick lashes—they were all Su, physical traits from the Sudlands that set him apart from Estinger commoners. I took in his plain but well-crafted clothes, and I thought of the way he spoke, a bit more formally than Caro did, a bit like what I'd learned to expect from the minor nobles I knew, like Fitz or the Steps, or well-bred commoners as I myself had been, before Mother and Father died.

Of course. I understood then what I must have known, in some way, all along.

"Oh, Fin—your father is a noble, isn't he?"

I wondered if my question would offend him. A noble father who did not recognize his child could only mean that child was illegitimate. The Brethren frowned on any union outside marriage, and illegitimate children were barely people in their eyes. It was incredibly poor form to mention such a shameful notion out loud.

But there was no shame in it, I thought. It would only be Fin's father's shame, if he refused to recognize such a son.

Fin simply nodded. "Yes," he said, "my father's in the court. I work at the palace; I suppose that's clear enough.

Caro works there too, and her family; we grew up playing together."

"So you're a servant." Something else we had in common, besides working with our hands, besides our ability to climb trees quickly. Besides hiding.

"Yes," he said. "I go to the stables too, whenever I get the chance. I love horses, and the ones in the palace are the finest anywhere."

"I love horses too." Something else. "I have one of my own—"

"You do?" Fin's eyes sparked in delight before I could explain that my horse was about the size of my two hands, made of steel and glass, and ran on coal. "Don't you love riding? Isn't it just—" He laughed. "Isn't it better than anything?"

I sighed. "I haven't ridden in a long time," I admitted. The Steps hired a carriage when they had to go out, so that they wouldn't have to pay for horses or for the servants to keep them. I was too busy with their other chores, and anyway, their suitors usually came to them. But I remembered the horses from my childhood with such fondness. Once you get up to a good gallop, riding gives you an unmatchable feeling of freedom.

I had Jules, at least, whom I loved more than any person in my life right now. But . . . I'd forgotten again . . . Jules was gone. My dream that he'd come back to life had been just that.

Fin's eyes narrowed. "You have a horse and don't ride him? You have to know how wrong that is, Nick."

I couldn't bear for him to think ill of me. "I meant to say, I had one. He was . . . put down."

It was utterly the wrong phrase, of course, for what had happened to Jules. Chastity's boot crushing him, alone in my room, when he had only been trying to help me, trying to find me for some reason I still didn't understand.

"I'm sorry." Fin looked sorrier than most people would have. "I've never . . . one of my—one of the horses is getting very old. He was the first horse I rode as a boy. Someday we'll have to . . . but I've never lost a horse yet. Oh, Nick, I'm sorry I said anything."

"No, you're right." Though it was easier to look at him now, his beauty still startled me. "A horse should be ridden. They go so bored otherwise, and then they're not fit enough to jump, and . . . even if I still had a horse, though, I've been so busy with my chores and the sewing—I make all their clothes—and the work I'm doing for my inventions, you know."

Fin shook his head. "I don't know how you do it all," he said. "All these things. You're amazing, Nick."

I winced. I'd spent so long trying to make the world think I was unremarkable; I realized now that I needed people to think of me that way. If anyone really thought I was special, they would ask things of me, things I didn't think I could give. Better if Stepmother thought me simple and stupid, and better if everyone else thought that too. Fin saying I was amazing threw off that balance inside me. There was space and darkness and color there now. There always had been, I supposed, but I had managed to ignore it.

I told myself that it was a thing to be proud of, that I worked so hard. "Thank you, Fin," I said with my exhale, and my tongue lingered a little over his name, though I didn't want it to.

But then I frowned. "You do about as much, I suppose," I said. "You're a manservant, and you care for the horses, obviously very well." He grinned again at this and ducked his head, a few curls spilling into his eyes. "And you still make those sculptures. Oh, they're gorgeous, Fin. They're like life."

He raised his eyebrows, his grin spreading, and then he slipped off the platform and jumped to the ground. I held back a small shriek—we were at least twelve feet up—but he landed in a fluid crouch, and his shirtsleeves were covered in a cracked film of powdered snow. I thought of how cold he must have been up there with me, with his coat spread under us.

A gentleman, I thought. It was a word I used to announce Chastity's and Piety's callers, but rarely thought of in its true meaning. A gentleman.

He vanished into the shed and came back a few seconds later, bearing something small and brown. He loped over to the tree, climbing with only one hand and his feet as he carried it with him.

I smiled at him as he settled down gracefully next to me. Was there anything he didn't do easily?

He gave me the sculpture he held.

It was a horse, a gorgeous roan, moving through some unseen wind—or no, standing still, with wind streaming back through its mane and tail and the longer hair toward its fetlocks and hooves. It was almost exactly the same size Jules had been. Its bright eyes did not hold Jules's life or intelligence, but through Fin's artistry, they almost seemed to.

"I knew this one was yours. I don't know how," Fin said, laughing a little, "but I did. I thought you'd like the horse best, much as you admired the Forest Queen back at Market."

"Oh, I do. I do like this one best." He couldn't know how perfect it was. There was no way he could know.

"But the Forest Queen," I said, recalling the questions I'd wanted to ask him, "these are really her ruins?"

"We're in them right now," Fin said, touching his hand to the platform under us. "Imagine that. These trees, right here, are where Silviana built her haven for . . . for anyone who needed her help."

I looked around, trying to picture the ruined tree houses at the height of their glory. "I always loved her," I said, hoping to keep him talking.

He hardly needed the encouragement. "I did, too," he said with a smile. "She isn't a popular figure up at the palace, you know; well, at least not with the court. Most versions of the tale make the king—it was King Dougray III back then, one of the worst in a long line of tyrants leading right up to today"—a muscle in his jaw twitched—"into a buffoon, if not an outright villain, and you can see why that's a dangerous story to tell." He looked at me. "It's actually banned, you know. Her story. You can't find it in print."

That detail shocked me for a moment. But I'd never read anything about the Forest Queen in our library, and it did sound like something the king would do. . . .

"The servants like to tell it, though," he said, "perhaps even more these last few years. Ever since those laws against Faerie came in, you see."

I was surprised he hadn't said *since the quarantine,* the way Fitz or the Steps might have done; but then, Fin had given me rhodopis berries. I was starting to see where his sympathies lay.

His voice had grown a touch deeper and faster as he spoke about Silviana, and now it sped forward again. "She did a remarkable thing, Nick: she saw a wrong and made it right. She kept the people of Esting from suffering. It didn't last, I know, and Dougray thought he'd bested her in the end, but . . . Well. The tree houses are ruins, but they're still here, aren't they?"

I nodded, looking around again, loving the place even more than I had last night.

"They're still here!" Fin cried. "And people still tell her story. The servants at the palace; people all over the country.

The Forest Queen is one of Esting's heroines, for goodness sake. Like the Wolfspeaker, or Ebony and the Gnomes, but—but *real*."

"She was always one of my favorites," I said quietly. Pleased as I was that I'd learned more about the Forest Queen, I was a little stunned by the power of Fin's love for her. "Still," I added, "wouldn't she be a dangerous subject for a sculptor like yourself? Rebellious, since her story can't even be printed?"

The hardness in Fin's eyes was replaced by his customary good humor, and he shot me a crooked grin. "Not rebellious at all," he said, as if the very notion were shocking. "Silviana represents the best of Esting. She was brave enough to do what was right, no matter what the law said. *That's* patriotism. Not following a tyrant lord, but dissenting, and putting real action behind your dissent."

"The way you tell it," I said, amused, "you nearly make me want to dissent, myself."

He laughed. "I imagine it's clear," he said ruefully, "that I've debated on this subject before."

"I had an inkling," I replied. We both smiled; but even though I knew he was laughing at himself, in truth I had to admire his passion.

"In any case," Fin went on, "maybe I'll sculpt another Silviana, since you love her, too. But this chap," he touched the nose of the horse I still held, "he might as well have spoken to me, and told me he was yours."

I looked down, still smiling, but the sculpture's resemblance to a certain other small equine form sent a tremor through me. Remembering Jules, it hurt to hold this heavy, inanimate horse in my hands. But it was beautiful, and Fin had made it, and now he had given it to me. I imagined him with his brush, lost in concentration, his eyes crinkled at the edges from squinting at his work instead of from smiling, his dark skin and hair lit by the steady glow of a gaslight—I supposed candles flickered too much to be of use to artists.

"It's wonderful, Fin," I said finally. "It would sell for so much at Market, though. Why would you give it to me?"

His answer was better than I'd even hoped. "I like you, Nick. I wanted to give you something." He smiled again, but there was some sadness, some hardness behind it that I didn't know how to place. "It's not charity, if you're worried about that. I know you and Caro are the same that way."

I blushed, but stood my ground. "I want to get things on my own merit," I said. "Is there anything wrong with that?"

He shook his head. "Of course not. I suppose I could have used a little more of it in my own upbringing."

I imagined his childhood, the illegitimate son of a noble father, how the servant children must have teased him and told him it all came too easily to him.

"But, Nick—what if someone you knew, someone you loved . . . someone in your family . . . really needed it? Would you take . . . help . . . for their sake, so they could get what they needed?" His smile had vanished. "Wouldn't it be selfish not to?"

I remembered Mother, who died of a Fey disease that only Fey medicine could have cured, illegal medicine Father refused even to look for. "I would have taken help for my mother before she died. Anything that would have made her well again. But the kind of sickness she had . . ." I shook my head. "The only help was lovesbane, and it was already outlawed here."

Fin nodded. "People still get Fey's croup, and they almost always die now. With enough money, though, one can still buy lovesbane—through less-than-legitimate means." He spat out the last few words; I supposed "less than legitimate" was a phrase that had been applied to him a few times too many.

"The Night Market? They sell lovesbane there?" I had heard Fitz mention the illegal-goods market that opened at midnight, once a week, in Esting City and changed its location every time. It was his father's pet project to shut it down, but no one from the court had found it yet—or if they had, they weren't speaking up.

"Any kind of Fey goods, Nick, almost anything you could have gotten before the quarantine. The price is exorbitant, but"—his face darkened in an angry flush—"if you have the money, and the knowledge of whom to ask, you can . . . It's a curable disease, you know. Or it was."

"I know." Why were we talking about the disease that killed Mother? I didn't want to, and it certainly didn't seem as if he wanted to, either.

"If I—if I had any power, really, the first thing I'd do is make lovesbane legal again," Fin said. There was real passion in his voice, real anger. "All the Fey goods, for that matter. It's wrong, the way it's done now. Wrong."

I remembered Caro refusing charity at Market and how sensitive both she and Fin had seemed on the subject of her lack of money. I remembered what she'd said about her mother. "That's what Caro's mother has, isn't it? That's what's making her sick."

"Yes." Fin shook his head. "She's had it for months now, a slow, lingering case. It will kill her. Not quickly, so Caro pretends it's not true. But it will kill her, unless she gets the lovesbane."

"Like it killed Queen Nerali."

Fin looked up at me, and something in his face had changed. "Yet it was lovesbane, too, that killed the Queen."

I considered this: lovesbane, both a poison and a cure. It had been the first Fey import to be outlawed in Esting, and it became the symbol for the whole quarantine. There wouldn't be an Exposition this year were it not for those laws and the demand for Estinger technology to replace the magic we'd lost.

"But could we afford it, Fin? Even if she'd let us help her, could we?"

"I could." Fin spoke quietly, and I could tell I shouldn't ask him how.

"Well." I flashed to an image of Mother's funeral, the itchy black dress that was too tight on me because Father had given my old measurements to the dressmaker, the long lines of strangers telling me they were sorry. "You have to help her, then, Fin. Anything is better than—well. Yes. You have to help her."

Fin pressed his gloved hand over mine. "I know."

His hand was warm, and suddenly I didn't have anything else to say, but it seemed all right this time.

We sat side by side, quiet, our hands slipped together. Until it grew late and I had to go home.

I WALKED back through the forest quickly, every once in a while touching Fin's sculpture where it lay in one of my coat's roomy pockets. I found myself lingering over the image I'd conjured of Fin sculpting the horse, sketching from life first, perhaps, then working through prototypes, molding parts, making the cast for this piece, pouring the metal and waiting and unmolding, polishing, and finally painting. I pictured his hands holding a paintbrush.

I'd come to the edge of the forest. I touched the horse's nose once more, smiling, and hurried across the clearing to the cellar window.

I slipped in with no trouble this time, my coat barely catching on the window's rough wooden edge. Enough times in and out this way, I thought, and I would wear it smooth . . . so long as the Steps didn't find me out again. I could only guess what they might do if they discovered the studio again.

But I was sure that the ombrossus oil would work, at least for a while. After the Exposition, who knew if I would even need it anymore? I could have a patron, and enough commissions to rent a room in the city, away from them, and I could start the long journey of saving enough money to oust the Steps from my parents' house once and for all.

The thought set my heartbeat into a skitter. *One step at a time,* I told myself. *One small, small step at a time.*

Caro's letter, I remembered, was still waiting unread in my coat's other pocket. Feeling a bit ashamed for my fixation on Fin's gift, I sat down in my desk chair to read it. I put my feet up on the desk; when the Steps had ransacked the studio, they'd knocked my chair over and destroyed the adjustable screws Mother had built into its legs. The chair was stuck too low for me until I could find time to repair the mechanisms, but I couldn't do that without taking it apart at great risk to its old, ornately carved witchwood frame. I couldn't bear to damage any more of Mother's things, given how much had already been lost. In the meantime, it felt pleasantly rude and rakish to put my feet up on the desk, even if no one but the insects saw me do it.

The letter was a thick one, and I wondered how a girl I'd met only twice could have so much to say to me. I slid my finger under the cheap candlewax seal on the envelope, remembering my search for the key behind Grandmother's portrait. I'd hidden the workshop key under my mattress since my birthday, but considering recent events, I made a mental note that it would probably be wiser to keep it on my person.

Dear Nick,

It's possible that I ought not to write you a letter as long as I already know this one will be, or any letter at all until we've been friends for years, and probably I shouldn't hug you so tight the next time I see you as I did the last. Certainly I shouldn't feel as fond of you as I already do. For, oh, in my mind we are such good friends already! Already you are dear to me!

My mother says friendship should be slowly and carefully cultivated, like a rose garden, like a romance in a story. That every reason you care about someone should be rational. She says I care too quickly.

I suppose she is wise; I know she has been hurt fewer times than I have, though she has twice as many years to her credit. But friendship has never been something I could do halfway. When I met Fin, he was scarcely more than a baby — and I a toddler myself, not far from my mother's eminently logical apron strings — and I announced that very day that he was my favorite person. Our mothers thought it was *only that he was such a lovely baby; Fin does insist on being obnoxiously beautiful, doesn't he? But no, it was simply that he was already my friend, or, to be more precise, that I was already his. And it was the same, Nicolette, with you.*

Nicolette, so baffled at Market and yet so brave, with such marvelous things that you've made, such marvelous hope in your eyes. Who could not wish to be your friend? It was beyond my small capacity, at least.

I had to laugh. I'd thought that all my eyes showed was loneliness, or perhaps a certain hard desperation, a determination to continue my mother's work. To hear that someone else had looked at me and seen something else, something better than what I saw in myself, was like a reassuring hand laid on my shoulder. I could hear every word of the letter in Caro's cheery, laughing voice too. It was like having her here in the room with me. Father's letters had always been cordial and stiff. Mother's journals were thoughtful and informative, but they were in an inventor's voice, not a friend's, and they had always been, above all, a reminder of her catastrophic absence from my life.

Caro's letter went on for ten and a half crowded pages, mostly stories about the scrapes she and Fin got into growing up (*. . . and would you believe it, his brother never found out where we hid them! It was in the ruins, of course . . .*) and, more recently, the scrapes from which she was continually trying to rescue her younger cousins (*. . . thirty-seven first cousins, just first cousins alone, Nick, and all but two of them working at the palace — you can imagine how busy that keeps a girl . . .*).

Busy indeed, I thought. How on earth did Caro find time to write a tome of a letter like this, with all her troublemaking cousins underfoot?

Really, though, she continued, *I'm glad I dive headfirst into caring for people. There's so much warmth in anybody, if only you reach out to find it. As pretty as Fin's always been, even, and as privileged as some people think he is, he can be overserious and a bit melodramatic sometimes. There aren't enough people who know how thoughtful and kind he can be. You brought that out of him at Market, you know, Nick. That's one of the reasons I liked you so well straightaway.*

And, oh, please understand that this isn't pity, but I think you might need someone to talk to . . . or, as is the best I can do in these letters, someone who can talk to you. I think most of the voices you hear are cold.

Anyway it is nearly morning now, and I have to get back to my chores, but I will send you more stories and — I hope! — laughter soon. You see, I can't stop talking even when my mouth is shut. Mother says I must make music boxes because I'm never content unless I have some kind of voice — talking, or music, or reading stories, or writing letters. So this letter is in fact very selfish and a welcome outlet. Do forgive me.

Whatever Mother might say about my foolishness, though, I have to believe it's right to be a warm voice, a companion if I can be, as soon as ever I find a friend. However I can be that friend to you, Nick, I hope you believe that I will do so.

All best of the best from,

Caroline Hart

PS: The ribbon is a little favor the servant girls like to give to each other here. Blue is for courage. You have plenty of that! But they are called friends-ribbons, and I thought you would like one.

I wound the ribbon around my wrist absentmindedly, imagining Caro as she wrote this letter: probably by the guttering light of the cheap candle she sealed it with, probably blinking with exhaustion from finishing one long day's work and getting ready for another. Much as she claimed to not be able to help talking all the time, I knew she was doing me a real kindness, taking time out of her harried day to give me a warm voice, as she called it.

I was grateful. I would tell her so, I promised myself, the next time we met.

I took the blue ribbon off my wrist and looked at it: it was thin, and long enough, perhaps, to . . . I looped it around my neck. It hung down to my sternum, and if I kept it under my dress, it would hide the workshop key perfectly.

And there was something else I could hide too. I'd placed Jules's fragments in a glass box I'd made a few weeks earlier; I couldn't bring myself to throw them away, or even to reuse the few parts that would still function.

I picked up one of his largest gears; it had been attached to a piston that moved one of his hind legs. I took the biggest piece of glass, too, the almost-round fragment that read *II*. I brought both of them, and the ribbon, into the back room, and I turned one of the iron wheels on the left side of the furnace. It rumbled into a higher heat, and I selected the smallest, thinnest poker, more a needle than anything else, from the wide selection hanging next to it. This would be a delicate, fiddly operation: I had to melt the edges of the glass fragment without ruining the etching in its center.

I strapped on my heavy smith's apron, goggles, and work gloves, and I pulled the now-glowing poker from the furnace. I ran it slowly along the edges of the glass.

An image of Jules twitching on my bedroom floor, Chastity's foot coming down to finish him off, flashed suddenly through my mind and made me wince. I flinched and the poker shook in my hands, dragging a hot line through the glass.

I wanted to cry. Even this, even this, I had ruined. Mother's workshop, Jules—I had let the Steps damage all of them. I pressed the glass into the gear quickly, before it could harden again, before I could ruin it further.

And yet . . . yes, they were damaged, the workshop, the last piece of Jules. But they were not ruined, not beyond repair. I had fixed the workshop again, the best that I could, and I was going to keep working. That was all I could ever do.

I straightened my back and took a deep breath. Looking down at the charm I'd just made, I saw that the damage was not so bad after all. The line I'd made when my hand slipped was small; it was just enough, in fact, to slide a ribbon through.

I picked up the charm with a small pair of tongs and hurried back into the studio, where I placed it on the windowsill so that it could cool in the frosty air. My broken window—damaged, but not ruined. Damaged, but more useful now, because it let me come and go from the house undetected.

Damaged, but somehow better, nonetheless. I started to smile.

The charm was still warm, but safe to the touch, and I strung Caro's ribbon through the line I'd accidentally made. The glass was perfectly clear and glinted in the light; the small weight of the charm made the necklace spin a little, back and forth. I tied a neat knot in the ribbon and hung it around my neck.

I turned back to the workshop, broken but not ruined, and thought about my next task. I still had to decide what to show at the Exposition. . . .

My coat was flung carelessly across my desk. I picked it up and hung it on the door, so as not to forget to bring it upstairs; I would have to haul in fuel in the morning.

The sculpture Fin had given me was in the coat's right pocket. The Steps were likely to find it, eventually, if I kept it in my room. . . . I remembered Jules's stable-box, still empty and waiting in its place on the shelf. Suddenly the box seemed like the perfect place to keep Fin's gift. It could be a sort of memorial.

I took up the box and placed it on my desk, running my fingers reverently over its seams, then undid the leather buckles at its clasp and opened it; the carved lid's heft always surprised me. I tucked the horse gently inside, touched its nose once more, and closed the lid again.

I turned back to the shelf—and saw a seam in the wall, where the chest had been. I ran my hand along it, recognizing Mother's way of keeping secrets by now.

There was a catch at the end of the seam, just by the bookshelf's corner. I pushed down, and the back of the shelf creaked open.

Of course I thought of Jules, and of the insects, and I

closed my eyes and reached my hand inside, wishing, wishing there might be another automaton sleeping there.

Instead my fingers brushed dry paper and leather. Lifeless.

With my other hand, I touched my new necklace, the relic of my old friend, the ribbon from my new.

I opened my eyes and shivered, forcing my hand to drop. I had no time for mourning today. I looked at the clock on the wall—one of Mother's designs, large and ornate, always a few minutes fast—and cringed when I saw the time. I had to move quickly before the Steps came home.

Reminding myself not to expect too much, I plunged both hands into the secret compartment and pulled out its contents. The leather I'd felt was binding for a journal, stuffed with so many extra papers and notes that the top cover jutted up at almost a thirty-degree angle.

I returned to the witchwood chair and sat down. Mother's handwriting was spidery and sometimes nearly illegible, but I'd seen enough of it by now that I could make sense of her entries quickly.

The first pages were fairly standard measurements and formulas and temperatures, and the drawings were a series of pistons. A few pages in, though, I had to stop.

I gasped and took a few deep breaths to slow down my heartbeat.

The series of mechanisms on this page had a definite

shape. I cast about in my mind for other things it could be, not wanting to give myself false hope. But there was no other possibility.

It was a leg, a decidedly equine leg, with a pattern of gears and pistons and chains that I knew well.

My hand flew up to my neck again, clutching at Jules's gear. I hugged Mother's journal to my chest and laughed, hardly believing my luck. I owed Fin yet more thanks: if he hadn't given me this new horse, I might never have moved the box.

I wanted to start reading right away, but I had so little time left, and I had to work on my knitting machines. There were enough supplies left in the furnace room for at least a few more. When I returned tomorrow, I would still need to decide exactly what I would make to show at the Exposition. My whole future depended on that one event, and I needed to save all my machine and bead proceeds toward putting together something truly spectacular. My loneliness for Jules, much as it howled behind my every thought, would have to wait.

Minutes later, as I welded the knitting needles onto their base, I stopped and gasped again. My torch slipped in my hand and nearly burned through my thick gloves.

I'd had my revelation after all. I needed a showstopping Exhibition piece, and I desperately wanted Jules back—could I not combine the two?

I dashed to my desk, poring through Mother's notes again.

Yes, I thought, it would be easy enough to scale—some changes to the weight-bearing structures, of course—and I'd need quite a lot of charcoal . . . I laughed again, and felt the muscles in my face start to ache from smiling so wide. I imagined myself at the Exposition—the entrance I'd make!—and I saw Fin's face in the crowd, his eyebrows raised with admiration, that easy grin on his face.

I shivered again, though the workshop was still warm from my metalwork.

Then I went upstairs, knowing I had little time to spare before the Steps' return. I'd burned my wrist in my haste, but it was a small price to pay for the day's wonders.

Just as I closed my bedroom door, I heard the crunch of the Steps' carriage wheels on our snowy driveway. One of the horses whinnied, and I thought of Jules, and of Fin's sculpture, too. I pressed my necklace to my throat, imagining things to come.

The Steps were often gone in the next weeks, attending teas and parties, touring the palace, and hoping to catch a glimpse of the Heir. They went out daily, to town or on social calls, or on Saturdays, to Market.

I couldn't resist my amusement when Piety returned from Market with a satchel full of glass beads—my own handiwork, that I'd have recognized anywhere. She poured a dozen or so into her hand and held them up to catch the light—"Look how fine, Chas!"—and while Chastity and Stepmother ignored her, I hid my sniggering in the crook of my arm. When Piety shot me a cold look, I told her the beads were "very fine, indeed," and I would happily sew them into her next gown.

I could produce a basic knitting machine, start to finish, in only an hour now. The beadwork went quickly too, and I began experimenting with finer glass craft: more intricate boxes and bowls, covers for my machines, and floral pendants. Thinking of the Steps' Heiress fantasies, I created a delicate headpiece of clear glass, not quite a tiara, not quite a circlet.

I told myself I would sell it later, but I kept imagining myself at the ball, spinning in the arms of some dark-haired lover I wouldn't let myself clearly picture, the headpiece twinkling in my hair and a full skirt swirling around me. It was a dream I knew my stepsisters often indulged. Could I not allow myself the same luxury?

My favorite dream, however, was still of the Exposition that would follow the ball. I worked on my masterpiece every night, leaving the creation of my Market wares for the days, when the Steps were gone. In between, I found myself smiling more and more, humming while I cooked breakfast, singing while I fetched wood.

I was singing to myself one night when I heard a knock at the cellar window. I jumped and squinted at the slat I'd put up to block any intruders—not that I needed to worry about the Steps, who minced from parlor to carriage to parlor, avoiding sunlight for the sake of their complexions. But I did worry about mice. Besides, the ombrossus oil was old, and I wanted to give it all the help it could get.

"Oy, Nick." The voice was cheerful, young, female. Caro. "It's only me."

I sighed and pulled the slat down, revealing her smiling, plump face, gold curls escaping from that same red knit cap she'd worn the last time I'd seen her.

"Can I come in?" she asked. "I've grown devastatingly curious about your gigantic orders from Market. I had to come see your work for myself."

I looked around at my cluttered desk and the walls covered in layers of sketches and notes. It always felt like something just teetering on a state of barely controlled chaos to me, but looking at it as I imagined she would, as someone who had never seen it before, I knew it must look interesting. Exciting.

"All right," I said, and found that I was almost shy again. I hadn't thought of myself as shy, in all the years I'd lived with the Steps. I had been forthright and talkative enough with Mr. Waters, hadn't I? But it seemed with people my own age, I was nervous. I didn't entirely like that about myself, but I wasn't sure if there was anything I could do about it.

Then I realized there was a more pressing problem with letting Caro into the workshop than my reticence.

"If I can't enter from inside, I have to go through the window . . ." I said carefully.

Caro examined the narrow window frame before her. "Well, there's no way I'll fit through there," she said with an easy chuckle.

I smiled; I hadn't known if I would offend her. If I'd implied there were some narrow space Chastity couldn't fit through, she would have thrown a tantrum—and Chastity's figure was not even as generous as Caro's.

"Hmm." I stood on tiptoe to look out the window at the sliver of dark sky I could see beyond her. Then I glanced back at the large cuckoo clock on the wall behind me, the one I had unearthed only a week ago. Mother had built it full of nesting mechanical birds, and they tweeted and chattered with no regard for any particular time.

"The Steps are in bed, but I'd like to wait a bit longer to be sure they've gone to sleep," I said. "Can you wait until midnight?"

Caro rapped a bag she kept at her side, which made a flat, wooden sound. "I've my book here," she said. "I can wait forever and be just fine—got the whole night off. Right near had to beg Cousin Louisa to cover for me, but she owed me the favor—well. I'll tell you the story when I get in." She glanced back toward the forest. "Shall I come tap on the window again?"

"No, I'll come out to you, and then I can sneak you in."

She nodded, another curl escaping from her cap. I glimpsed her brown skirts and boots for a moment, and then she was gone.

I looked around the workshop again, and decided a bit of cleaning triage was in order before I had my first-ever guest. I shuffled the papers on my desk into some semblance of neat stacks, grabbed a dustpan and collected the tiny grommets that had fallen onto the floor, and poured them back into the little tin storage box where they belonged.

Then I went back to the furnace room and finished welding the needles to my newest sewing machine. After that, just over half an hour had passed, and I supposed the Steps must surely be deep asleep. I took my coat and crept up the cellar stair, into the hallway. All was still.

I opened a disguised servants' door in the hall, covered in the same simply patterned paper as the walls—after Mother's death, Father had covered over the Fey wallpapers she had loved so much, the ones with flowers that grew and faded to match the seasons—and slipped into a narrower, plainer hallway, this one with bare wooden walls. From there, it was a quick journey out the back of the house and across the snow-covered lawn.

I thought I would have to walk all the way to the Forest Queen's ruins before I would find Caro, but she was perched on a low-hanging tree branch just at the edge of the forest. The snow that had accumulated on the branch was swept into neat little drifts on either side of her, and she sat with her back curved and one hand under her chin as she read, utterly intent on her book. It was a bulky pink volume, and the title—stamped in black on the cover, in a fanciful font—simply read *Stories.*

"Caro?"

It seemed she didn't hear me; her brown eyes continued to flicker over the words, and she chewed her bottom lip. She was entranced.

"Caro?" I repeated, a bit louder. "It's midnight; you can come inside now, if you like."

She looked up then, finally, startled. Her eyes widened, and the book slipped in her hand.

"Oh! Hullo, Nick, I'm sorry," she said. "I just go some other place when I read, I guess."

I smiled at her. "I'm the same way," I said, "though I don't get to read much but engineering texts these days, and my mother's old journals. The Steps took most of my books away years ago."

Caro's mouth twitched; the sympathy in her eyes was far deeper than I had anticipated. "Goodness. I'll bring you more novels from Market, then. There's a traveling peddler due back next week who sells wonderful books." She tapped the one she held before earmarking its page and stuffing it back in her patchwork bag. "I must've read this twenty times already, but they're some of my favorite stories from when I was small. Just silly little things—what people used to call Faerie tales before the quarantine. Magic stories. You can't get much magic in stories anymore—but I can lend you this one for a bit, if you like. It's that good." She pulled the book from her bag again and held it out to me.

I knew it was a dangerous offer, a sign of trust. I felt sure she and I would like the same books. I took it happily and tucked it under my arm.

She smiled fondly at it. Then her eyes narrowed as she looked at me, though they never lost their good humor. "Just be sure you give it back, now."

I made my face as serious as I could and crossed my heart. "I swear it," I said, as if I were vowing knighthood. "I shall defend it with my very life and treat it most reverentially until I return it to your ladyship."

She giggled. "Oh, no need for reverence," she said. "You'll see I've folded and unfolded every page in there to mark my place, and written in it too. Books are meant to be well-loved. So long as I can still read it when I get it back, you can be a bit rough with old *Stories,* if you like."

I grinned; we understood each other still better than I'd thought. "I do the same to my books," I said. "Nothing like a good argument in the margins with someone who's already said all they have to say on the subject."

She nodded, smiling broadly, and we set off across the lawn together.

I took Caro in through the servants' entrance, and together we crept through the night-dark hall to the cellar door.

"I didn't want to take a candle in the halls, lest Stepmother see us," I explained, "but I have some stashed at the bottom of the stairs. The treads are uneven; you'll need to be careful. Just put your hand on my shoulder, and I'll go down first—you'll feel how to follow."

"All right," Caro whispered in assent. Then she giggled quietly and said, "I'm not worried about your Steps, you know. They don't scare me."

I laughed a little bit, wishing I could say the same. Soon, I hoped.

I opened the cellar door and felt her gentle touch at my back.

We crept down the stairs together, our steps in perfect tandem. At the bottom, I tapped Caro's hand. She let go, and I fetched my candlestick. Her eyes and hair glinted in the flickering new light. I took out my key.

As the door began to ratchet its way open, I heard her catch her breath. "Oh!"

I grinned, remembering my own wonder when I had first discovered that entrance. If the door alone impressed her, I thought, I could have faith in the workshop to carry the day.

Inside, Caro kept darting around the room, looking first at a pinned-up diagram, then the huge tome on my desk that was spread open to some particularly long and obscure-looking formulae, then to a large metal sheet I'd leaned against the far wall, where she saw herself reflected back in absurd lines and whorls, her beaming, pretty face distorted past recognition. Then she approached the cuckoo clock, and as she did, one of the starlings popped out of its perch and tilted its head at her curiously. It cooed and ruffed its metal feathers, and Caro lifted a cautious finger to it, then glanced back at me.

"Can I?" she asked.

I shrugged, then nodded.

"I mean—is it safe?"

"They won't hurt you." I started to smile.

Caro stroked one careful finger along the bird's head. It cooed again, then warbled and nuzzled against her finger.

"Oh!" she cried. "Oh, Nick, it's lovely!"

I laughed, glad she wasn't frightened, glad she understood.

Envious of the attention she gave the starlings, I supposed, one of the beetles buzzed up to her, hovering goldly in front of her face before perching on her shoulder. A dragonfly looped past them, the red glass in its wings glittering in the workshop's gaslight.

I felt a small twinge of jealousy, for a moment, that Caro received a warmer welcome from the menagerie than I had. I'd had to find Mother's animals; they flocked to Caro as if she were a shepherdess.

"Nick." Caro turned back to me, stroking a caterpillar

that had nestled in a coil in her palm. "This is wonderful. Remarkable. If I didn't know better, I would say these things—this place—are full of magic."

I laughed, and the sound was harsher than I expected. "Magic?"

Her smile faded and she nodded, somber again.

I set my mouth and nodded back. "Yes, at least a little. I know it's not quite legal, but, well—I can't bring myself to think there's anything really wrong with it either. At least not with this sort of magic."

"Of course not," she said firmly. "And you should see all the little spells we use in the servants' quarters, even at the palace. King Corsin hasn't scrubbed the place of magic half so well as he'd like to think."

I was intrigued, and I knew it showed on my face. "Magic at the palace? Really?"

"Oh, certainly." Caro laughed. "Just yesterday my cousin Jamie nearly got caught with it. He was polishing some silver, you see, which isn't the worst work, but long and monotonous, and just the kind of thing an eight-year-old boy would hate to do and would be trusted with, too. Crystal, for instance, is prettier, but the children will break it, sure as I stand here. Anyway, Jamie's friend Mell told him about this spell she'd been using to clean some of the copper at the stables, and Jamie figured it could help him speed up the silver cleaning. He said just the words he'd been told, but the metals are different, of course, and the silver turned green—just as green as you please. He had to scrub twice as hard and twice as long as before to get the color out, and he was up long past his bedtime too . . . or he would have been, if some of the other cousins hadn't stepped in to help him. We'll all have green fingers for the next week, I swear it."

She wiggled her hands at me. Indeed, the pads of her fingers were stained a weird, mottled green.

I laughed, and so did she. "It was kind of you to help him," I said. "If I'd made a mistake like that when Mother was teaching me something, she'd have had me clean it all up myself, no matter how long it took, just to be sure I'd learned the lesson." I paused. "She wasn't cruel, though. Just—she wanted me to learn."

Caro nodded, but the way she looked at me made me feel almost uncomfortable, as if I were being disloyal to Mother. "It's just the way of things up at the palace," she said. "So many of us, and someone always getting into scrapes. If we don't look out for each other, who will?"

"Who will?" I repeated. I didn't know, really.

Caro walked over and squeezed my hand, then pulled me over to the desk. "Now, I want to hear all about everything you're doing," she said.

I found my throat had caught, and I took a breath. "Well, I've been working on the knitting machines a lot," I said. "They're the first things I've been able to make entirely by myself. I've been making repairs in the house for years, working out of the kitchen and the servants' quarters, but I didn't find the workshop until my birthday, back in the autumn. Everything my mother did started here. She made machines too—especially sewing machines, things like that. She said she had no talent for what she called feminine handicrafts, so she wanted to make machines that did. That's what gave me the idea for my knitting machine. I'm a little bit better at sewing and things than she was, I think, but not by much. I wanted to try to give myself a way out of the chores I like least—a bit like Jamie and the silver polish, I suppose. I haven't turned anything green yet, though."

Caro laughed. "And what of the birds? And the insects? Your mother made those, too, surely. Oh, Nick, they are wonderful."

I nodded. "Those are what she was best at," I said. "Father traded them at really exorbitant prices. But they're magic, at least a bit, and I think Mother couldn't make them anymore after King Corsin started the embargoes. I still don't know how she made them. But there are"—I hesitated for a moment, but I already knew I would tell Caro everything—"there are these drawers in the other room, full of ash, with pictures of animals on the labels. I'm sure the ash has something to do with making the animals come to life, but I don't know what it is yet. Sometimes I think maybe she found it dangerous, after the quarantine, but—" I stopped.

Caro nodded, listening intently. "But there is magic here, isn't there? In the insects themselves. I might not even recognize it if I weren't used to the secret magic in the servants' quarters. The machines themselves are so clever that most people would believe they are only automata. If she really wanted to get rid of all the magic in her workshop, she would have had to get rid of those, too."

"Right." I sighed. "And there are other things. I found the workshop on my birthday—that has to be magic. I got a letter from her that day, and a hidden key. She must have chosen that spell before she died, so the letter would come to me on my birthday, and only to me. Stepmother . . . well, I changed rooms after Mother died, several times, actually. When I found the letter, I thought at first Stepmother must have left it for me, but now I know better; she wouldn't have done that. She wouldn't have given me anything my mother wanted me to have." I looked around at the workshop, the one part of Lampton Manor I really felt I owned.

Caro nodded. "Nothing wrong with magic, not really," she said. "It's blessed useful at times. Not even the whole royal family hates it the way Corsin does."

I brightened. "Really? Do you hear them talk about it? I heard a caller tell Stepmother the other day that Heir Christopher is campaigning for a Fey ambassador, even."

"Aye, that's so." Caro nodded. "The Heir has lots of notions his father doesn't approve of. You ask me, I'd say that's one of the reasons King Corsin doesn't let him meet the people. I mean, he's scared of another assassination, of course, but I think it frightens him even more that the Heir *isn't* scared. You know?"

"I do." I knew about the fears of parents all too well, both from Stepmother's fawning over Piety and Chastity and from the evidence of my own mother's continued protection. Now that I had found Mother's workshop, I wondered if there weren't other cloaking spells on the place—or on me. I wondered how much Mother was still helping me.

The cuckoo clock started acting up again. I glanced at the time: it was nearly one.

"I ought to go, I suppose," Caro sighed.

"Will you be safe walking back through the woods this late?"

She laughed. "Oh, of course. My whole family knows those woods almost better than we know ourselves. The Forest Queen was my so-many-times-great-grandmother, you know."

"Really?" I wanted to hear more about this, but I knew it was time for Caro to go.

She grinned at me. "A story for next time, maybe. Now, can you sneak me out the door again? I don't think my hips will ever make friends with that window."

I laughed and walked back with her, all the way to the edge of the woods.

My blossoming friendships with Caro and Fin made me happier than I'd ever been. I didn't see Fin in the forest again, but I met Caro there several times. She was more verbose than he; minutes at a stretch went by with her talking, and I hardly had to say a thing. And sometimes we just read together, mostly in silence, occasionally sharing a special line with each other.

Caro even gave me one of her Market creations, as Fin had done: a little music box. I sang its sweet, dreamy tune to myself often during the day. I didn't know the proper words, so I made up nonsense or, when the Steps were gone, sang about melting glass and turning gears.

Caro's music box was wonderful, but I treasured the letters she left for me even more; I kept them in a desk drawer that would soon prove too small for the stacks of pages filled with Caro's friendly chatter. Before long, I thought I knew her friends and cousins as well as she did.

She mentioned Fin sometimes too, but not as often or in as much detail as I thought she should. But perhaps, I had to admit, nothing she wrote would seem like enough. I would want to learn more about him no matter how much I already knew.

Fin's horse, though, remained the most precious gift of all. I had to keep reminding myself not to stroke it too much, lest the paint wore off.

I planned my own gifts in return. For Caro, I made a hinged round vessel of swirling red and clear glass, to cover one of her music boxes. I wrote my own letters back to her too, though they could never be as warm or as interesting, since she had so many loved ones, and I none. It was still a relief, though, to be able to share the small troubles and joys of each day with someone I knew would listen.

I left Fin a note, early on, promising that he would get his present soon enough. But day after day, night after night, I couldn't think of anything to offer him that would express what I felt.

October 7

Mr. Candery has stopped buying new Ashes for me—I spilled a packet in front of him, fool that I am, and he started going on about spirits, about how he didn't know. All ridiculous, of course. At least I have plenty left. It takes so little for each of them: only the smallest pinch, and the wish.

Wishing is a frustrating business. There are far too many variables, infuriating for the scientific mind.

Mother went on about the lack of science in wishing for a full two pages. I read her rant fondly, remembering similar diatribes she'd spouted about magic while we repaired insects or wound clocks. But even when it frustrated her, she loved it; I had always known that. I liked to believe that her ability to love things she didn't understand was what made her such a great inventor.

I loved without understanding, too. I had loved Jules, and I still loved the workshop and its other occupants. And somewhere, pulling at the edges of my heart, was the beginning of something else I didn't understand—something I felt whenever I thought of Fin.

But I tried not to think of him too much.

The most intriguing part of Mother's designs for Jules was her notes on the Ashes. Several times, it seemed she was beginning to describe where they came from, but always she stopped herself and scribbled out her notes. I knew at least that I would have no chance at completing my Exhibition piece without the Ashes, so even without understanding them, I tried to love them, too. And if I didn't *know* they were magic—if there was no *proof* that they weren't just some astonishing chemical compound, that I wasn't controlling Jules with some secret panel or lever—then no one could charge me with Illicit Magical Activities. Surely not.

I knew I had to start designing my Exposition outfit, too. At first it seemed wasteful to take time away from what I thought of as my *real work,* but as I sketched out designs, I began to grow more and more excited about how I would look. Father had been the one to sell Mother's inventions, not only because he was a man, but also because he was a trader, a salesman by profession and, it often seemed, by vocation. He was slick and persuasive and charming, and nearly everyone who met him liked him. Few people could say they liked my prickly mother, or even knew her. I needed to emulate both of my parents in order to obtain the kind of patronage I wanted. My clothing had to be a part of the idea I was selling, the idea of not only my inventions as good investments, but also myself.

And besides all that, it made me happy to feel that I would, for perhaps the first time since my childhood, look *nice.* I'd scarcely looked in a mirror since Mother died. When I left to seek my fortune, though, I wanted to look like a daughter who would make her parents proud.

What time I had that wasn't devoted to my chores or spent in the workshop, I passed reading Caro's letters, the novels she'd brought me, or, despite the vague feeling that I shouldn't, telling myself my own tales about Fin. Sometimes he still worked in the palace in my stories, and I lived with the Steps, but more often I was a successful inventor or a noble lady, and he an artist or a knight errant or a lord, recognized by his father after all.

But it was easiest for me to picture him at the palace, going through his daily chores and spending what time he could riding the palace horses or reading or working on the sculptures he and Caro sold at Market.

I knew he must spend a lot of time with Caro, but she didn't mention him much at all in her letters anymore, and I preferred to picture him alone . . . or at least, alone with me.

I held whole conversations with him in my mind, telling

him about the Steps' inanity, or their coldness, or the transparent fawning of whatever beaux they had entertained that day. I told him about my work as I made it, explaining the movements and turnings of the knitting machines, the temperatures and mixtures I needed for my glass beads, the delicate clockwork that went into replicating Mother's mechanical insects. I still didn't know *why* the Ashes made them come to life, though the *how*—the wishing—at least seemed simple enough. I spoke more with my imagined Fin than I did with the real Caro in our letters.

Every once in a while, I would remember that I could count my actual interactions with him on one of my hands, but the thought would skitter away as soon as it came. I certainly didn't welcome it. Besides, I didn't think it mattered much. I knew we could talk to each other, knew we liked each other—and it seemed I *would* talk with Fin in my mind, whether I wanted to or not.

Besides, it made my days easier, having someone to talk to . . . even someone in my head. I found that Fin's voice, asking me questions, laughing, shut out the more critical voices that used to fill my mind: the Steps, great inventors who'd come before me, even Mother. I could tell my imagined Fin about my inventions, and he'd be impressed, proud, whereas once I'd only heard my mother's voice telling me how much more I had yet to learn.

I knew it was only another story, but I could not help telling it, any more than I could help pulling a novel from under my mattress at night and rereading before I went to sleep, even so tired as I was. They were each, in their own way, things I needed. I was not sure why, but I couldn't resist them.

The stories I read in Caro's book were my favorites, and I found they took my mind away from worrying about whether I would finish my Exposition piece in time, whether the Steps would find the workshop, whether Fin was really as wonderful as the boy I talked to in my head every day. I read stories of Fey and humans, of the different kinds of magic they could give each other—clockwork and coal power were as foreign to the Fey as their magic was to us. Mr. Candery had always said we would be stronger if we helped each other, and Caro's Faerie tales seemed to agree. But mostly the stories in her book were adventures, romances, and tales of family. The Fey were not men and women, as humans are, but all alike. They loved as humans did, though, and it seemed the tales of how they came to love each other were just as fraught and frightening and immersive as they were for humans. I often found myself imagining one of the characters as someone like me, and the other as just a little like Fin.

Three weeks before the Exposition, I started moving the pieces of my project out to the forest. Once assembled, it would be so large, I could never get it out of my workshop, so I had to design it in such a way that I could finish it outside.

I put an oversize wheelbarrow to use, carrying the parts one by one from the back of Lampton Manor, across the lawn and into the woods. I used the ground-level shed among the Forest Queen's ruins to keep my work out of the snow.

I wouldn't let myself think too much about the finished product; whenever I considered how much work I had to do in the few remaining weeks, it all seemed impossible. Instead, I made myself focus entirely on each individual step as I took it. When I pounded steel and copper in the furnace (my arms growing even stronger than my chores had made them), I thought only about each shape, how to match it to my calculations and blueprints. I didn't think, *This is his hoof . . . This is his ear . . . This piston goes where his heart would be.* If I thought of those things, my hands would inevitably start to shake with love and hope, and with fear. I wanted so much to see Jules again, and I wanted even more for this huge, impossible experiment to be a success. What if no one noticed it? What if it wasn't good enough to be noticed? Lord, what if it didn't work at all?

I couldn't think those things. I made one part, and the next, with the cold distance I thought a surgeon must feel cutting into a body. I knew it was the only way I could manage.

The workshop soon grew too small, and besides, looking at the collected parts reminded me too much of the whole that I still insisted on thinking about only in the vaguest of terms. I visited the forest nearly every night, bringing out springs and wheels and joints and panes of glass that were either too big for the workshop or too intimidating for me to look at.

So it was that Fin found me one evening pushing a large wheel through the shed door. I was struggling; between smithing, glass blowing, all my chores, and heaving parts out to the forest, I was the strongest I'd ever been, but the wheel was an awkward, cumbersome height and the door was narrow.

"Hello, Nick," he said, nodding his head in an almost-bow. He grabbed a spoke as he greeted me, and with his help, it rolled inside easily, as if of its own free will.

I hadn't expected him to be quite so strong, so I'd overestimated how much I still had to push. I tripped after it, losing my balance, the wheel rolling away from us both, where it came to a wobbling, slanted halt on the other side of the shed. For a moment, I felt only relief that the wheel hadn't dented somehow—it had taken several nights' work to make it—and then I realized that Fin had caught me as I stumbled.

It was horribly embarrassing, looking up into his face with his arms around me. Since the moment I'd met him, I'd wanted him to think me capable, stable. And since that moment, I'd felt as if he'd only seen me at my most incompetent.

"I'm sorry," I managed to say, looking into his eyes, not sure what I was apologizing for.

He shook his head, but didn't let me go. His mouth played with the beginnings of a smile.

Then . . . oh, I had no business doing it, but I thought of the sculpture he'd given me, all his kindness and help, the warmth of his arms as he held me up—all the conversations I'd had with him in my mind . . . I kissed him.

I kissed him.

His lips were warm, warmer than his hands, and softer than I'd thought a man's lips would be.

For a sweet moment, he kissed me back.

Then I felt his arms turn stiff, and he let me go, almost dropping me after all. He was still looking at me, but I couldn't read his face. "Nick . . ."

"I'm sorry!" I said, knowing exactly what I was apologizing for this time.

"No, I . . ." He stepped forward. He looked at me with those dark eyes.

There was nothing I could do but look back.

He stepped closer, and with the careful steadiness of someone performing an experiment, he touched his lips to mine again.

His kiss was thoughtful now, and curious, and his arms wrapped tentatively around my waist.

I brought my hand to the back of his neck and leaned into him, sliding my fingers into the curls at his nape. His arms clasped tighter around me. I sighed just a little against his mouth, feeling that it was almost too much, all this newness, this feeling that there was space and light inside me I was only just learning to notice. Every part of me down to my fingertips felt like warm glass, melting into some new shape, my edges beginning to glow. I wanted to do nothing but change this way, pressed against his body, his warmth and goodness, forever.

Fin pulled away.

He looked down at the snow that had scattered over the floor. "I . . . I brought the supplies you asked for," he said, motioning toward a large oilcloth sack leaning against the shed door. "And Caro said to—Caro, she—" He glanced outside, his face unreadable. "I have to go," he said. "I won't be able to come back for . . . a while. I'll see you at the Exposition." He looked at me again, finally, and offered me a smile that was too quick and bright.

Then he turned and left, almost running, and the dark woods hid him from me.

I should have called after him, spoken with him, so that maybe we could have come to understand each other, before everything that happened later. But I was still standing there, shocked, probing the empty space in my heart and wondering if I could fill it with anything but Fin.

I had gone somewhere far away. When the shadow of an owl swept suddenly across the ground, I blinked and the world around me came back into focus. I had been looking somewhere else, somewhere inside myself, and at the same time,

I had gone back to the palace with Fin, had wandered with him through the cold, snowy forest, where so few people are permitted to walk.

But I could not walk back through the forest with Fin, even if he had wanted me to, even if he hadn't pushed away from our second kiss.

And even if (the most important reason, I reminded myself) I didn't have work to do.

First I checked to make sure my runaway wheel hadn't done any damage. Thankfully, it had continued the trajectory I'd given it before Fin joined in, and it had rolled to the shed's far wall to join its twin. I inspected each wheel, running my hands over their rubber rims, testing the resiliency of their steel spokes. These wheels each came up to about the height of my shoulders; while light for their size, they had still been a challenge to roll up the cellar stairs and out to the ruins. I was glad that the next time they moved, they'd be attached to an axle and carrying *me* instead of the other way around.

There were two other, smaller wheels next to these that didn't even come up to my hips. I'd been able to carry them easily, hoisted over my shoulders, and I only checked them again now to make sure the cold atmosphere in the shed hadn't done them any harm. But they, too, were sound; I'd have been a poor designer if I hadn't considered changes in temperature. Mother had told me so in one of our very first engineering lessons. *Nothing exists in your mind the way it does in the real world,* she'd said. *One must always account for the vagaries of truth.*

But I had. I had designed these wheels to survive fire or flood, drought or blizzard. She had taught me well, and I had done both of us proud.

I settled into the work, trying to pretend that my skin wasn't still glowing with remembered warmth, that it didn't matter that Fin had kissed me like that and then left. It was hard, at first, but the physical effort of joining the wheels to their axles and the axles to each other, and then hammering on the base of the carriage frame, soon distracted me well enough. This was still something I wanted more than I wanted Fin.

The bottom of the carriage's steel frame unfurled between the wheels like a spiny gray flower. I had to step into it to finish the top, and it felt strange to do so; I had never been *inside* one of my creations before. There was an intimacy about it, an intimacy with my own dreams that I hadn't quite expected. Even though there was only the darkness of the shed around me, I could almost see the admiring crowds, and through the silence of the forest, I heard their whispered murmurs of appreciation, their applause as I swept by. I lifted a hand to wave back at them, and I started to smile; then I laughed at myself and returned my hand to the steel spacer I was trying to place.

Finally the frame was complete, the skeleton of a sphere.

The next step would be to install the curved glass panels I'd started forging the other day. I had at least one more trek out of the forest and back before my day would be over.

I hopped out of the carriage frame and made for the door—but a thin brown package on the floor caught my eye. It was too small and light to be one of Fin's sculptures, to be anything but a letter. . . . What if he'd written to tell me about his feelings for me? To tell me he was dreaming up stories about us, just as I was? I told myself I was being foolish, but even so, as I unfolded the letter, my heart gave a quick leap. . . .

And then I recognized Caro's handwriting. After all, I chided myself, when had Fin ever left me more than a brief, businesslike note? Foolish indeed.

Still, holding Caro's letter was like holding her hand, the hand of a friend, and even in my disappointment, I found myself comforted. I couldn't stand in the light of her friendship without feeling warm.

This was a much shorter missive than her usual:

Nick—

I've finally managed to scrape together what I think is enough money for a course of lovesbane, and I'm going to the Night Market to try for a bargain. Come with me? The Night Market is a sight to see, and safer by far for two girls together than one alone.

I won't have time to check for your reply, so meet me here Wednesday night at ten if you can. We'll have lots to talk about too, I'm sure.

—Caro

Wednesday; that was tonight. I tried to consider the work before me, everything I still had to do if I wanted to get to the Exposition in a few short weeks. But as soon as I read Caro's note, I knew that I would go; I'd wanted to see the Night Market ever since Fin had mentioned it. Fey goods and magic trinkets, trading with Faerie going on right under the King's nose, in Esting City? It sounded marvelous, and who knew what helps to my inventions I might find there. Why, I might even find out what the Ashes really were. . . .

And I could go with Caro, my new friend who felt like someone I'd known all my life, my friend who was almost the sister I'd longed for. That reason was the best of all.

When I returned home, I counted the money I'd been able to save from my Market earnings: I had fifty-two crowns and an odd assortment of the smaller silver half-crowns and brass pennies.

Though it was nothing to what Mother used to make, I felt shockingly wealthy. I allowed myself a brief daydream about the kinds of wonders I might buy at the Night Market; perhaps there would be something that could inspire my next project, after the Exposition was over. I put thirty crowns—a hefty sum, but this was a rare opportunity—in a bag and tied it into my sash, where it rested with a pleasantly heavy weight against my hip. I tucked ten pennies in another part of my sash and tied it again. After I'd wrapped myself in hat, shawl, and coat, the evening had darkened to night, and it was time to leave.

That night, Caro and I walked up to a moldy-looking pub door on the outskirts of Esting City. Caro lifted one hand, clad in red fingerless mitts that were badly frayed, up to the moldy wood. She knocked four times.

A voice, seemingly close enough that the speaker's lips could have brushed my ear, whispered in a low, menacing grumble, "What are you?"

Beside me Caro shivered; the voice must have sounded too close for comfort to her as well. She squeezed my hand, and we answered in unison, "Friends of the Fey." The words seemed somehow to hang in the air after we spoke them, to echo and twist as if they were being tested.

Finally, the disembodied voice spoke again. "Then enter." I had to try hard not to wince away from the closeness of it, the way it seemed to linger and caress my ears, my neck. It took me a moment to notice that nothing had happened; I'd expected that the door would open after we spoke the password Caro had told me in the woods, or at least that we would be given further whispered instructions.

I looked to Caro, but she simply nodded and strode forward . . . straight through the wooden door.

Our hands still clasped, I felt myself being dragged, and I followed her. I had just enough time to wonder if the door was an illusion before my hand entered the wood and I felt a curious squeezing sensation, one that slithered up my arm and over my whole body as I struggled to stay with my friend. I felt hundreds of large, blunt splinters digging into my shoulders, my legs, my hips, my face. The smell of mold and crumbling wood overwhelmed me, and the pressure reached my torso, pushing the air from my lungs. As I gasped, my mouth and nose filled with dry, tasteless dust.

I coughed and sputtered, but suddenly the dust vanished, and the squeezing, splintery feeling passed to my back and was gone. I could breathe again, and I did so in frantic gasps.

As my eyes adjusted to the low light, I looked down the dark, crowded passageway before me; it seemed to go on forever, receding into blackness. The air was hot, almost oppressively so, and everywhere there were sounds of people chattering and of laughter, some friendly, some incredibly sinister. I coughed again.

I saw that Caro was watching me. I thought I must look ridiculous, gasping and coughing to rid myself of invisible dust, and that she would laugh. But her face was concerned.

"Hold your breath next time," she said. "Sorry, I should have told you. The last time it was under a bridge, so there was no need."

"When you went through it like that, I thought . . ."

"That it wasn't real? Fin thought the same thing when I first brought him. It's real enough, just with a passage charm put on it. Goes a bit funny when there's a solid door instead of just a space. Not sure how they work, myself, but they're none too pleasant, anyway."

I managed a chuckle. "That's one way to describe them."

Now that I could breathe again, excitement at seeing the Night Market welled up inside me, drowning out the brief panic I'd felt. Everywhere I looked there were memories, things Father used to trade before the quarantine: paper patterned with flowers that blossomed and wilted and blossomed again; Fey wines and food and drink that Mother used to order, even clary-bush tea; small lights in glass spheres that thrummed like heartbeats; teapots, platters, and plates that held heat indefinitely; glamours for beauty and wisdom and luck. A small distance away, I saw a small booth covered entirely in narrow vials filled with viscous, whiskey-colored liquid: ombrossus oil. It was shockingly expensive. *Thank you, Mr. Candery,* I thought, eyeing the sign that priced the oil at fifteen crowns a gram. I wondered if I'd ever finish learning the extent of what he'd done for me.

There was a heavy, sweet smell of sinnum in the air, spun through with traces of yeast and burnt sugar. I looked around for sinnum buns like Mr. Candery used to make, although it wouldn't have surprised me if at least some of the dark, spicy scent was coming from the ombrossus booth or from a potion already in use. Everyone at the Night Market had something to hide.

I thought I should probably help Caro look for a loves-bane vendor, or at least try to find some Ashes, but it had been hours since my meager supper, and the scent memory of sinnum was overwhelming: the soft round buns, spice-flecked and tender inside, and coated with a dark, bitter caramel glaze . . . but even if they were here, they could never be as good as Mr. Candery's. . . .

I followed my nose, pulling Caro along with me, and there they were: stacks upon stacks of sinnum buns, ensconced in a sourceless, rosy light and presided over by a part-Fey woman with golden eyes and a quick smile.

I thought of the money I'd tied into my sash that evening; I'd never had extra coins of my own and a place to spend them before. I'd been too young when my parents were alive, and until recently I'd been afraid to use my Market money for anything but supplies. But I had everything I needed now. . . .

Caro and I could both use a treat, I thought. I approached the vendor, and the spicy sweetness in the air around her stall filled my mouth and nose. I sucked my lips in hunger, forgetting even to smile or say hello.

"Two of those," I muttered, only just barely remembering to add "please" as I reached for my sash.

Caro yanked me away. "What d'you think you're doing?"

she demanded, her face flushed, her curls starting to frizz in the hot, dark air.

"I—what?" I blinked, the enticing cakes still pulling at my senses, demanding their attention. "Are they poisonous?" There was a tale about poisoned sweets in Caro's book; I tried to remember the details. But it had been humans who'd poisoned the Fey in that story . . .

"No, no, Fin and I have had Puff's cakes a hundred times—they're the grandest things. But Lord, Nick, what do you mean going for your money in full view of everyone like that? You'll have your pockets picked before you can reach them, and Puff's as likely a thief as any. Don't think she doesn't know what she's doing, spreading that scent around the place, turning everyone addlepated and drooly. It's the same as the day Market. Everyone's after the same thing, and that's your purse. Keep your wits about yourself."

It was only the pennies I'd reached for, not the whole crowns tied deeper inside my sash, but I still knew Caro was right. I went with her into a quiet corner between stalls, and Caro stood in front of me to block the view as I pulled out two brass coins. I tied it extra tightly, too, though this small amount of money—strange thought!—wouldn't be catastrophic to lose, with my Exposition supplies all bought and paid for already. But I had worked too hard, for too long, to be careless of even a single coin.

Money in hand, I returned to the booth, Caro glancing around me protectively. Puff had already speared each bun on a wooden stick, and she held them out to me, smirking. I thought I saw her wink at Caro.

"Thank you," I said quickly, depositing the coins in her blue-freckled hand. I gave one cake to Caro and brought the other to my lips, taking a last breath of that heavenly smell before my first huge bite.

The top of the bun had crystallized in the hot light of Puff's display, and it crackled pleasantly; the rest of the glaze was still sticky, and it oozed as I bit down. The dough was light, pillowy, and tender, flecked with bits of sinnum that tingled on my lips and tongue.

I sighed with delight. "Thank you," I said again, smiling stickily at Puff, whose golden eyes crinkled with amusement.

The sinnum's heat spread through my whole body. I felt revived, alert, awake. Beside me, Caro had a similar spark in her eye.

"Let's find that lovesbane," I said, and she nodded.

We progressed down the seemingly endless row of stalls lining the passageway, pausing now and then to examine a shelf of leather-bound Faerie books or a collection of self-inking quill pens, with the Fey scribehawk they came from sitting morosely in a pewter cage, indigo dripping from its beak and the points of its claws.

I didn't see Ashes anywhere.

Finally we came upon a stall covered with medicinal Fey flora: silver orchid, cap-o'-rushes, and rhodopis berries covered most of the table. I had assumed that lovesbane, the most infamous Fey import, would not be on display, and it seemed that Caro had thought the same: she approached the old man behind the stall with a knowing look and lowered voice.

She said only two words: "Fey's croup." The man nodded and raised his eyebrows. "One course," Caro added, "please."

He shot her a quizzical look, then ducked down and rummaged under the table for a moment. He stood again, his two hands clasped together like a seashell, and cocked his head to tell us to move closer.

We bent over his hands, and he opened them slowly, carefully. A single, three-petaled flower rested in his palm, the size of a small butterfly. Its petals were jet-black, but just at the center, one of them was starting to blush red. "In a few days," he said, "the whole flower'll be the color of blood, and in another week, it'll turn white as bones." He chuckled. "White as snow."

The life cycle of the lovesbane bloom. I'd never seen one before, only read about them. It hurt to look at the flower now, remembering Father's prejudice, remembering Mother's preventable death. If I'd known about the Night Market back then, I would have gone, even as a child. I was glad that, at least, I could be with Caro now.

"Pluck one petal when it's black, one red, and one white. Brew them up strong in a cup of boiling water. They'll drink a mouthful, and no more. No more, you hear?" The man's voice was gravelly, and his expression fierce. "I know who you'll blame if they drink it all." He paused. "Of course, if you're after a poison, there are easier options." He smiled unpleasantly and his hand wandered back to the storage under his table.

"A mouthful, no more." Caro said quickly. "I'll remember." She looked up, into the man's eyes, and I could hear how hard she was trying to sound indifferent when she said, "How much?"

I bristled at once, waiting for this man to dare to cheat my friend. I glared hot pokers into his head, but he wasn't looking at me. He squinted at Caro as if he was trying to read her mind, and then, slowly, he nodded.

"Two hundred crowns," he said.

I realized I didn't know if this was a fair price. I looked at Caro to see if I needed to defend her. I thought I saw tears start in her eyes, but in the next moment, they were gone.

"I have a hundred," she said. "That's my offer."

He scoffed. "Hardly an offer, my girl."

She drew herself up to make the most of her small height and looked the older, taller man square in the eye. "I can't afford to bargain with you, sir," she said, and only someone who knew her could have noticed the tremor in her voice. "My mother is ill, and this is what we can scrape, my whole family."

I thought of her legions of cousins.

"We need it now," Caro said. From nowhere, it seemed, she produced a heavy-looking sack of coins the size of my two fists. She placed the bag on the table, and I saw the man's hand twitch. "There's no more time. I can give you a hundred."

I saw compassion flicker in the man's eyes, but then it left, and he shook his head. "I can't do it," he said. "Got my own to think of. Would be a loss, and Lord knows this stuff's hard to come by nowadays. Would be a loss."

I looked from Caro to the merchant. "A hundred and twenty," I said. I didn't know much about bargaining, but I could sense that I shouldn't offer everything on the first try.

"Nick . . ." Caro's voice was a warning.

"No. No, Caro." I found myself growing angry. "I'm doing this."

We stared each other down. "I never let Fin . . ." she said, but her voice trailed away.

"I'm not Fin," I said gently. "And you said there's no time." I cast around for a way to explain what I was feeling, this hot anger and protectiveness. "You said your family was helping. Can't you see—don't you—" I wanted to say, *Can't you see that's what I am, what I'm doing?* But as I said it I thought she might push me away even so, push away that idea that I was part of her family. I thought I couldn't bear it if she did.

Caro looked hard at me, and just as my fear of refusal was starting to sink into my bones she said, "You're right, Nick." She took a breath. "Thank you."

The thank-you made me nervous; that wasn't what this was about. I shook my head briskly and turned to the merchant.

"So, then?" I asked. "A hundred and twenty?"

He frowned. "Anything less than one fifty would be shockin'," he said.

"So be shocked," I replied. "I don't mind."

He snorted, but said nothing. Silence tightened the air between us.

"One thirty." I tried to stare pokers at him again. "That's all."

I had only thirty with me; as the merchant frowned and thought, I wondered desperately whether I'd have time to get back to the workshop to get the rest of my money if he said no.

Finally, almost imperceptibly, he nodded. "Go on, so," he said.

I undid my sash; I was taking all my money out, so I didn't mind if anyone knew where I'd kept it. I removed the purse with my thirty crowns inside and started to lay it on the table, among the weeds and flowers, but the merchant scooped it up in one broad hand and hefted it, along with Caro's larger purse, onto a rusty-looking pair of scales behind him. It swung for a long moment, balancing. I looked back at Caro; she wore a shaky smile. I smiled back, and we waited.

"Grand," the merchant finally announced. He placed the

small black flower into a tiny glass vial filled with something smooth and dark that didn't quite look like soil, wrapped it in a white tissue, and gently pushed the package into a tiny red velvet pouch. Caro held out her hands for it eagerly, and once more, I couldn't see where she hid the pouch before her hands were free again.

"You're a good girl," said the merchant, still eyeing her speculatively. "Be careful what you do with that bloom, now. Let no one know you have it."

Caro nodded solemnly, and if the look he was giving her made her uncomfortable, she showed no outward sign. "Thank you," she said. She took in a deep, steadying breath, and then turned to me. "Come on, Nick, it's getting late."

I took a step away from the booth with her, but the temptation was too great. I turned back. "Um, pardon me, sir," I said to the merchant, who had busied himself with rearranging a spray of luminous silver orchid leaves. "There's something . . . something else I was looking for . . ."

He swept the same piercing, appraising look over me that he'd given Caro. "A sleeping draft, perhaps, my dear? Or a poisoned apple?" He gestured over his crowded display. "A potion for undying love; surely that's the one. Your lover will never know what hit him—or her." He nodded furtively in Caro's direction. "What'll it be, princess?"

"No." It took me a moment to pluck up the courage to ask; I couldn't figure out why I felt so nervous. "It's . . . it's Ashes I'm looking for. Do you know what they are?"

Before I finished speaking, his face had gone as gray as the Ashes themselves. "Don't know anything about them," he managed to say, his gravelly voice a croak. "Don't know what a young one like yourself would want to do with them either. Nobody wants that cursed stuff around here."

"What do you mean?"

He glanced from side to side, refusing to meet my eyes.

"No one'll sell you them here. There aren't many as know what they are in the first place, and those that do would hurt you for asking." He glared at me for a brief moment, accusingly, before breaking his gaze again. "Don't mention them again, if you know what's good for you."

I felt a tug at my wrist; Caro had come back from petting the scribehawk. Blue ink dripped from her fingers. "Come now, Nick. Remember, it's getting late," she said.

"Right," I muttered, "we should go." I turned back to thank the merchant, even though he'd more frightened than helped me; but he'd rolled down cotton blinds all around his booth, closing him in and me out.

I followed Caro back through the passageway lined with booths, and I remembered to hold my breath against the dust and mold as we crossed through the door. My mind, though, was still on the merchant, how drawn and frightened he'd become just because I'd spoken of the thing most of Mother's inventions relied on. My mind was spinning, unable to rest.

Cursed?

*

In the hushed darkness of the forest, snow whispering beneath our feet, I tried to let go of my worries about the Ashes. There were other things I wanted to talk about with Caro, other things that were pressing on my heart.

The whole time we'd walked toward the Night Market together, I'd wanted to tell her about Fin's and my kiss—our two kisses. But I couldn't. I couldn't even bring up his name, only hope that Caro would do it for me.

She didn't. On our way there, she had been quieter than I'd ever known her to be, though she'd seemed cheerful enough once we arrived. Now, while we trekked back to the Forest Queen's ruins, whenever I glanced at her, she wasn't even looking at the path ahead, but at the small velvet pouch in her mittened hands.

I felt practically evil for begrudging her her silence. If I'd had the cure for my own mother in my hands, I wouldn't have been able to tear my eyes from it either.

But then, finally, she spoke. "I've been thinking about charity," she said.

I knew this was dangerous ground. "Caro, I—"

"No, don't." She looked up, reluctantly, from the lovesbane she held, and her eyes were bright. "I've been thinking I was wrong. All these years I wouldn't take anything from Fin that wasn't . . . wasn't my due. I kept such careful track of everything my friends did for me, so that I could do for them in return, so that the scales could be balanced." She shook her head slowly, and I heard her take in a shallow breath. "But then, all of my cousins coming together to save Mum, and you, too . . . it's not about balance, I know that now." She closed her eyes briefly and nodded to herself. "It's about taking care of each other."

I wished I could hug her, but she seemed just a little defensive, a little shaken, and I thought I should let her be. "I knew what you meant, though," I said quietly, "at Market, the day we met. There's a kind of pity that makes you feel less than human. But you and Fin never treated me that way." I laughed. "Not at all."

"Exactly." We had reached the ruins now, and we stopped walking. Caro smiled up at me. I could see months of fear for her mother, and years of frightened pride, sluicing off her like water. She smiled as if she'd been carrying a weight for years, and had finally set it down.

I remembered that I still hadn't managed to tell her about Fin's kiss, but I decided that it could wait. Instead I simply hugged her goodbye.

I made sure my hug was a good one, at least. I tried to impart some strength to her with it.

"Good night, Nick," said Caro. "I hope you liked the Night Market. And—and thank you."

I hugged her again. "It was fascinating," I said. "It really was. I . . . I hope the lovesbane works." I didn't want to say "you're welcome," because that would mean I wanted her thanks. "Good night, Caro," I said instead, with all the warmth I could find in myself.

It was very dark, with no moon, and within a few steps, Caro had vanished as if she'd never been there at all.

Cursed. The word haunted me all the way back to the workshop. It whispered around my neck and nipped at my ears while I tried to work, so that I couldn't focus on the umpteenth knitting machine I'd made since that first Market day. It made me twitch and scratch at my skin, made me look away from the insects that came to greet me or offer their assistance.

I knew I should look at the Ashes again—but even the thought made me cringe. And if a man who sold lovesbane was afraid to speak of them . . .

My hand found the charm around my neck again, Jules's glass and gear on Caro's ribbon.

I couldn't believe Jules was a curse.

I chose the drawer with the horse label again, and it opened silently, smoothly, and the Ashes inside flowed like water. I crouched over them, forcing my eyes to look. There was no reason to be so frightened. No reason.

Still, when the ghostly shape rose up, trembling, I had to work hard to keep from recoiling. I watched carefully, but the form was still too vague to identify.

It didn't look *evil,* I thought. Just . . . in pain. And somehow that was worse.

Finally the shape winced back into the drawer and the Ashes were still again, but it was the stillness of quiet water that even the smallest movement might disturb.

I'd put on my closest-fitting work gloves. I couldn't bear to touch them directly, somehow. *Please, don't let me hurt it, whatever it is,* I thought, and I slowly pushed my fingers into the Ashes.

They rippled and flared around my hand, and I tried to sift through them as quickly as I could, though I also knew that I had to be gentle.

I didn't want to think about what else I might find in the drawer beneath the ash, although somehow the merchant's words about the white lovesbane petal kept swimming through my mind.

White as bones, white as snow. . . . The color of blood . . .

There was nothing else there. Only Ashes.

I withdrew my hand quickly, and not a single speck adhered to my glove. The next breath I drew was deep and shuddering, as if I'd just walked out of a tomb and into fresh air again.

I looked at the little label, at the horse that seemed, somehow, so much like Jules.

Oh, Jules. Whatever the Ashes were, I would bring him back with them. I had to.

I closed the drawer. I didn't want to know.

I SPENT most of my nights without sleep in those last weeks before the Exposition. Jules and the insects had finished the Steps' gowns, thank goodness, before his demise. Chastity had recently demanded a ridiculous abundance of lace be added to her dress; I was more grateful than ever for my knitting machines, and with harnesses and pulleys for the insects, they could produce yards with a few minutes of simply cranking a handle.

I still labored endlessly on my Exposition work, both my finest and my largest invention yet. Finally, I stomped through a fresh layer of snow the night I planned to put everything together, preparing for the delicate, strange work still before me.

I'd combined Mother's miniature-scale design with the vision of Jules I'd dreamt of the night he was killed. I'd worked retractable stirrups into his sides, remembering the thrill of riding him in my dream, but he was also built for pulling a carriage now. For the Exposition, I'd decided a carriage was more dignified—and I needed every scrap of dignity I could pull together if I was going to find a patron.

The Exposition was only two days away, and I knew the hardest part of my project had arrived. I wished I'd given myself more time, but I'd had extra work helping the Steps prepare for the ball, and I had to admit that I'd shied away from this last and most daunting task.

I'd just finished the carriage itself, and its glass walls glittered in the darkness at the back of the shed. It was almost spherical and quite small—I had neither the budget nor the time to build a carriage that would hold more than two people, though most seated at least four. I hoped it would still look respectable.

I reached down to Jules's belly and unhitched the clasp there. I pushed his glass hide up and out of my way, and I reached in to adjust his clockwork innards for the thousandth time. I paid particular attention to the thick chains that ran between his hocks and his hip joints, and I rubbed a bit of extra oil between his vertebrae. I wanted to make sure he would walk both smoothly and silently at the Exhibition.

I spent more time than was necessary, really, checking his every cog and piston, and making sure his belly was brimful with charcoal. I could only give him enough to last a few hours; a furnace any larger would distort his proportions.

Finally, however, I had to close his hide again. The time had come to bring him to life.

I opened Mother's journal to the bookmarked page and

read her instructions again to make sure I'd gotten everything right. It seemed too simple—deceptively simple, to create a life this way. The only thing that gave me confidence was the knowledge that even Mother had not fully understood what made these animals live.

I tried not to think of the look on the Night Market merchant's face, on the face of someone who sells lovesbane and readily offers "easier poisons." I tried not to think of the fear in his voice.

I reached up to open the hatch under Jules's copper ears, and I removed the packet of Ashes from my pocket.

There was only one drawer labeled with a horse among all the hundreds of insects and spiders and other animals. I knew Mother had written that only a pinch was needed, but dividing the Ashes seemed violent somehow. Even they felt like Jules to me, in a way that I still didn't want to understand. I reminded myself that all I had to know was that I wanted Jules back, and Jules was good, and surely he would want to come back too. That was all I had to know. That was all.

I poured the Ashes into the box I'd built under the hatch, then closed and locked it again. My fingers lingered on the seam there, and I stroked Jules's new ears.

I pressed my hand over the place I'd hidden the Ashes, closed my eyes, and focused on how very much I *wished* Jules would come back to life. I felt slightly ridiculous—and I knew well that what I was doing was magical, highly illegal, and even, possibly, somehow *evil*—but Mother's journal was very specific about this step too. And, oh, I wanted him back. So I wished.

Nothing happened.

I groaned and leaned my head against Jules's body, exhaling a cloud of steam onto his neck in the frosty air. After all my fear about the Ashes, what if they did nothing? All my work hinged on this—I should have known better than to think I had the skill to bring him back. What would I bring to the Exposition now?

I heard a click.

Raising my head, I squinted at him.

All seemed still.

The click sounded again, and a tiny movement flashed at his knee. I ducked under him, thinking maybe I had deluded myself, maybe it was only my longing that had made me see him move.

When Jules brushed his steel nose gently against my hair, I didn't notice at first—I'd been searching too hard for that one movement to notice anything else.

He nudged me again, and I jumped, knocking the crown of my head against his chin. "Ow!" I cried, flinging my arms around him. I laughed and laughed, and Jules craned his neck into a sort of embrace, nuzzling my cheek with his.

"You're back, Jules," I whispered, struggling to compose

said. “I’ve looked for you many times since our encounter at Market.”

I looked up.

“Your friend sells your wares, but you’ve never come back yourself. I wish you had.” He frowned. “I’ve a grave matter to discuss with you regarding your machine.”

Horror drew the warmth from my skin. A man like Lord Alming could ruin my professional reputation; if he found my work unsatisfactory, he could easily make sure every potential patron at the Exposition knew not to bother with me.

But before I could respond, he swept into a far deeper, more intricate bow than the one he had offered me. I spun around, knowing that whoever commanded Lord Alming’s deference would require mine as well.

I found myself face-to-face with the Heir himself: the medals on his black dress uniform, the thin platinum circlet on his head, and especially the Heir’s crest near his heart, told me the young man before me could be no one else.

It was several more seconds before I realized that he was also Fin.

No; it wasn’t possible. Christopher—that was the prince’s name. I frowned and recited his full title to myself, which I’d inadvertently memorized during the Steps’ many repetitions: His Highness Prince Christopher Dougray Fadhiri Anton Abdul-Rafi’ Finnian—oh . . .

I felt my eyes widen as I stared at him. He looked so much like his mother, Queen Nerali, with her wide, deep brown eyes, dark skin, and curling hair. How could I not have seen it? I told myself it would have been ridiculous to think someone I had met at Market was the Heir—but I still felt like a fool.

Royalty suited Fin. He stood straight in his dress uniform, seeming somehow taller than he had in his plain clothes. His hair, which I'd always seen in unkempt curls, was pulled back into a short queue.

Still, the mischievous quirk in his eyebrows and the open kindness of his face were just the same as they had always been. His eyes glimmered with good humor, and their utter familiarity threw me off. I felt a blush simmer over my face.

He offered a fluid, formal bow, and I stupidly attempted to curtsy in response. My hard, slippery shoes wobbled under me, and I had to spread out my arms to catch my balance.

Fin chuckled and took my hand. "Hello, Nick," he said.

My shock was fading, and annoyance and embarrassment took its place. "Why didn't you tell me?" I rasped.

But I already knew why, of course. The Heir never left the palace. King Corsin kept him even more closely guarded than the borders of Faerie—or so, at least, he'd let his people believe. An alias would be the only way for Fin to come out of hiding.

He shook his head—*not now*—still smiling. "Care for a dance?"

I pulled back. Of course I wanted to dance with him, but I wasn't feeling particularly graceful, and I didn't want to embarrass myself in front of him ever again. "Didn't you see me curtsy? I can't possibly dance—I'm here to find a patron for my workshop. Which I was about to do, by the way, until you turned up." Talking to him almost made me forget he was the Heir; I'd imagined our conversations so many times, that with the real Fin finally before me again, I could hardly help but talk to him naturally. I could see him again as the boy laughing at me at Market, murmuring seriously up in the trees . . . kissing me in the shadows of the Forest Queen's ruins.

I pulled my thoughts back to Lord Alming. "If you don't mind, I'd like to find him again."

Fin nodded but didn't drop my hand. I looked around for Lord Alming, but he'd vanished. As I wondered desperately if I'd lost my chance, I realized that quite a few people were staring at us.

My mortification grew. I wondered if my dress was all wrong: most of the other ladies had chosen white gowns, as had Piety and Chastity, or barely there pastels. My midnight blue ensemble stood out like a deep bruise.

Then the circlet on Fin's brow caught the light of a passing chandelier, and I remembered why people were staring. Every woman here hoped to gain the attention the Heir was offering me.

"Don't you want to dance with me?" he asked.

I remembered the note in the forest, the real reason I'd come. Of course I did.

There were so many things I wanted.

My face burned still hotter. "All right," I said, "but something simple, please, Fin."

He made a small motion with his white-gloved hand. A servant near the wall nodded and strode away, and a moment later the music slowed. I might almost have called the song gentle, if the prospect of dancing with the Heir while everyone watched hadn't set my heart careening against my ribs like a steam engine.

Fin led me to the center of the dance floor, and the couples around us backed respectfully away.

He turned to face me and smiled again. His hand found my waist.

I slipped my own hand onto his shoulder. I crimped the corners of my mouth into a smile, and Fin laughed outright.

"It'll be fun," he said. "Just let me lead."

His hand tightened ever so slightly around mine, then the music swelled and he stepped forward and we were dancing, spinning over the floor, my skirt swirling around us, and the chandeliers drifting and sparkling overhead. So much space opened inside me again, space exploding into something bright and rare that, in that moment, I knew must be love.

I don't know how long we danced; in his arms, I had no sense of time. We simply moved together, on and on through the music . . . until Fin stopped in the middle of a step. "She's here," he said, so softly that no one but I could hear him.

The momentum of the dance spun me against his chest, but even my slamming into him didn't distract him from where he was looking now—off toward the dark pit devoted to the mechanical orchestra. He stepped toward it, leaving me in the center of the dance floor.

I heard a few scandalized murmurs behind me, but I tried to ignore them as I followed Fin. Once we were beyond the silver drapery that surrounded the pit, none of the courtiers dared to follow.

The air was warm in there, the same metallic-friction warmth I knew from my workshop. A heavy woman in a red gown, the color of blood or roses, was standing in front of the orchestra, her back to us, quietly asking questions of a man in a conductor's tuxedo. She watched as he moved a series of levers on a panel set back against the wall. There was a moment of silence, and then the music changed, the dance Fin and I had shared becoming a minor-key saraband.

I didn't want to know who the woman was—I knew only that Fin had spoken of her with reverence, relief, adoration, and I'd never heard him speak of me that way. The space he'd made in my chest collapsed, and my muscles and bones went metal-cold.

Then the woman turned, and I saw that she was Caro.

Her dress was almost exactly in a style my mother used to wear—very much in vogue a decade or so ago. The full, rounded skirt had no bustle, and the neckline plunged into a deep vee. The old-fashioned gown suited her, though: its low neckline showed her creamy skin, and its tight bodice molded her torso into a thick hourglass. Even through my misery over Fin, I knew she looked beautiful.

"Oh, Nick," she said, reaching toward me, "I hoped you'd come, I really did—I asked Fin to leave you a note. Do you like the music? I gave Mr. Kinsworth here an idea or two, from my music boxes, you know." A flush of pride colored her skin all the way down to her shoulders.

The conductor nodded a brief greeting to me, then bowed to Fin and discreetly made his way out of the orchestra pit, leaving us in private.

"Yes, Caro. It's wonderful."

My voice was quieter than I would have liked it to be. I hated this. Tonight ought to have been thrilling, perfect, the beginning of the Exposition and the portal to my future. I was supposed to be utterly happy, and yet here I stood, wretched and confused, unable even to congratulate my friend properly.

I asked myself if I was jealous of Caro. I glanced at Fin again, then tore my gaze away, unable to bear the way he looked at her. Yet I cared for Caro as well—I cared for her too much to resent her happiness.

She was looking back at Fin now, and their smiles showed all the years they'd known each other, all the experiences they'd shared, and most of all, a secret they'd kept far too long . . . even from each other.

Watching them, I realized I'd known they were in love ever since I'd met them at Market.

I expected them to embrace, but neither of them moved. So much love shone on their faces that I was sure they couldn't help but recognize it in each other.

And I could not watch that happen. I looked from one to the other of them, and I could not bear it. I shook my head, and as Caro began to reach toward me, I drew open the curtains and walked back into the ballroom. Dozens of courtiers gaped at me, but I kept my shoulders straight and my head high. I knew they were only looking for Fin, and sure enough, as soon as I passed they gathered around the orchestra pit again.

I prayed Lord Alming would still be there and that I could fix whatever was wrong with my machine. I paced around the edges of the room, searching, but I could see no monocle-wearing men with huge mustaches anywhere. I began to walk more swiftly, and I felt my heart quicken.

Not looking where I was going, I ran headfirst into one of the guards. "Ah—sorry!" I gasped, still scanning the room for my lost patron.

"Never mind, miss, never mind," he grumbled, straightening the hem of his coat.

I wondered if he might be able to help me. "Excuse me," I said, "but have you perhaps seen Lord Alming? He's a very tall man in a purple jacket, and he has a monocle, and—"

"And a great gray mustache?" He nodded. "Yes, I believe

he left just a few minutes ago—went out by the main staircase, I think."

"Oh—thank you!"

I only narrowly avoided crashing into the guard again as I dodged toward the stairs. I picked up my skirts and rushed for the doors, but when I'd almost reached the top of the staircase, I stumbled. One of my shoes slipped off and tumbled down the steps.

I turned back for a moment, wondering how far I could chase Lord Alming through the snow in stockinged feet, but the shoe had fallen all the way to the bottom of the stairs, and I hardly had time to fetch it. There was nothing to be done—I dashed down the dark entry hall and out the doors, hobbling lopsided.

Snow was falling. It covered the palace, the courtyard, and the winding path down to the city square with its quiet white glow. The valets were gone, or at least inside.

I took out my pocket watch: it was exactly midnight. The courtyard looked entirely deserted.

My unrequited love suddenly seemed like a small disappointment indeed, compared to my loss of Lord Alming's approval and, with it, his patronage. I'd wanted my independence long before I'd ever wanted Fin.

I covered my face with my hands, and my lace gauntlets scratched at my cheeks. All I wanted now was Jules, and to go home.

The doors behind me groaned open, and I turned to see

one of the valets coming out. "Do you wish me to call for your carriage, miss?" he asked.

"I wish—" My voice caught. I closed my eyes and nodded. "Yes, please."

The valet nodded and strode into the snowy darkness.

I leaned against the wall and couldn't make myself move even when the snow melted and seeped through the back of my gown. I opened my eyes only when I heard Jules's metallic gait draw near to the palace doors.

He was glorious in the snow, his glass hide gleaming, puffs of smoke from his nostrils lingering in the freezing air. He followed the valet calmly, as docile as a child's pony, but the man still glanced back at him every few moments, frightened and awed.

I could see a thousand questions about to spill from the servant's lips, with only his palace training keeping him silent—and even that, I supposed, might not hold out for long. I didn't think I could bear much more human interaction just then, so I slipped past him quickly, murmuring my thanks.

"And thank you for waiting, Jules," I whispered. He shook his head in response, and his ears pricked forward.

I took my place inside the carriage and pulled the levers that were my reins. Jules set off quickly, and we left the palace behind.

I took Jules down small side streets until we left Esting City, and then back through the forest. Soon everyone would see him, but for now, he was a secret to all but the palace servants—and still a secret from the Steps.

I worried that they would be waiting for me, ready to punish me for leaving the house. Or worse, had they seen me there, despite the ombrossus? Had they seen me dancing with Fin—with the Heir?

Had they seen my heart crushed?

Seen me run?

Jules slowed when we approached the shed beneath the ruins, and as he plodded into his makeshift stall, I could sense that he was tired too. But he still steered my little spherical carriage expertly through the door. A new snowdrift had edged its way in; I'd been so distracted by the idea of the ball, I'd left the door open behind us. I lit one of the lamps I kept inside the shed, scraped the snow outside with a length of steel that was lying against the wall, then turned back to close the door.

Fin's note was still pinned there. I stared at it for a moment: *I'll look for you.*

I tore down the paper and walked into the shed again, slamming the door behind me. What could he have meant? I now understood the leap my heart had made when I read his words—a precursor to the plunge it had taken tonight. I'd thought his heart was leaping too.

But Fin loved Caro. Not me. He loved Caro.

I prodded at the part of my brain that knew that, while the rest of me—the part doing the prodding—watched, puzzled and fascinated. Such a strange-looking, squishy little idea; it couldn't be real, could it?

But there it was. The one I loved loved someone else.

As I thought of it in those words, it seemed silly and melodramatic. Did I even love Fin, really? Had I had time to love him yet?

Oh, I knew I had. Time didn't matter. And I loved him still, whatever he felt. I loved him for his kindness to me, for his easy happiness and laughter; I loved the imagined conversations and stories that had brought so much light into these last narrow, dark months after Jules's first death. I'd had the insects, to be sure, but Fin's friendship had made my life less lonely in a way they never could.

But then—another part of my mind chimed in—Caro had given me all those things too, and I had never fancied myself in love with her.

He had kissed me. The kiss had spun me silly. He'd smiled at me many times, charmed me, laughed in a kind, close way that made me believe things that perhaps I should not have believed. My skin felt warm when I thought of him; there was always something empty about my hands when I remembered that, on a very few occasions, they had held his. My waist still remembered the feel of his glove as we danced.

And he loved Caro. And he loved Caro.

And he didn't love me.

I closed my eyes.

I had hoped that he loved me—but it was more than

that. I had hoped I was loved. Mother and Father and Mr. Candery had each loved me well enough in their ways, but they were gone now. Stepmother, Piety, Chastity: they certainly didn't love me. And Mr. Waters thought kindly of me, but that wasn't the same at all.

Caro's friendship had helped to sustain me just as Fin's had. She loved me, in another way, and I loved her, too. I had felt certain since we first met, long before we should have known any such thing, that we would be friends for the rest of our lives. That, at least, was a kind of love I could count on.

And then there was Jules, of course. Jules loved me. But as much as I wished otherwise, and as intelligent and kind and sweet and as good a friend as he was, Jules was not quite a person. His was not the kind of love I thought I'd found in Fin.

All the things I'd learned from novels, from Faerie tales, from Piety and Chastity's gossiping and storytelling and swooning, silly as they were, had taught me that the love I'd thought I'd found in Fin was the best kind to be had. That the reason behind all of life and all of love in the first place was to find someone, love him, and let that love become the foundation for the rest of your life.

And I had found not only a kind, charming, handsome young man whom I could love, but also a prince, the Heir to all of Esting! No story could have asked for a better ending than the one that—just for a moment—I'd thought my love for him would give me.

But what was I, without that ending?

No less me, no less myself. No less loved than I had ever been, not really.

And of course Fin did care for me in his way, in a way that I tried to tell myself might be better, if I could only learn to see it so.

My head collapsed back against the cold wooden wall. All this thinking was well enough, but it did not give me the love I'd hoped was mine.

Worst of all was the small part of me that thought I was wrong about what I'd seen, that Fin could still love me after all. It was only a look between them. One moment and one look. Almost nothing.

I turned to Jules, waiting patiently in the flickering, low light for me to unhitch him from the carriage.

He nosed his cold muzzle against my shoulder.

I circled my arms around his neck. Jules was with me. I had friends. I was still loved.

I let myself lean against him, and for a few minutes, I let myself cry.

Then I raised my head and smiled at him, swiped at my eyes, and rubbed my handkerchief across the cloudy tear and breath marks on the shining glass of his neck.

I took up the oil rag and a wrench from a bin I kept inside the shed, kilted up my skirts, and covered them as best I could with my overcoat. I spent twenty minutes—ticked out on the clock in Jules's flank, and the pocket watch at my hip, in perfect synchrony—rubbing the residue of snow and grime from his legs, his hide, his face.

"You did so well," I told him. "And I could only go at all tonight because of you—" My breath hitched; I pressed a hand to my stomach. "I'm so glad to have you back, Jules. I couldn't lose you again."

Jules shook his head, and once more I found myself wondering how he could understand so much more than a real horse could.

"All right," I sighed. "Good night, Jules." I took off my one glass shoe and slid my feet back into the overlarge work boots, where the ache of spending the night in heeled dancing shoes compounded with the rough wear of leather on my thin-stockinged feet. I winced and limped my way back through the woods, but I knew I had to hurry. I didn't want to linger on my own thoughts anymore—and I knew I had probably incurred enough of Stepmother's wrath as it was.

My gown was mostly hidden beneath my long men's coat. I pulled off my gauntlets as I walked, stuffing them into the coat's roomy pockets. I unwound my glass fascinator from the hair I'd curled about it, nestling that into a pocket too. How practical men's clothing was! I promised myself my next dress would have pockets aplenty hidden amongst its skirts.

Lampton Manor, I saw with surprise, was completely dark as I approached.

I decided I might as well go in the front door. Even through my heartbreak over Fin, over my loss of Lord Alming's business, something about the ball had made me momentarily brave. So I held my head high and sailed through into the foyer with all the dignity I could muster.

All was dark and still. A few steps inside, I paused, surprised that Stepmother had not yet sprung herself on me.

I pulled off the long, heavy coat and stashed it in one of the vestibules, trying not to drip too much snowmelt on the floor. I couldn't make any more housework for myself than was absolutely necessary, not with the Exposition still ahead.

I smoothed out my skirts before walking—quickly, I admit—to the servants' staircase. If I could at least make it upstairs and change into my rags before Stepmother saw me, I might almost be safe. Where could she possibly be?

Once inside my room, I twisted around to undo the row of small buttons at the back of my gown. I had to shove the skirts toward the floor to step out of them, the fabric was so thick and rich. I had the extra silk from Piety's and Chastity's wardrobes to thank for that. I'd dyed them myself in my experiments, and Jules had known, had used the rest of my clockwork menagerie to gather them all together and make this dress, this gorgeous dress.

All the things he had done for me—I was still amazed.

The gown continued to stand after I stepped out of it. I lifted it carefully by the shoulders, feeling its weight in my hands. I knew I had to return it to Stepmother's closet by morning. I was sure, too, that any luck I'd had that evening had long since run out; I couldn't imagine getting in and out of Stepmother's room without being discovered.

This was not a night for blessings.

Still, I had to try.

Dressed in my brown flannel skirts and blouse, my sootiest apron tied around my waist—for the suggestion, at least, that I'd been cleaning fireplaces after all—I stepped back into the rear hallway, closing the door as silently as I could behind me.

I padded over to the main hall, where the Steps' rooms lay. I crept along for several moments before I heard it: Piety's telltale snore.

I clapped both hands over my mouth to stifle my laughter. They were already asleep!

Sure enough, Chastity's high-pitched gibbering shortly followed.

Stepmother's room was silent, but then, I'd never heard her make noises in her sleep.

I wondered if I really dared to go inside. She might be up reading Scriptures, or doing any number of things—or she might be waiting for me.

But perhaps she wasn't in her room at all. Perhaps she was out searching for me, even more furious than I'd imagined.

I held my breath as I opened her door. It was very dark; she slept without even the light and warmth of a banked fire.

A worldly foolishness, she said, to keep the sleeping body warm while the dreaming mind communed with the Lord.

Or, of course, the fire could be out because she wasn't there.

I prayed—and I rarely prayed—that she would be asleep and that I would not wake her. And perhaps the Lord heard me after all, because the door opened silently the rest of the way, and my feet padded equally silently over to the closet, where I managed to rehang the gown. Or perhaps it was just that the ombrossus still concealed me.

I crossed the room to leave, passing by the huge bed Stepmother had once shared with Father—the bed, I realized exactly then, that Mother must have died in.

I'd made Stepmother's bed every day for years, of course. But I had never thought of that moment. I'd turned down and changed and washed her sheets, and I knew now that I had not let myself think of it.

Mother had died there.

And Stepmother slept there now. As if suddenly entranced, I slowly approached the bed.

There she lay, her brown hair coiled in a long braid and pinned on top of her head, little streaks of gray showing at her temples where the soft side-rolls she wore during the day usually concealed them.

Stepmother never let me do her hair. I straightened Chastity's and curled Piety's after every wash, and I had the burn marks on my hands to prove it. But Stepmother insisted she needed no help with her ablutions. She sailed downstairs every morning looking as cold and perfect and iconic as ever.

Was this why, this bit of gray at her temples? It was beautiful, a bright silver gleaming under my candle and in the thin moonlight coming in between her curtains. The snowstorm must have been passing, if moonlight could get in.

She turned in her sleep. I backed away from the bed, suddenly terrified I'd woken her.

"William," she murmured, barely a sound, barely a movement of her lips. Her hands on the pillow dug deeper.

Her breath evened again, and she kept sleeping.

My father's name. William Lampton. William.

How many times had I woken, knowing I'd called Mother's or Father's name in my sleep, and knowing no one would come to me?

Stepmother was calling Father too, and no one would come.

I told myself to back away. If I stayed, I would start to care for her. If I stayed, I would start to think about how alone she would be, with only the silly daughters she'd made, after I left. I couldn't begin to think of Stepmother that way. I had to be able to leave her.

My heart hammering as hard as it had all night, I turned and fled her room.

IN the morning, I donned the sky-blue day dress that Jules and the buzzers and I had sewn months ago, years and years, it seemed now. My hair curled and pinned by my own hand, the work boots on my feet after all—in the aftermath of last night's storm, I had no other choice and could only hope that my long skirt and the thick snow on the ground would hide them when I walked—I went to the kitchen. The last drop of ombrossus waited for me in Mr. Candery's cupboard. I was a little frightened of using it, this final smidgen of disguise and protection that he had left for me. I kept telling myself that I wouldn't need it anymore after today. But that wasn't necessarily true. It was just another part of my great gamble, the one I decided to make as soon as Stepmother had read the words on that filigreed invitation . . . as soon as I'd found Mother's workshop, really. I had to gamble on my own escape.

I tipped the last drop onto my finger, trying not to let my hands tremble. *The Steps,* I thought, closing my eyes . . .

"So, it's true." Behind me, Chastity's beautiful voice was light and mocking. Even before I turned to face her, I knew exactly the cold smirk that would be on her face. And I was right: it was the same expression she'd worn when she told me about stomping on Jules.

Oh, no, I thought. *Oh, please.*

Chastity stood there triumphant in a yellow morning dress, her hair half tumbled down from last night's elaborate updo, kohl smudged under her eyes. My shock at her being awake at this dawn hour, the night after a ball, was exceeded only by wondering how she'd managed to dress by herself.

"I didn't quite believe Fitz, even though he insisted it was you."

Fitz! I thought. When I'd applied the ombrossus and thought of my enemies, I'd only pictured the Steps . . .

"I have to admit, Nick, I didn't recognize you. You just don't *fit in* at a ball." She looked around the kitchen, which had fallen into a slightly grimier state than usual in the last week or so; magic can only do so much without your own elbow grease to help it along, and Lord knew I'd been busy.

I looked at Chastity then, really looked at her. Any passing stranger would have said she was a beauty. Even a suitor besotted with lust and money might not notice what lay behind her blank and lovely expressions. The callousness, the cold in her eyes . . . but that inner frost was not what I saw as we faced each other in the kitchen. It was that girl I'd first seen at our parents' wedding, who I'd thought would become a new sister, who I'd dreamed of and planned for over those lonely childhood months, decorating her bedroom, choosing her books.

It was this, still, that frightened me, that hurt. I looked down at the floor.

"You're pathetic, Mechanica," Chastity continued. "You can't even look at me. Too scared. Too scared even to run away, all this time, eh? At least before you'd found someone rich enough to run to."

"What?"

"Please. How else could you have gone to the ball? And why else would you be sneaking out this morning? And"—her eyes flashed even colder—"how old and ugly is he, to take on someone like you? What do you let him do to you?" She sniffed contemptuously. "You've never had any mettle. Whoever's stooped to rescuing you must be just *embarrassing.*"

I don't know what did it. Maybe it was the strange experience of seeing one sister without the other as backup; maybe the early hour and my lack of sleep lowered my tolerance for the Steps' absurdities.

And of course Chastity was far, far off the mark, something I articulated to myself only just then. I had rescued myself entirely. I'd had help, certainly: Mother's workshop, Jules and the minions, Mr. Candery's gifts. Fin and Caro, and everything they'd done. My heart healed a little, just thinking of their goodness. But *I* rebuilt Jules, *I* made the carriage;

when I decided I wanted to go to the ball, the products of my own hard work took me there.

Yet it wasn't until I caught sight of the patent boots that had crushed Jules adorning Chastity's feet that I moved, that I stepped forward and slapped her as hard as I could across the mouth.

I'd just finished building the vehicles of my self-made salvation. I'd spent months hammering metals and carrying hundreds of pounds of horse and carriage parts out to the forest.

As hard as I could slap was hard indeed.

Chastity stumbled sideways, clasping her jaw. There was blood on the red of her lips. I could see my last brown drop of ombrossus clinging to her cheek, but it didn't matter. My gamble would succeed. I would never need it again.

"Nick . . ." Chastity mumbled, prodding gently at her cheek, which was already beginning to swell. "Nicolette . . ."

I stared at her; she hadn't used that name since we'd first met. It was strange, but she was looking up at me now with something like surrender, something that in a less proud girl I might have thought was jealousy. "The Heir couldn't really . . ." she whispered, then trailed into silence again.

I didn't want to wait for her to finish. Whatever she was trying to say, I was sure I didn't need to hear it.

I laughed at her and left.

Instead of going through the forest and back roads, as we had on our way to and from the ball, Jules and I made for the main thoroughfare right away. Today, I wanted to show him off as much as possible.

The road was crowded with other people on their way to the Exposition, most in carriages and carts drawn by real flesh-and-blood horses, some traveling on foot, a few on bicycles or other contraptions. No one else I saw had transportation as fine as Jules, but I knew the most wonderful inventions, those commissioned by the crown and built by court-backed inventors, would already be in the main square.

At first I was lost in the swelling crowd as we approached the city. But then a few people began to make way for us—for the carriage, for Jules.

We were a sight, to be sure, the glass walls that surrounded me gleaming like a bubble in the clear winter sunlight, shining bright enough to blind me when the sun hit at the right angles. Jules's glass shone too, as did the brass and steel and copper of his framework. I was so proud of him—of my work. We were everything the Exposition stood for, everything new and progressive . . . and we were a few things *I* stood for too, the magic melded with technology, the coexistence of Esting and Faerie, the affection and gratitude I still felt for Mr. Candery and my mother. Those parts had to be secret, of course, but I was proud of them nonetheless.

I was thrilled to see people's mouths drop open as we

passed, to see them stop and stare and point at the marvel that drew my carriage. It didn't matter what I had been before this moment; I could hold my head high as one of the finest inventors in Esting that day, if our arrival attracted such attention.

A lively group of young people not much older than I had kept a close pace with us on the road. They smiled and waved at me several times. It would have been easier for me to duck my head, to turn away—so many years of loneliness still made me frightened around people my own age.

But I thought of my inventions, of Jules, of all the things I wanted, and I smiled and waved back. I told myself I could be brave, if not for my own sake, for the sake of my dreams.

The procession slowed as we neared the palace; people and carriages bottlenecked into the city square. The young group and I halted next to each other on the road. One of them, the boldest, I supposed, broke away from his companions and approached me.

He was perhaps twenty, and rather stunningly handsome: tall and broad-shouldered, with hazel eyes and the dusky skin and hair—and expensive clothes—of a Su-descended nobleman. His confident stride certainly indicated a life of privilege, a life in which no one had ever turned him away.

He rapped three times on my door.

"I beg pardon, miss," he said, "but my friends and I"—he

indicated the ornate carriage he'd emerged from, where two curl-covered feminine heads leaned out, staring at me in brazen curiosity—"we'd just like to know if it's true."

"I'm sorry?" Somehow I felt as if I already knew what he was going to say. My heart sank.

He chuckled at my question. "I see, miss." He tapped the side of his nose. "You'd like to keep it discreet for now. I don't blame you. But—just between us . . ." He leaned in and gave me a smile that had no doubt stolen a dozen young hearts. "It's a wonderful story. You and the Heir. I'd just like to say, well"—another lightning smile, which thrilled me; I knew a beautiful man when I saw one—"I am happy for you, miss." He winked knowingly, and when he turned away, he gave the same knowing nod to his waiting friends.

This, oh, this, my heart could not bear.

"Ah . . . sir?" I called after him.

He turned to me and bowed—actually bowed, deeply. He smiled as he did it, but it was a kind smile. I did not think he was teasing me.

I wasn't sure how to begin, how to ask him the question that tore too much at my heart to form itself into words. We regarded each other for a moment, his eyes warm and thoughtful, and mine, I was sure, only searching.

"Please don't worry, Mechanica," he said gently. "I won't tell a soul."

Mechanica? Where on earth had he heard that name?

He jogged quickly back to his waiting companions, and I could already see him starting to tell them what he'd gleaned from me—which I hoped was not much, but I couldn't be sure.

I didn't know what to think, but at the mention of Fin's title, something inside me had woken up, shaken its feathers . . . something like hope. I felt a tug at the levers I held; there was space ahead of us on the road, and Jules wanted to move forward. I urged him on.

But as the minutes passed and Jules and I neared the square, more and more people began to whisper when they saw us. I kept hearing the name "Mechanica," and my pulse skipped every time.

I still wanted to think it was Jules and the carriage that spurred their talk. But then I began to catch more fragments of words as we passed, murmurs that wove in through my carriage's open vents.

"The Heir himself . . ." said one.

"The last one he danced with!" another exclaimed. "Oh, no, the *only* one!"

And, finally, the phrase that nearly made me halt Jules in his tracks: "Such a romantic story."

My heart clattered at my ribs. People were talking about the Heir—Fin—and me, together, and they were calling it romantic? Had they seen something I hadn't, something I'd told myself I couldn't dare to hope for?

I sat up straighter, leaning forward in my seat so I could hear them better. Fin and me, a love story after all . . . That was a story I was desperate to hear.

But there was something else, something that did not sit so sweetly with me. These people didn't care about my inventions at all; most of them were looking at me, not at Jules or the carriage. And they weren't even talking about *me,* not really; they were talking about Fin. About a story that—I still had to admit—probably wasn't even true.

Jules and I encountered group after group that started pointing and talking to each other excitedly as we passed. He looked back at me, nervous, but I nodded at him and sent a gentle prod through his rein-levers, and he straightened his neck and kept walking.

He was braver than I. There was no glass wall between him and the staring and pointing. At least I could feel somewhat enclosed, somewhat protected.

The murmurs and gestures and conspiratorial smiling only increased as we reached the palace. At last, at the edge of the square, I began to feel truly lost in the crowd. I felt the burn in my cheeks subside, and I began to look up and around me, out the sides of my faceted glass bubble, to see the other wonders of the Exposition.

And, oh, there were wonders to see.

A huge puppet theater, festooned with green curtains, caught my attention first. It had already entranced many of the children who milled about. The scene was a familiar one: the Forest Queen's village at the height of its splendor, the platforms and sheds I knew not ruined, but flourishing as a whole, lively community. The set was at least ten feet high, a labyrinth of two-dimensional trees painted almost like life, but brighter, richer. Their leaves seemed nearly to move—no, they *did* move, metal leaves on clockwork mechanisms tinkling against each other, apples and pears crafted from small bells. The tall queen and her man-at-arms swung through the branches on ropes, climbed them like squirrels. I could see wires glinting off the ends of their jointed limbs, but there didn't seem to be a puppeteer above them—just a pretty woman turning a crank at the side of the stage. Was the whole show automated?

I watched for a few more moments, as delighted as the children who gathered in front of the theater. Much as I admired the artistry and invention of the show, however, I had to wonder at the puppeteer's choice of subject. Finn had told me, after all, that it was illegal even to print her story. I couldn't imagine King Corsin, or the powerful advisors who depended on his favor, would want to offer further funding to such a project.

Of course, that could well be an issue with my own magic-dependent display too, but I was not looking for money from the crown. I only wanted a private investor, one who would help me set up my business. Besides, it wasn't *obvious* that I was using magic. I told myself that I, at least, did not need the King's approval.

I wondered if anyone else at the Exposition had decided to snub him as the puppeteer had done. But when I looked around again, I could think only of the wonder of the inventions all around me.

Since the Steps' invitation had described the Exposition as a celebration of Esting's achievements, I had not expected to see so many inventors from other countries. Yet there they were, one display booth after another. The Su aesthetic, with its sharp, elegant angles and warm, bright colors, jostled against the elaborate curls and aurora borealis shades that Nordsk designers favored. Yet they were both exuberant, vividly colorful, and I could not help but think that Esting's simple, grayscale style looked a bit prudish in comparison.

There was a raised stage in the middle of the square, covered with gray curtains. I wondered at first if something especially grand might be hidden there, but then I saw the palace guards posted around it. The Exposition judges, I decided, must be waiting behind the curtain. Perhaps even the royal family . . . but I wouldn't devote more energy to confusing thoughts of Fin than I could help, especially when there were so many other fascinating places to direct my attention.

I was not the only one who had built a mode of transport; that much was clear right away. None of them seemed really alive the way Jules was, but they were still incredible.

There was a many-legged contraption like a centipede, clomping along low to the ground with great clanking and screeching sounds, a grinning conductor at its head and flower-decked baggage filling each of its five jointed sections.

There was a vaguely triangular boat of sorts, blasting steam out of a small chimney and puttering around the square in an oddly comical fashion. It was operated by a young man in a caricature of a sailor's costume, a beautiful man, his smile wide and roguish. In his ease and assurance, he reminded me of no one so much as Fitz. Fitzwilliam Covington, who had revealed me to Chastity. I might have seethed a bit about that if I'd had more attention to divert from the Exhibition.

A low, animal rumble from above drowned out my thoughts. When I looked up, I forgot about Fitz, my machines, the other inventions in the square, the burgeoning gossip about Fin and me, even my broken heart. All I could do was stare, mouth open with wonder, as was every other mouth in the square—every other mouth in Esting City, I had no doubt.

There was a ship in the sky.

I did not know what else to call it, but *ship* hardly did it justice. No word I knew, no word I might have learned, even from Mother's books, could describe the great vessel high above us. I could not guess accurately from my place on the ground, but I thought a seafaring ship of similar size could hold at least fifty sailors. It had portholes, like a sea-ship, but I could not see the top to know whether it had a deck or merely a roof. And above it, hulking even larger than the vessel itself, was a great black balloon, emblazoned with the silver triple star and cross that was Esting's emblem: our national flag, hundreds of feet wide, sailing across the sky.

Black spikes, needle-thin from so far away, began to protrude out of the portals. I squinted at them in confusion for a few moments, then realized—cannons!

And they exploded, all at once, in one round and then another, spirals of gray smoke following their volleys into the sky. Fireworks cracked and blossomed around the ship, green and blue and pink and gold, starbursts and flame spikes burning through the air. Fireworks that glowed in the daytime—these were a marvel in their own right, and I couldn't stop watching them.

We all gasped, and took a collective breath, and gasped again at the next volley.

I had never been so close to fireworks before. I had seen them only a few times in my life, when Mother and Father had taken me to the city for Empire Day, the anniversary of Esting's discovery of Faerie.

After they died and all my time was occupied working for the Steps, I would climb the servants' steps to the roof on Empire Day, and over the tops of the trees, I could see the distant flicker and glow of the fireworks in the city. It was a lonely thing, sitting there by myself in the heat of summer, but it was lonelier to scrub floors and think of the fireworks without being able to watch them at all. On the roof, I could at least imagine all the other Estingers who watched with me and pretend I was lost in the crowd, or perhaps with a group of friends. The first year, I let myself imagine I was a small figure snuggled between Mother's and Father's tall shoulders. But it hurt too much to come down from that dream when the fireworks ended and I had to go back inside and finish my chores before the Steps returned from the city. After that, I simply pictured myself among strangers.

And in this moment, with every mind turned toward the ship and away from Fin or me or anything else in Esting City, I felt the same way I'd imagined then: one of many. All of us the same, lost in our collective wonder.

A dozen trumpets blared their sudden brass voices. An announcer cried, "Welcome, citizens of Esting, to the first annual Royal Exposition of Art and Science!"

I looked toward the gray-covered stage. The curtains were still closed, but for a moment, I saw the announcer we'd all heard standing before them, a short, round man with a red face. A second later, my view was blocked by a huge white mare—and by Fitzwilliam Covington, in a black military jacket, riding her. His auburn hair was slicked straight back from his forehead, emphasizing the strong lines of his cheekbones and jaw. He looked forbidding and handsome. I swallowed.

"Miss Nicolette Lampton," he said, dismounting. "If you would accompany me. You've been summoned by the Heir."

I stared. "Fitz, I—" I groped for what to say next. "Why does he want to see me?" Then a better question came: "Fitz, *why did you tell Chastity about me?*"

He grinned and leaned in close. "I told everyone," he said. "It's perfect; I even told them that fanciful name the Halvings gave you. You'll see. It's a perfect story."

He mounted his horse again and moved ahead of the carriage, waving for me to follow. Dozens of spectators pushed each other aside, making a wide clear lane for us. I followed him, too overwhelmed even to think about what I was doing.

He led me to the stage. I worried for a moment about leaving Jules alone while I followed Fitz—while I went to meet Fin—but as I cast my eyes around for potential meddlers, two of the palace guards who were standing by the stage stepped forward to guard the carriage. I could see that I didn't have to worry about thieves anyway: the multitude of faces regarding us were full of only awe, of something almost like worship. They looked at me as if I were not just a girl, but a heroine.

I opened my small glass door and stepped down, trying as best I could to hide my work boots under my skirts. I was embarrassed to see that more than a few people were peering down at my feet, as if they expected to see something unusual; glass slippers, no doubt. I wondered how much everyone knew.

I pressed my forehead to Jules's to gather my strength for whatever these next moments might bring. He whuffled against me, hot coal smoke and the sound of springs, and at least for that moment, I could feel my pulse start to calm down.

"I told the story, Nicolette," Fitz said again, beckoning me toward the stage steps. "It'll help you, I promise. It'll help us both. I can't begin to tell you how delighted King Corsin was to hear of how his son fell in love with a hard-working, well-born, but self-made Estinger girl. It's just the kind of thing the kingdom needs to bolster up Esting for the coming war."

"Fitz, how did you know that we—that I—" I started to ask. But before I formed that question, a more frightening one took its place. "War?"

Father's bloodless body on some frontier, girls like me everywhere left without families . . .

"Fitz." I made my voice as hard and authoritative as I could. "Fitz, what war?"

He looked at me disparagingly. "The Faerie revolution, the one that's been brewing for years. Don't be naïve."

A thousand questions sprang to my lips, but Fitz continued talking before I could ask them.

"First things first," he said. "I saw you and the Heir

dancing at the ball—as did everyone else of importance in Esting, I have no doubt! Those ninnyish sisters of yours didn't even recognize you so clean and made up in a lovely gown like that. I always knew they were idiots."

I knew enough not to mention the ombrossus. Still, I remembered all of Fitz's fawning over Chastity. I knew he was a charmer, but I'd thought at least that he was genuine about his admiration for her. "But, Fitz, you always said Chastity—"

He cut me off again. "Ah, she's a beauty, that's certain. But you and I both know that's all she is." He winked at me, and I was flustered, as always. "I'm sure when you're Heiress, you'll be flocked by lovely women who can hold a conversation . . . and hold their high places in court, too." He smiled, and there was something in the smile I didn't like. "You and I, Miss Nick, we're both going places. I helped you, you see?"

It echoed between us, unsaid: "And you in turn will help me."

He had always called me Miss Nick, and I'd always been glad. But now I wondered: had he only been making me like him in case the liking ever became useful to him?

"Right," he continued when I did not reply. "We had better go in."

I hesitated at the bottom of the steps, not quite willing to follow him.

He took my hand and pulled me forward, so I did not

have any more time to be frightened of what waited behind the curtains. To my chagrin, a smattering of applause broke out when I reached the top of the stairs. Fitz stopped, turned, and waved at the crowd, nodding and grinning. He squeezed my hand, hard, and I knew he was telling me to do the same.

I still didn't quite dare to hope, to believe that what Fitz had told me about Fin's feelings for me was true. But what else could I do? I smiled and waved along with him, and for a moment, with the people of Esting smiling back, I let myself believe that this happy ending was mine.

And then Fitz opened the curtains, and I stepped backstage alone.

It was dark, a darkness too much like the one in the orchestra pit the night before.

I wondered briefly if my life would be defined by a series of miseries in places like these—dark, gray, heavy-curtained rooms. Backstage areas, when everything outside was clean and bright.

But I thought of my dark cellar workshop; I was not afraid of shadows. I stepped forward to meet my fate.

As my eyes adjusted to the dim light, I was surprised to see only one other figure in the space with me. I thought they would both be there, the King and his Heir, but it was just Fin. He leaned against a heavy ebony chair, almost a throne, its back tall and carved with a lattice of sharp angles. He didn't sit on it properly, as I supposed a prince should sit on a throne, but rather leaned one hip against it, his ankles and arms loosely crossed. As always there was that smile on his face, that grin without a trace of malice, that radiant kindness.

"Hello, Nick," he said. "Will you marry me?"

FOR a moment, I thought I could say yes.

When I tried to part my lips to speak, though, nothing happened. I stood and stared at him, blank-faced and blank-souled, my heart in free fall. I knew I could, should, catch it. But I could not move.

Fin's smile faltered; it was only the second time I'd seen it do so. "Well," he said, more softly this time, "will you?"

At last I found my voice, a voice that would not deny him, yet; a voice full of questions rather than answers. The voice I had always had. "Why?" I asked. "Why, if you love Caro?"

Now it was his turn to be stricken, to go blank. "I—"

"I know you do," I said. "I know it. I could see it in your face in the orchestra pit last night. Don't do either of us the injustice of denying it."

"So that's why you left . . ." He blinked, twice. "I've never denied it," he said. "It's just that no one ever asked me, till now. No one even thought it was possible. But you—"

"They must not know you very well." Not that I knew him so well either—something I'd told myself a thousand times since last night. But I knew him well enough to see the light in his eyes when he looked at another girl. I knew him well enough to see that light was not there when he looked at me.

He nodded, then laughed a little, and some of his natural ease came back. He took in a breath, and I knew he was going to tell me the truth. "I've loved her forever," he said, more quietly still. "Since we were children. I loved her long before I ever met you that day at Market. Sometimes I wondered . . . sometimes I got angry, that I had loved someone so long, before I even had the chance to fall in love in the first place. I fell in love with her before I could speak, before I could think. My first memory is of her, of making her laugh. Even then—I was probably two—all I wanted was to make her laugh, always.

"Of course," he went on, "there hasn't been a single moment in my life when I haven't loved Caro, but sometimes I . . . sometimes I've wondered if it would still have been that way, if we hadn't been friends our whole lives. I know she's wondered that too. There are other people she . . . but none of them last. And for me, well, the only person who's made me wonder is you."

He took three steps toward me and clasped my hands

in his. He leaned forward to search out my eyes. "You," he murmured, "a girl who had brought herself to Market of her own volition, a girl clearly of the kind of, well, the kind of background my father is hoping for, and a girl who is also intelligent and sweet and beautiful . . . How could I not have wondered? My father has lectured me for years, ever since Philip died, that the only girl for me would be an Estinger maiden of proper background, of proper birth . . . but I was never allowed to meet anyone at all, of course. And over the last year, when I've met a very few . . . well, they've all been like your stepsisters: vapid and stuffy, named after virtues that are usually an absurd clash with their personalities. But you were fresh and real, Nick, and I admired you from the start. I wanted to make you laugh too, the way I did with Caro. And when you laughed, then I started to wonder what it would be like to kiss you. And then I—I hoped—oh, Nick, wouldn't you have hoped, as I did?"

"I did hope," I whispered, tears stinging my eyes. I swatted my fingers across my face, embarrassed, and I had to pull away from his grip to do so. "I hoped too."

Fin looked horrified; his other hand dropped mine of its own accord. "Oh, Nick. How incredibly cruel you must think me. How incredibly cruel I have been."

"No—you didn't—" But that denial died on my tongue too. "A little, maybe." A laugh broke its way through my tears.

"Oh, Nick, I never thought. You were—you were a

hope, for me, of a different life. A change in fate when my fate was already designed." He glanced down at his hands, clenched and released them. "But my story was decided a long time ago."

I heard a murmur from the crowd outside, at some miracle or other passing by. "The people out there don't think so. They think your story—our story—began last night."

Fin took a long breath, and when he spoke again, his voice was clearer, steadier. Somehow I knew he'd rehearsed these words. "Yes, exactly," he said. "They believe the story is ours, yours and mine. They believe in us, Nick. That's why we have to get married."

I stared at him; I ogled. Just seconds ago, ticked out in the beat of my own heart, I'd heard him tell me all about how he loved someone else. Did I know him at all, this person I thought I loved, if he could propose such a thing?

"But I—but Caro—" It seemed the mechanisms of my voice had seized up again.

"I know," he said. "I think . . . I think I am glad I told you after all. If we marry, we should at least be honest with each other. And if you—bound as my heart is, it would only be reasonable for you to find someone else to love too, Nick. I wouldn't blame you, not in the least. And there are plenty of brilliant young men in court, in Esting, in the realms abroad—genius inventors, poets, men far more handsome than I, men with a thousand more virtues, and I say this as a prince who has never counted modesty or humility among the particularly worthwhile virtues. And, oh, Lord, you should meet those two demons-in-gowns. Modesty Dulac and Humility Covington make your stepsisters look like turtledoves."

I had a sudden image of Piety and Chastity as preening birds, stuffing feathers from other species—peacocks, perhaps—amid their own gray plumage and cooing over the results, and I had to laugh again.

That was the first moment of hope I had for my broken heart. At least I could still see the humor where there was humor to be had.

"Anyway, Nick . . . we can use this story. Remember the Forest Queen? The whole country is in love with you right now—and not just because they believe I am too. They're in love with your ingenuity, your beauty, your grace; they love that name they're calling you. You are everything Esting longs to be, and this story, falling in love at first sight at the ball—my father's councilors couldn't have constructed something so perfect if they'd tried. This story will build us up, Nick, you and I, until the whole kingdom follows us. You'll be Mechanica forever, with a happy-ever-after people will tell each other for generations, countless generations yet to come. You'll be the story girls tell themselves at night, girls who hope for a better life. You can become that, Nick. Think of how a story like that would inspire people." His eyes were bright, and there was a faint sheen to his skin. His words had sped up until they were hurried, fervent.

I thought of all the long nights spent in my lonely bed, reading Faerie stories and romances, imagining that a happy ending waited for me, too, preconstructed as perfectly as Mother's machines. Having to believe that, just to keep on going.

But with Fin, as Heiress—as the story Mechanica—my bed would still be lonely. I would still lie there and tell myself stories instead of living them. The only difference would be that every girl in Esting would be telling herself the same story, my story, and wishing her life would have as happy an ending as mine.

And then, finally—with a feeling in my chest that was a sinking and a rising at once, a drowning and a stirring of wings—I knew my answer. I could not fit inside a story someone else had built.

"No, Fin," I said. "I can't marry you. I love you; for a few moments, I even thought I was in love with you. But I can't marry you."

I touched his cheek, and we smiled at each other, gently, sadly.

Fin reached his hand up to cup mine. "I thought you might say that," he said.

That fervent look in his eyes had dimmed a little, but it

was still there. He looked like an Heir now, truly, a young man who would someday lead a country. I thought he must love Esting more than he loved either Caro or me; in a strange way, the thought was a comforting one.

He released my hand. "You may be right, in the end," he said.

I nodded, and because my heart asked it, I kissed him for the last time, under his right eye, then his left.

And then I turned, and I left my love behind.

Fitz was waiting for me just outside the curtain, as I expected him to be.

"Well!" he said, grinning at me. "Are my best wishes in order?"

I laughed, and I was surprised to hear the sound, not so soft or sad as I'd thought it would be. I really laughed.

"Always, Fitz," I said, and nothing more. However he chose to read my answer was fine with me; I didn't think I owed him the truth.

Thankfully, he took this as all the confirmation he needed of Fin's and my impending nuptials, and he winked slyly at the tall, muscular guard who stood by the stage stairs. To my startled amusement, the huge man let out a squeak of glee, and I saw the kind of happiness spark in his face that I'd thought was reserved for young children listening to a Faerie tale.

And I found I was happy too. My heart was free, and there was the Exposition to take in, still. So many things to take in.

People made way for us again as Fitz escorted me back—and not just in front of us, either. There was a clear cobblestone path leading all the way from the stage to my carriage, to my beautiful Jules, who stood patiently waiting for me, nickering at passersby, clearly enjoying the awed and admiring glances he received. I couldn't help admiring him myself, as well as the faceted bubble of the carriage. No one dared to come near him—or rather, only one person: a tall man in an acid-green top hat, who stroked Jules's nose in a way I found all too intimate. And Jules, guileless showoff that he was, leaned happily into the man's gloved hand.

I bolted toward him. The man turned, and I just had time to recognize the monocle, the serious, freckled face, and especially the huge gray mustache that curled up most of the way to his hat, before I collided with him headlong. He was holding a round, lilac-colored hatbox, and he fumbled and nearly dropped it.

"Lord Alming!" I panted. "I'm so sorry! Just a . . . just a moment of your time . . ." I'd come to think of myself as very fit, especially in the last few months; I thought it must have been my panic that had winded me, rather than the short sprint to my imagined patron.

"Ah, Miss Lark," he said. "I have been hoping to find you. You waltzed off with the Heir last night, and I must say I was a bit put out with you, but I hear you have plenty of reason. Ah! Romance, drama, youth. How any of you enjoy it entirely escapes me, but I am sure you must be pleased. The whole kingdom is delighted with you, at any rate."

Suddenly he frowned, and his mustache angled perilously downward. "But love stories are not what I have come to discuss with you. Ah, no. We must talk about your machine."

My heart skipped, not in love or hope this time, but in fear. I still didn't know what had gone wrong with the machine I had made for him, but I would set things right if I could. "I don't know what's wrong with the knitting machine, sir, but whatever is broken, I'll replace it, repair it, I—I usually do quite good, quite reliable work—"

He stopped me with a raised hand. "The machine's perfect, lass," he said. "I'd wanted to discuss a further order with you, last night. But now . . ." He opened the hatbox he held and withdrew what was inside. "Now I'd like to talk about this."

In his hand was my slipper—the one I'd lost at the ball.

It was still whole, perfect, steel gears glinting their delicate circles inside the shining glass exoskeleton.

"I nearly went home early last night, before I'd decided to forgive you. I am relieved that I returned; the food alone was spectacular. You'd gone by the time I came back, but you'd left this in your wake. There's remarkable workmanship there," Lord Alming said, following my gaze. "A dancing shoe, a real one, made of glass and gears! A wonderful thing in its own right, and a beauty too. I imagine every lady in Esting will want a pair, with this grand romantic tale circling about." He winked at me. "Mechanica and the Heir. It's a lovely story."

I studied Lord Alming's smiling face, wondering if I'd lose this chance too. Would he still want to sell shoes made by a nonprincess?

"Oh, sir," I said, "the story's not—the story's not true."

I was close to tears, but Lord Alming chuckled and waved his gloved hand. "Does it matter? Will it matter to the ladies paying a hundred crowns for these beauties?"

"A hundred crowns?" I was startled out of my self-pity, and I looked at him incredulously. The exorbitant price reminded me of the lovesbane bloom at the Night Market; a pair of shoes, for nearly the same price as lovesbane, which could save a life, or end one . . . "For one pair of shoes?"

Lord Alming nodded. "More, perhaps, once the trend sets in. I'd like to put these into large-scale production, Miss Lark—I'd like us to be business partners. I believe you are going to be a very rich woman."

He handed me the slipper, and I looked down at it, rubbing my finger over the rounded toe. Lord Alming watched me, his face serious and professional, that of an investor making a business proposition.

He began to talk of the details: seed money and commissions and royalty rates. Because of Mother's journals and the economics books I'd read, I was proud to say I could understand all of his terms. The rates he offered seemed more than fair, but he still insisted I get quotes from other potential investors before I signed an agreement with him. He'd seen young people swindled before, he said, and he wanted to be sure he was doing right by me.

I gathered myself together, the parts of my heart that still worried about Fin, and Caro, and Jules and the Ashes, and even the Steps and how I would deal with them, how I would manage to leave them. What Lord Alming offered here was no Faerie-tale ending, at least not the kind Estingers all over the country were dreaming up for me. It was simply a step, albeit a valuable one: a step in the right direction. But a step was all I wanted. The rest I would do myself.

He held out his hand, and I shook it. "Yes," I said. "I believe I'd like to work with you."

He smiled that wide-cracking smile again, the one that made his mustache brush his eyebrows. "Excellent, Miss Lark, excellent." He winked. "Or would you prefer that I call you Mechanica?"

I held my slipper up to the light, where it glimmered and flashed. I flexed my toes in my old, cracked work boots, considering. I placed the glass shoe gently back in the box.

"You can call me whatever you like," I said, "but I should tell you my real name is Nicolette Lampton."

"Lampton." His eyebrows rose halfway to his hairline. "Not Margot Lampton's daughter?"

"Ye—yes, sir." Blood rushed through my ears.

"Well, I'm more confident in your abilities than ever. I've more than one of your mother's creations in my study. Fascinating, wonderful work she did . . . though I know most people believed the work was your father's. The more fools they."

There would be time, I was sure, to discover how Lord Alming had known my mother. So much time. I smiled more widely than I ever had in my life. I couldn't find my voice, so I could only hope that all my gratitude and happiness showed on my face.

"Well, Miss Lampton, we certainly have a lot to discuss." He gestured toward the carriage door, looking hopeful. "If perhaps we might try a spin in this delightful contraption?"

I shook my head. I'd just caught sight of a very round, very golden sort of girl, wearing a red wool cap and stroking Jules's nose. "I have to talk to a friend first."

I felt a weight press down on my buoyant spirit as I remembered all the things Caro and I had to talk about, all the ways I might lose her friendship before we were done.

Lord Alming smiled in a way that suggested he was bemused at my youthfulness again. "Well, you have my card, Miss Lampton. Please do call upon me at your earliest convenience; after the show closes today, perhaps."

"I will," I said. "Oh, thank you again." I looked up at him. I'd never been close enough to notice before, or perhaps it was the brightness of the winter sunlight, but I saw that the freckles on his face looked faintly blue.

He tipped his green top hat and vanished into the crowd.

I turned back toward my friend; I thought it would be best to get this over with quickly.

"Caro!" I cried.

She turned and beamed at me, and all the complicated feelings I'd had about her since last night were swept away in an instant. She ran toward me with her arms open, I opened my own, and we wrapped each other up in such a strong embrace that I lifted her off the ground.

"Oh, Nick," she said, a little breathless, "I've been hearing all about it!"

There was no jealousy, no anger in her voice. She sounded, to my complete and utter confusion, happy.

"Er . . ." After my exhausting heart-to-heart with Fin and my unexpected encounter with Lord Alming, I was somewhat less than articulate. "What do you mean?"

"Oh, come on now. You know." Caro squinted at me, and whatever she saw in my face made her smile fade. "Here," she said, in a softer tone. "Let's go in your lovely carriage and talk about it. Fin'll be stuck in there all day, but the three of us can talk together later on."

"All right." I suddenly wondered why on earth I hadn't at least tinted the glass I'd used for the walls; we'd be as plain as day talking in there. And yet, what other option did we have?

And would there be a "three of us" at all by the end of the day?

I opened the door for Caro and followed her in, then shut the vents.

"The glass does block a fair bit of sound," I said, looking around us, "and at least people seem to be keeping some distance."

"Well, sure," Caro said with laughter in her voice. "Due deference to their future Queen."

There was still nothing in her face but cheerful amusement. I had to ask her outright, I decided. We all had to keep being honest.

"Don't you love him?" I asked.

Caro shot me perhaps the most sardonic look I'd ever seen, and I'd lived with Stepmother for years. "Course I do," she said. "What's that got to do with anything?"

I stared at her. Was she leading me on? "But surely—surely you know how he feels about you."

As soon as the words left my mouth, I wished I could take them back; honesty on my own behalf was well enough, but what if Fin hadn't meant Caro to know this secret?

Caro shook her head. "Fin can be so *dramatic,*" she said. "Ask him where his heart belongs most days, and he'll say Esting. As he should . . . Lord, but I'm glad you know he's the Heir now. He should have told you a long time ago, I always said, but it was up to him. And anyway, it's true that he had to be careful, with his father so paranoid about everything." She rolled her eyes. "But the whole business about, you know, me. It's just that he gets a bit moony sometimes." She made a small, frustrated sound, and I had the feeling that she was struggling to explain in the right way, without doing a disservice to either of them. "The thing about Fin is this: he's wonderful, and I really do love him. But he has some growing up to do, and I think he'll always make me a better friend than he would a lover."

Caro's being so calm, so clearheaded about all of this, was what befuddled me. Was it really that easy? And didn't she ever . . .

"Sure," she went on, dismissing the question that still burned in my mind, "I've felt for him sometimes, only I'm not so . . . *exclusive* about it as he is. Remember how I said I make friends too easily?" She laughed. "I fall in love the same way. A few times a year at least."

I regarded her, a little bit in awe. To go through this—this summit and plunge, this love and heartbreak—*often?* And to be able to speak of it easily and laugh while you're speaking?

"But, Caro," I whispered, "how can you bear it? I feel exhausted just from this one . . ." I remembered Lord Alming's words. "This one drama. How can you bear the heartbreak?"

She looked at me as if I was the one who didn't understand. "How can you bear not loving people? Where does your love go?"

I blinked. Years with the Steps flooded my memory—hard years of drudgery and mutual scorn and the even harder first months, when I'd wanted so badly to love them.

That was all over now, I told myself. It had ended today.

Yet those empty years still echoed through me, and in them I could see Caro's question: *How can you bear not loving people?*

For a long time, I'd walked through a fog, thinking my love had died with Mother and then Father, obeying the Steps because none of it mattered anyway. When I found the workshop, I'd thrown my love into it, working and working, and I loved Jules and even the insects more than I could express.

I thought of how much I'd come to rely on Jules, how much I loved him. Had my bubbling, frenetic love for Fin been only an outlet . . . a place, as Caro said, for my love to go?

And finally I remembered the books I'd read about Faerie as a child, the descriptions of the friend-families the Fey could make. I remembered what I'd told Caro at the Night Market when I'd helped her buy the lovesbane.

Caro's hand pressed down warmly on mine. I found myself blinking back tears.

"I didn't mean that," she said, squeezing my hand more tightly, "I was just trying to explain . . . I think you just haven't met enough people worth loving. Not yet, anyway. You'll see, Nick. A year from now, I bet you'll be telling me all about some new paramour." She shook her head. "But even if it's still Fin . . . even if it's always him, or it's him for both of us at the same time . . . it'll be all right."

"How? How can you know that?"

She twined her fingers through mine and took a slow breath, looking thoughtful. "I suppose I can't promise beyond any doubt," she said, "though I can tell you that Fin and I have weathered many a worse storm, these nineteen years, than one of us being in love with an inconvenient person—even when we are those inconvenient people.

"But anyway, we're friends, aren't we? Fin and I, you and me, you and Fin, all the pairs that can be made of us, and the three of us together, too." She shrugged, and her smile broke out again. "I just don't see that changing anytime soon."

I turned this over in my mind, thinking of the Fey families with longing.

I looked back at Caro and shared in her smile.

Neither did I.

Epilogue

"It's not that simple, of course," I said over my shoulder. At the table behind me, Fin and Caro laughed.

"What isn't?" Fin called.

I took my kettle off the Bunsen burner and poured boiling water over clary-bush leaves in a glass teapot. Two silver spiders pulled a machine-knitted tea cozy around it for me. Mother's cuckoo clock chimed and twittered on the wall.

Outside, I could hear Jules nicker in his stable; since the Exposition, I'd kept him well supplied with the best charcoal. He mostly stayed there; he seemed to prefer the indoors. I'd asked him a few times if he wanted to go riding, but he always shook his head. I wondered if his new home was a comforting reminder of the stable-box he'd slept in for years.

I had to admit that I was still a little frightened, too: frightened that someone would realize he wasn't simply some technological marvel, but magic. There had been plenty of near miracles at the Exposition, and I thought he had seemed like one of them, but I couldn't bear the thought of losing him again.

And I still didn't know what the Ashes were. I'd brought them with me too—I knew, at least, that nothing so potentially powerful should be left in the hands of the Steps.

Someday I would have to find out their true nature. I had given myself the gift of waiting, though, the gift of time to do all the other things I'd dreamed of doing for so long: leaving the Steps, setting up my own workshop in Esting City, beginning to save some money. The day when I could buy back Lampton was approaching faster than I could have hoped for.

I would face the Ashes, and their meanings, in time. Thinking of them felt ominous in the same way as thinking of the oncoming war . . . and it seemed no one could deny that it was coming now. It hurt Fin more than he could bear, I knew, that he didn't yet have the power to stop it—and the thought of war made me almost physically sick.

But all of this was still in the future, and Caro always said that until there was something we could do to help, it did no good obsessing, or encouraging Fin's obsession.

Still, somehow the Ashes and the war were connected in my mind. My heart quailed when I thought of either of them. But I knew Caro was right, and there were enough other things to occupy our minds and hearts for now. Sometimes you have to put things away for a while.

"Tea getting cold there, Nick?" came Fin's teasing voice.

"Patience," I called back, rinsing three cups with hot water. "Don't be such a prince."

I brought the tea set to the table, where sinnum buns Caro's mother had sent me were set out on a chipped yellow plate that was considerably emptier than it had been when I'd gone to boil the water.

As I settled into a chair opposite Fin and Caro, a dragonfly swooped low over the table, glass wings sparkling, and cleared away a few crumbs.

"Lord, Nick, you've got them well trained," said Caro. "Hard to believe you've only lived here a month."

"Mm," I said, "one glorious month."

I'd left Lampton Manor the day of the Exposition, parading up to the house in Jules's carriage, not even thinking of ombrossus or hiding, not even thinking of fear.

It was still strange to remember how easy it had been just to . . . leave. I simply held my head high and walked through the front door, straight past the parlor and the Steps' gaping faces (Chastity's nicely bruised), and down into the cellar and the workshop to gather my things. The insects followed me back up like pilgrims, and I was pleased to see that they left tiny soot trails wherever they could. The Steps never uttered a word, and I hadn't seen head nor tail of them since I'd moved into Esting City, though a slipper-shaped sign announcing my name and trade stood outside my door for all to see.

However hard they'd tried to keep me, and to hurt me

when I was theirs, it seemed they didn't dare come near me now. It would have been anticlimactic if it hadn't been so oddly funny—or maybe it was the other way around.

Either way, I was free of them.

"What's not so simple, Nick?" Fin asked, talking through a mouthful of sinnum bun in a very unprincely fashion. Caro rolled her eyes and tsked at him, in just the same way I'd seen her reprimand her younger cousins a few days ago. Visits to the palace, and especially its great labyrinthine servants' quarters, were quickly becoming a favorite part of my new routine.

I gestured out the window at my cheery, brightly painted sign. "I can't sell people glass slippers without telling them the truth."

Fin groaned histrionically; Caro and I shared a private look. She'd been right about his tendency toward the dramatic. This was one thing, at least, that made him very different from the Fin I'd talked with in my mind so often: that Fin was steadier, more thoughtful, and gentler than this one. I was learning to pay attention to those differences.

"Lord Alming's having a whole new factory built, just for them," I said. "I don't want people to think I'm a liar, in the end. I don't want to *be* a liar."

"No one thinks you're a liar, Nick, for goodness' sake," said Caro. "You tell the truth to anyone who comes asking."

"Yes, but . . ." I wasn't sure how to explain. "But so few people come *asking*. They just want to stare, and giggle, and assume I'm betrothed. And so many of those who do ask refuse to hear the truth when I tell it to them."

Fin poured a cup of tea for me, one for Caro, and finally one for himself. "I told you they'd love the story," he said. "I can't say how many court ladies I've seen wearing those slippers, even the ones who know I'm still free for the taking." He shot a pointed look at Caro, who ignored him. She'd been chattering about a redheaded stable hand named Bex all morning, and I highly doubted that Fin's hints would have any effect on her.

"Ooh, did I tell you what Bex did on Tuesday?" Caro asked. She didn't wait for either of us to answer before she plunged ahead with a long story involving an unbroken horse, a very high fence, and a daring rescue. This time it was Fin and I who shared a private look, and the only tension it held was that of affectionate frustration. He smiled his charming smile and tapped a finger against the rim of his teacup.

His winks, his small flirtations, had affected me less and less in the past weeks too. My heart still fluttered or skipped when he smiled suddenly or touched me when I didn't expect it, but I no longer felt the sheer longing I'd developed before the night of the ball.

I couldn't call myself cured, by any means, but it was a start.

Another start: two friends at my table, in a home of my own.

Caro was right. None of us could truly promise the others that we would always be friends. But always, I knew, was a long time—a time in which mothers could die and fathers be killed, housekeepers be sent away, Steps come and go. A whole life could change, and change again, in the smallest fraction of forever.

That the love between friends could create life, I thought, remembering the Fey history texts I'd read as a child. I had a new life now: a life away from the Steps, a life of friendship and freedom.

Caro's hair caught a shaft of sun coming from my display window, and it shone as golden as wheat. Fin laughed at some detail in her story that I'd missed.

I leaned in to listen better, and the sun warmed my face. Here at the table, laughing, drinking tea, I knew I had found my family.

About the Author

Betsy Cornwell is the author of *Tides,* a YA novel inspired by selkie mythology. She graduated from Smith College and was a columnist and editor at *Teen Ink* before receiving an MFA in creative writing at Notre Dame, where she also taught fiction writing as well as film and television studies. She is currently living and adventuring in Ireland. Visit her website at www.betsycornwell.com.